tigers of the snow

# tigers of the snow

Eighteen Canadian
stories selected and
edited by
James A. MacNeill
and Glen A. Sorestad

nelson

© Thomas Nelson and Sons
(Canada) Limited 1973
81 Curlew Drive
Don Mills, Ontario

ISBN 0-176-33043-7

# contents

Tyger! Tyger! burning bright
In the forests of the night,
What immortal hand or eye
Dare frame thy fearful symmetry?

# introduction

This anthology is totally
Canadian. The book includes
stories which describe most
regions of Canada; these are
not 'regional' stories in the
limiting sense of the term because each has a definite universal appeal. Certainly the stories
in the science-fiction and fantasy
area are not 'regional'; instead,
they exhibit the superb ability
and imagination of Canadian
writers.

The collection is modern in
that all stories have been written
during this century; almost all of
them within the last twenty-five
years; many within the past ten
years. There are stories by the
premier snow-tigers — the
Indians and Eskimos.
Some of the stories are ap-

pearing in an anthology for the first time. Several have not been previously published in this country. In terms of story selection, we feel that this group of stories is new, fresh and exciting.

The writers themselves are as different and as interesting as their stories. The personality of each writer comes through vividly and clearly. Their exposure to the public varies; there are the widely known and respected authors, as well as the lesser known but equally adept contemporary writers. These Canadian writers have explored the range of emotions to include such experiences as love and hate, acceptance and rejection, cowardice and courage, humour and pathos, understanding and alienation, victory and defeat, and the ordinary and the unusual.

James A. MacNeill
Glen A. Sorestad

# man alone

In a matter of months the departures and arrivals of the late man and the fishing fleet have diverged to such an extent that the returning fishermen see the late man's boat heading toward them at dusk, on its way north toward open water. He stands huddled over his wheel, eyes staring unseeing at the darkening horizon as if in purposeful blindness. The fishing fleet parts to let him pass; though no one appears to understand, everyone sees the desperate undertow in his eyes and says nothing. When all the boats are secured and the gear locked away, the late man is a dissolving blotch against black evening. A few moments later he is gone.

from *The Late Man* by
Andreas Schroeder

"I hear the marigolds but not the daisies anymore. It's too late in the year for them."

What sort of man hears the flowers talking to him? What are the flowers telling him? Is this man crazy, or are the flowers telling him something important — some truth *meant for his ears alone*?

# the sound of hollyhocks

Hugh Garner

**t**wo young student nurses were shooting pool with a couple of the patients in the recreation room, but the TV set on the glassed-in veranda was turned off. It was almost time for late evening sedation, and most of the patients were sitting on the edges of their beds, wearing pajamas and dressing gowns. They were waiting for the registered nurse on the evening shift, accompanied by a male attendant, to bring along her tray of sleeping potions and pills.

Pinehills Clinic is now about evenly divided between alcoholics and what we called "head cases," which covers a bewildering variety of psychoneurotics and relatively harmless psychotics. The drunks tend to band together for companionship but most of the head cases, except those recovering following treatment, live in their own loner's world.

I gave a wave to the professor and the Protestant minister as I passed the open door to their room and they waved back before continuing their conversation. The door to the next room was shut, as were the doors to the rooms across the hall, but the next one on the left was open. I paused in the hallway and looked in. One of the beds was empty, but sitting on the edge of the other was a tall good-looking young man who was a close neighbor of mine in the dining hall. He was staring at the floor, his chin in his hands and his head undulating with the forlorn despair of a caged polar bear.

Somebody, before my arrival, had nicknamed him "Rock Hudson," which fitted his tall good looks and his movie star air of disdainful

quietude. He did not look up but continued mumbling to himself. I
made my way back to the dormitory where I had been sleeping for
three nights since my arrival at the clinic. While we waited for the nurse
I listened to the grandiose plans of the young man in the next bed, who
bubbled with the excitement of one who has almost reached the top of
his manic cycle.

After breakfast the next morning one of the attendants stopped me
in the hall and said, "Mr. Armstrong, we're moving you into one of the
rooms." He took my bag and clothes from a dormitory locker, and I
followed him along one of the bisecting corridors that formed an L
through the ward, lined with single and two-bed rooms. He entered one
of the semi-privates and hung my clothes in a closet. I wasn't too
happy to discover I was to share Rock Hudson's sleeping quarters.
My roommate was out, having been taken downstairs with the others
for his tri-weekly electric shock treatments.

During the first two days we shared the room not a word passed
between Rock Hudson and me, he seemingly content to sit on his bed,
staring out of the window or down at the floor, while I sought companionship among my fellow drunks. He occasionally muttered a few
words to himself, but most of his time seemed to be listening to
sounds pitched too high for others to hear, like an unheard noise that
wakens a sleeping dog.

On the third afternoon I lay down in my bed to grab a short nap.
Most of the ward's patients had gone for a walk through the grounds
with a pair of attendants, while others were down in Occupational
Therapy making their moccasins, wallets and ceramics. Rock was sitting on the edge of his bed as usual, staring at his shoes. Though I
knew he was aware of my arrival he didn't look up. I was just dozing
off when he spoke to me for the first time.

"I hear the marigolds but not the daisies any more. It's too late in the
year for them."

I turned my head sharply and stared at him. He was looking at me
and smiling.

"I suppose daisies *are* a springtime flower," I agreed, not wanting to
ignore him but feeling foolish for allowing myself to be drawn into
such a kooky conversation.

"They're not necessarily a springtime flower," he corrected me.

"Well—no, I guess not."

"They tell me everything. Especially the hollyhocks. They're a funny kind of flower in a way, tall and gangling, but they've got good ears."

I sat up, as casually as I could.

"They were Sandra's favorite flower. I could never understand why. Most people like roses or 'mums or even petunias, but not hollyhocks."

I agreed.

He turned away and stared through the window at the red tile roof of a building across the courtyard, nodding now and then as if somebody or something was talking to him.

He spoke to me quite often from then on, though he didn't make much sense at first. By the end of my second week however his shock treatments or something had seemed to snap him out of his earlier mental isolation, and he talked quite sanely for short periods of time. From what he told me I was able to piece together a two-dimensional sketch of what his life had been up to then.

Rock was the only child of one of my city's leading bankers. He had attended the right prep school, and later had taken a business admin. course in university. On graduation he had gone into one of the downtown branches of his father's bank as an assistant accountant, and from then on his promotions had been foreordained.

One evening as we sat smoking in our room, and I listened to Rock do most of the talking, he suddenly exclaimed, "She's the Bitch of Belsen!" We hadn't been talking about women at the time, but I presumed he was talking about his wife.

Sandra had been a teller in the bank, and their romance had been the old familiar one of a young man and woman brought together through office propinquity. He had taken her to lunch a few times before they had an evening date, but after that he began visiting her apartment, which she shared with another girl. When her roommate married and moved away he half moved into the apartment with her, paying a share of the rent. Though Sandra was a high school dropout he was sure she was intelligent and pretty enough to hurdle any social barriers his family or friends might raise against her. They were married secretly one afternoon at City Hall, and shortly after the wedding he took her home to meet his parents.

The meeting between his bride and mother had been a disaster, though he avoided confessing this to me openly. His father had proved friendly enough to Sandra, but the old gentleman's family and social decisions were generally ignored by his wife. The first meeting between his wife and his mother proved also to be the last, and Sandra was never again invited to the house. One time he told me, "Mother's a take-over woman, great in a crisis but sometimes unbearable when things are normal."

He was not happy as a banker, and he began to question what would be waiting for him when he reached the top. The thought of the emptiness of the achievement frightened him, and once he told me, "I could see my father sitting at his big empty desk down at head office, staring through the window at something far off that he had lost or overlooked when he was young. At home I saw him going through the ritual of two pre-dinner cocktails, later either watching TV or getting dressed to take Mother to the symphony or a theatre first night or some other social do. It's all a charade, Armstrong, don't you see? They're only puppets being maneuvered by strings from their Presbyterian heaven."

Rock and his bride had continued living in her bachelor-girl digs, but they rented and furnished a small apartment when he received his promotion to accountant in one of the bank's suburban branches. Their daytime separation and his refusal to let his father help them out financially soon drove them slowly but inexorably apart. There had been long acrimonious squabbles about money, about his parents' attitudes towards her, about what she called his rich-boy mentality.

One evening she had phoned home to let him know she was staying at a girl friend's place overnight, and another time had disappeared for a whole weekend. When he had called her at the bank on Monday morning she told him blithely that she had accompanied another girl and her husband to their summer cottage. He had checked and found her story to be true, as far as she had told it to him.

After that, however, he knew their marriage was on the skids. The next time she stayed away overnight he did not bother to call her, but through his father arranged a loan, packed a two-suiter, and flew to Las Vegas. There he threw away his money on the tables, and also on a couple of would-be Hollywood actresses, whom he described as "Wampus Baby Stars of 1944." He returned home to find his wife had moved, and his clothes and belongings placed in storage. Two weeks later he received the news that Sandra had been killed in a highway traffic accident, along with a young married man who was driving the car.

He said to me, "I had to play the broken-hearted husband at the funeral, but that part of it was easy. Believe it or not, Armstrong, but I *was* broken-hearted. Mother, of course, took me back home where she could treat me as her little boy. She never mentioned Sandra's name again. I moped around the house and garden all summer, and it was then that the flowers began telling me the things I wanted to hear."

Rock's continued improvement seemed miraculous to me. I awoke one afternoon from my nap to find his psychiatrist sitting in our room talking to him. I kept my face turned to the wall, pretending to still be asleep.

Rock was asking, ". . . and in your opinion, Dr. Kellock, how long does this usually take?"

"It's hard to say," the doctor answered, in the vague way of doctors and lawyers. "I think the shock treatments are doing you a world of good, and you tell me your blackouts aren't as frequent or of as long duration as they were; certainly I've noticed that they are not constant as they were when you were first admitted. If things continue improving as they have over the past two weeks you could be ready for discharge perhaps in another month or so."

"I'm anxious now to get back to work, Doctor."

"Now, Mr. Ranson, I didn't say anything about going back to work just yet. You'll need a couple of months, at least, of convalescence after leaving here. Just take things easy, get plenty of rest and try to get rid of your memories of your wife. Let the medication do the rest."

"I'm only twenty-five, Doctor," Rock said. "I realize now that I was ill for months before coming here, and you tell me I've been here at the clinic for seven weeks. That's an awful long time for a young man."

"I know it is. I'm quite pleased with the improvement you are now showing, and if your recovery continues as it has over the past couple of weeks I see no reason why you shouldn't be discharged in a month or so. These blackouts, as you call them, will probably continue for a time, but will continue to diminish in both length and frequency. When they disappear completely we'll be able to talk of going home."

"I hope so, Doctor."

The doctor stood up and said, "Just take things easy. Recovery from

any illness seems slow and tedious, but there are times when it can't
be hurried."

"How many more shock treatments do I need, Doctor?"

"Perhaps only another week. It all depends."

"I don't hear the flowers talking much any more," Rock said with a
laugh.

"Good. It's not uncommon for a person with your illness to have
auditory hallucinations. You may have short infrequent returns of these
but they'll disappear as your condition continues to improve. Don't
let them worry you."

I heard the doctor walking to the door.

"Thanks, Doctor," Rock said.

"Just remember to take things easy, Mr. Ranson."

After the doctor had gone I turned over and said, "Things are looking up for you."

"Yes. Were you listening?"

"For a while."

"I've only got three more shock treatments, the doctor said.
Did you hear him telling me the way I used to act when the treatments
first started?"

I shook my head.

"It used to take four attendants to get me into the room, and they had
to hold me down until they knocked me out with the needle. Now I
don't mind taking the treatments at all, for I know they're doing me
good. What I hate most is missing breakfast three mornings a week."

"How do you feel afterwards?"

"Woozy for a while, and I can't remember recent things very well.
When I wake up an attendant brings me back here, and I usually sleep
until lunch. When I wake up my memory has mostly returned."

"The shock treatments have sure done you a lot of good."

"They seem to. You know, Mr. Armstrong—"

It was the first time he'd called me "Mister." I said, "Please call me
Wilf."

"Okay, Wilf. You know, I once tried to commit suicide."

"Oh."

"It wasn't long after Sandra was—after Sandra died. One night I went
down to the kitchen and tried to slash my wrists with a carving knife.
I cut one of them and then fainted I guess. The next thing I remember

was waking up in the hospital with my forearm bandaged. Maybe I
didn't faint but blacked out. I know that when I was sent home again I
began blacking out regularly, which threw a hell of a scare into them."

"Them?"

"My parents."

"How long did this go on?"

"I don't really know, Wilf. I don't remember much of the summer."

"Rock—" I smiled. "You know I've shared this room with you for
more than two weeks and I still don't know what to call you. I've
known all along that your last name is Ranson, but I don't know your
first name."

"It's William. William Cornish Ranson. The Cornish is my maternal
grandfather's name. Everybody calls me Bill."

"Around here they call you Rock."

He laughed. "I know. I'm beginning to answer to it."

"Somebody named you that before I got here. After Rock Hudson the
movie star."

"That's pretty flattering, but undeserved," he said. He swung his feet
to the floor and pulled up his pullover sleeve. "Here's my scar," he
said, as I leaned on my elbow to look. Across his left wrist was a faint
white scar bordered with the close elliptical marks of the stitches.

"You were lucky."

"Yes. I guess I realize that now. At the time I tried to kill myself I
was still suffering from the shock of Sandra's death and the breakup of
our marriage. It takes quite a while to get over something like that."

"Maybe you were lucky there too."

He shot me a quick look. "How do you mean, Wilf?"

"Well, one day last week we were sitting here talking, and you called
her The Bitch of Belsen."

"Not Sandra," he said. "I wouldn't call Sandra anything like that."

I stared at him, wondering if he'd forgotten.

"When do you expect to leave here, Wilf?" he asked, as if to hurry
away from the subject of his wife.

"I'm leaving here next Monday."

"You're lucky. All you alcoholics are lucky. Maybe I'd have been
better off going on a binge myself than trying to bottle everything up
inside me."

"I'm sure there's legitimate arguments both for and against it."

"There's arguments, legitimate or not, against everything," he said, laughing and jumping up from his bed.

For the rest of the week Rock—I couldn't get used to calling him Bill—acted quite normally, going out with the gang for walks through the grounds, talking to the attendants and other patients, glancing through some picture magazines we had in our room, and even going downstairs to Occupational Therapy once or twice, where he was making himself a wallet. One evening he came with us to a bingo game in the auditorium, where he sat opposite a young student nurse I'd seen him talking to in our recreation room.

She was a stunningly pretty girl, who, like the other students, was attached to a general hospital in another city, and was taking her psychiatric nursing training at the clinic. After the bingo they walked back to the ward together, and as I followed them along the corridor I thought to myself how perfectly matched they seemed to be. I guessed however, that her friendship with him was merely professional sympathy and friendliness, though perhaps part of his therapy.

I became afraid of what it might do to Rock when the current group of young nurses was replaced in a couple of weeks, and the pretty student left. Her attraction for him might be building up to an awful let-down, which might set him back to the way he had been at first.

That evening he had another "blackout" as he called them, and I heard him talking once again to the flowers, as we lay on our beds waiting for the ten o'clock medication. He said, "Yes, I know," which was followed by some mumbling I didn't understand. Then he sat up and shouted, "I don't believe it! From now on I'll only listen to the hollyhocks!"

I too sat up. "Take it easy, Bill," I said.

He gave me a dreamy smile.

"You had a nightmare that's all."

"What do dandelions know about anything?" he asked, staring into the darkness outside the window. He remained seated on the edge of his bed, staring outside and muttering to himself.

When the evening shift registered nurse brought our pills and sleeping potion, she and the attendant stared at Rock for a moment. I knew she would have to place his regression in her report, and it would delay Rock's discharge.

She handed me a small paper cup containing my pill. "Your sleeping potion has been discontinued, Mr. Armstrong," she said. "I suppose you'll be leaving us soon?"

"On Monday."

"That's fine. That's why they've reduced your medication."

I pointed to Rock, who was oblivious to us. "He was all right until a few minutes ago," I told her.

The nurse shook her head sadly. The attendant said, "He's improved a lot lately. I wouldn't want to see a young man like that moved down to A3 among the chronic cases."

The nurse handed Rock his small paper cup and said, "Here, Mr. Ranson. Here's something to make you sleep."

He gave her his blank smile and swallowed the bitter-tasting draught and the paper cup of grapefruit juice handed him by the attendant.

"Get into bed, Mr. Ranson, please," the nurse said, and he did as he was told.

The nurse and the attendant bid us good night, shut off the light and left, closing the door behind them. I fell asleep before Rock did, even without my sleeping potion.

When I awoke the next morning Rock was shaving himself with an electric shaver that one of the attendants had taken from his locker for him.

"Good morning, Wilf," he said. "You'd better get up. We'll be going down to breakfast pretty soon."

He had changed completely from the young man of the evening before.

There were three discharges from our ward on Saturday, and a couple of the alcoholics were allowed to go home for the weekend. The dining room was only partly full, and after breakfast Rock brought his coffee to my table, where we sat and talked until he was called out to join the rest of the "chain gang," as those who were taken to meals in a group were called.

"There's been a lot of improvement in that boy," said an elderly businessman who shared my table.

"Yes, he seems to be coming along fine," I answered.

"The first couple of weeks I was here he didn't speak to anyone."

"I know. I was his roommate for three days before he noticed me."

"I feel sorry for the kids in here with mental troubles," said the businessman. "I may be a damn fool sometimes, but I'd sooner be a drunk than one of them. I was afraid that boy was a hopeless case when I first saw him, but his improvement has been almost miraculous."

When I returned upstairs Rock was lying on his bed reading a magazine. He lowered it when I entered the room.

"What are you going to do this afternoon?" I asked him.

"Well, if Helen doesn't go away for the weekend I have a date to teach her how to play pocket billiards," he answered. "A pool table isn't quite satisfactory, but I can at least teach her the rudiments of the game."

"Is Helen the young nurse you walked over from the bingo game with last night?"

"Yes, Helen MacDonald. She's from Niagara Falls. She's engaged to a young doctor down there."

I was glad he knew that about her. Perhaps his interest was only a friendly one too.

"Don't let me interfere with your reading," I said. "I'm going down to A4 Ward to watch TV; ours will have nothing on but football all afternoon."

"I'm looking forward to getting my house privileges," Rock said. "I'll go visiting too. See you later, Wilf."

When I returned to A2 before supper Rock was shooting pool with an attendant.

"Who's winning?"

"He's skunking me, Wilf. That's what I get for having been brought up in a neighborhood that had no pool parlors."

"What happened to the young nurse you were going to teach to shoot pocket billiards?"

"Helen? Her fiance came for her, and she went to the Falls for the weekend." He seemed quite unperturbed by this, and laughed happily as the attendant made a run of a string of balls.

On Sunday there were quite a few visitors to the clinic, and some took lunch with the patients they had come to see, in the guest dining room downstairs. After eating my lunch in the half-empty dining hall I returned to my room and took my usual nap. I was awakened by the sound of male and female voices in the room and when I sat up I saw the voices were those of Rock and a man and woman in late middle age.

Rock said, "Wilf, I'd like you to meet my parents. Mr. Armstrong."

I stood up as Mr. Ranson offered me his hand with a smile and a friendly nod. Rock's mother half turned and gave me a curt nod.

"I'll get out of here and give you a little privacy," I said, pulling on my shoes.

"Don't let us drive you out," said Mr. Ranson. His wife turned away, ignoring me.

As I tidied my hair before the mirror above the washbowl I heard her say to Rock, "I'll phone our own doctor tomorrow. If you ask me you're completely recovered now from your breakdown, and I'm sure you'll be much better off at home, where I can take care of you."

"But Mother, Dr. Kellock told me just the other day—"

"He's already given you a wrong diagnosis. Why, you certainly weren't suffering from anything as serious as he . . ."

I shut off the rest of her harmful foolishness by closing the door behind me as I left.

Rock didn't speak to me at supper, and when I asked him later if he'd enjoyed his parents' visit he turned his face to the wall and didn't answer me. I spent the rest of the evening watching television on the glassed-in veranda, and didn't return to our room until it was time to put on our pajamas and bathrobes.

Rock was sitting fully dressed on the edge of his bed, staring through the window and talking to himself. I changed quietly so as not to disturb him.

"I know," he said, speaking to the unknown something outside. "They told me. The hollyhocks are the only ones who really know. Ask Sandra." He shook his head. "The Bitch of Belsen wants me back, but I won't go—never—never again!"

I lay down to wait for the medication to arrive, leaving Rock to himself. Every once in a while he muttered snatches of unrelated conversation.

When the nurse and the attendant arrived, Rock jumped up from his bed and made a lunge at the man, knocking him back into the corridor and spilling his jug of grapefruit juice on the floor. The nurse and I ran out of the room, as the attendant wrestled with the younger man. The nurse hurried back to her office, and in a minute or two a pair of younger attendants came running along the hall. They quickly overpowered

Rock, and then carried the swearing, sobbing young man back to his
bed. The nurse returned from the nursing station carrying a hypodermic
syringe. She entered our room, closing the door behind her.

When the nurse and the attendants came out again in a couple of
minutes the nurse said, "I'm sorry you were disturbed like this, Mr.
Armstrong. Mr. Ranson is asleep now, and probably won't waken
again until morning. If you like though you can take one of the empty
beds in the dormitory for tonight. There are a couple of empty beds,
aren't there, George?"

The elderly attendant nodded, as he picked up his spilled jug from
the floor. "It may be best, Mr. Armstrong," he said, straightening up.
"Sometimes a patient as disturbed as Mr. Ranson is pretty unpredictable."

"I'll sleep in my room," I said. "I'm sure Mr. Ranson will be all right
by morning."

"I think so," said the nurse. "I gave him a rather heavy sedation."

Despite my brave words in the corridor however it took me a long
time to fall asleep. The nurses and attendants could take such frenzied
flareups in their stride but I couldn't.

It was some time during the night when I awoke thinking that the
noise I'd heard in my sleep was Rock having another attack. I looked
over to his bed and found it was empty. The shouting was coming from
along the hall. I pulled on my bathrobe and slippers and hurried from
the room.

The watchman who sat all night at the angle of the two corridors was
staring into one of the toilets, wringing his hands.

"Get—me—a knife—the breadknife!" a night attendant was gasping.
As the watchman ran into the small kitchen where the juice was kept
and they made up the evening lunches, I looked around the toilet's
open door. Rock was hanging strangled in his belt from an overhead
pipe, the belt having been twisted around his neck. The attendant was
trying to push him up by the legs to relieve the pressure on his throat.
Rock's face was purple, his mouth twisted into an obscene leer. I tried
to help the attendant hold him up—After they cut him down they tried
mouth-to-mouth resuscitation on the corridor floor, but it was too late.
By the time the doctors arrived, Rock was dead.

I was discharged from Pinehills shortly after lunch, and my son
drove me back to the city. From our apartment window we can look

down on the back shed of an old private house in the next street. During the summer the shed is half hidden behind a row of tall flowering hollyhocks. Now the flowers were dead, their gangling stems dried and broken.

"What's the matter, Wilf?" my wife asked, as I swung away from the window.

"Nothing. Nothing's the matter at all. I just wish that old woman across the parking lot would get rid of her back shed. It's a real eyesore."

"It's pretty during the summer though when the flowers are out," she said. "What's the name of them again?"

"I forget," I answered.

*Hugh Garner has long been one of Canada's most industrious story writers and novelists. Many of his stories have been universally recognized. 'One-Two-Three Little Indians' has, according to Mr. Garner's most recent count, been anthologized no less than 28 times since its first appearance in 1952. 'The Sound of Hollyhocks' is from Garner's latest collection of stories,* VIOLATION OF THE VIRGINS (1971). HUGH GARNER'S BEST STORIES (1963) *gives us a good sampling of his story-telling talents. A Toronto native, Garner presents a frankly realistic view of contemporary life, particularly the urban scene.*

A submarine lies helpless at the bottom of the sea. Inside are twenty men—trapped.

Rescue will not arrive for seven days. There is enough oxygen to last twenty men *less than three days* . . .

But the same oxygen will keep five men alive for the seven days until rescue . . .

*You* are the captain. What is your decision?

# gentlemen, your verdict

Michael Bruce

"Next Witness."

"Call Torpedoman Preece."

Lieutenant Paull bowed his head and covered his face with his hands. Though the courtroom was tense and silent around him, all he could see was the long compartment with fifteen men lying dead on the floor and five men staring in stricken silence. Though the proverbial pin could have been heard drop in the courtroom, he could still hear the ghastly sound as fifteen men died and their cups fell with a clatter at their feet.

"Tell the court what happened, in your own words, please."

"Well, sirs, it was like this. We was on this trial cruise, and was running at about ten fathoms off Steins Point, when the mine got us . . ."

Lieutenant Paull tried to shut out the voice with his fingers in his ears. He had told that story first. Then Engineer Nordin had given his version. Speer had told his story next, followed by Jenvey. Now Preece was repeating it. Each story was the same yet a little different, and each sentence struck the lieutenant like the lash of a whip.

They had been running at ten fathoms at half speed when the explosion came. Probably it had been a drifted acoustic or magnetic mine which should have rusted long before, for a contact one would have finished everything and everyone at once.

It had been just 1430 hours when the submarine shuddered to a blow that felt like the impact of Thor's hammer. Her tail rose, she rolled half over and started down in a steep, swift dive. Men fell or were flung in scrambling heaps. Lieutenant Paull, half stunned, found himself under four heavy men.

Almost instantly, it seemed, Lieutenant-Commander Oram's voice rang over the uproar: "Stop engines. Blow one and two. Blow four and six."

The engines had been racing above top speed, and every man knew the reason. The blast had blown the propellers off. Now it was impossible to reverse and unless she were checked soon, the submarine's steel bow would crumple like tin as she rammed the bottom of the sea.

The noise of the engines died, and the bow began to rise as she rolled back to a level keel. But she still slid forward, deeper and deeper, from the initial impetus of the dive.

"Blow seven and eight. Hard arise with the bow planes. Hard aport," came Oram's voice again.

"Steering gears jammed, sir," reported the coxswain.

At that moment the submarine struck. Except for those who were holding something, the whole crew went down again, this time sliding to the forward end of each compartment. But the speed of her downward rush had been checked, she was almost on an even keel, and the bottom was the tip of the sandbank that extended from Steins Point, not the rocky ocean floor.

"... and he orders: Report your instruments." Preece's voice broke through the lieutenant's fog of memory.

They had reported. Bow planes immovable, apparently buried in sand. The radio was still usable, though damaged. The bow tanks could be neither blown nor flooded, their vents clogged with sand. At the stern the propellers were gone, the steering gear wrecked and the stern tanks flooded. All the hatches were hopelessly jammed. But by some miracle there was no leak in the ship itself.

The crew had come through fairly well. One man, thought stunned, was found to be dead, and two men had broken ribs. All had bruises and scrapes.

"Call the shore station," Oram ordered the radioman. "And let me know as soon as you have them, please."

"Shore station's calling us, sir," the radioman reported a second later. "Our tender got some of the blast and reported we were probably hit."

"Right, I'll talk to them," and Oram took up the radio telephone.

"Yes, sir, must have been a mine. Our steering gear is wrecked, propellers have gone, and she dived into the sands off Steins Point. The stern tanks are flooded, and she won't move at all. None of our hatches, even the escape ones, can be opened. Torpedoman Kimmel is dead, but the rest are all right . . . We're about thirty fathoms down. We can be reached fairly easily and we've enough air for almost two days."

The earphones rattled faintly for a few seconds . . . Lieutenant-Commander Oram's face paled.

"How soon can our second one be ready, sir?" he asked. There was a pause and the earphones rattled again. "How about planes then, sir?" There was a longer pause and the earphones sounded again for nearly half a minute. "I see, sir," he said, almost in a whisper. Then he laid the instrument down and for nearly a minute sat staring blindly in front of him.

"What's wrong, sir?" Lieutenant Paull asked at length.

Lieutenant-Commander Oram faced him: "As you heard, our tender got some of the blast. It jammed her steering gear for a minute. This trip was to test the new stabilizers in a storm, like the one top-side. That storm just drifted our tender onto those rocks—remember them? —and she is burning like a torch . . . The next nearest one is in dry dock, four hundred miles away, with half her plates off. She can't possibly get here for a week . . . Planes are grounded until the storm ends, and then they can't bring all the equipment they'll need to get us out. The shore station is doing all it can to find another ship."

Lieutenant Paull shuddered as he recalled his feelings. Their own tender wrecked and no other ship near meant rescue was impossible for five days, more like a week, and they had air for *less than two days.*

Then Oram roused himself.

"Have a drink served out all round, please, Mr. Paull," he said. "And send four bottles forward to me. When they have had their drink, send the five married men to me."

In some bewilderment Lieutenant Paull obeyed.

"We was glad to get that drink, sirs," came Preece's voice. "An' when we'd downed it, we five reported to the Old Man—beg pardon, sirs— Cap'n Oram. He told us he had special duty for four of us, what could only be done by married men with families, and as far as he knew, there wasn't nothing to choose between us. Would we draw lots? We did, an' Nordin, Speer, Jenvey and me got the marked ones . . ."

The voice faded out, and Lieutenant Paull tried to swallow the lump in his throat.

The men had gone back to their comrades. Oram called the shore station again. "Any luck with the ships, sir?" he asked. There was a slight pause and a faint sound from the earphones. "That's absolutely certain, then, sir?" There was a longer pause, a few more sounds from the phones. "Thank you, sir. I'll call again—later."

"Assemble the men, please, Mr. Paull," he ordered. "I wish to say a few words to them."

When everyone was gathered, Lieutenant-Commander Oram came in. He was carrying the four bottles of whisky and a tray with six white mugs; putting them down, he faced the crew.

"Men," he began, and hesitated. "Men, I have a few things to say and they're not all pleasant, nor easy. First, I'd like to say that I think you're the finest crew I've ever seen, let alone commanded . . . I know that you will take this news like men. You know what's happened. Well, we're stuck. And we're stuck until someone on top pulls the sub up, for all our hatches are stuck too. Now there is one very hard job to be done, but it's one that can be done only by men with families. You know them; they drew lots for the job just now and Preece, Nordin, Speer and Jenvey got it. I'll tell them what it is in a few minutes. I thank you for the quick, cheerful way you have carried out orders . . . That's all. Now all pass here with your mugs, married men last, and we'll drink a toast. No early sipping and no heeltaps and then we'll get on with our next job."

With a face white as death he poured a stiff drink in each man's cup. He gave Preece, Nordin, Speer and Jenvey four of the white mugs which were already charged. He gave the fifth one to Lieutenant Paull and took the last one himself. He raised his cup.

"God save our country and King," he said and drank.

The men drank; and drinking, died. Like one man, they stiffened, choked and fell. The cups clattered on the floor.

Only Lieutenant-Commander Oram, Lieutenant Paull and Preece, Nordin, Speer and Jenvey remained standing, white mugs in their hands.

Then Oram spoke, his voice harsh and clipped.

"Men," he grated, "the shore station reports our tender is wrecked and on fire. The other one is in dry dock, as you know, and can't get here for a week. They have contacted all the planes they can and the earliest any help can arrive is between six and seven days. We had air for less than two days for all of us. Now there will be air for all five of you for seven days. Obey my last orders. Mr. Paull, you will take command. Men, remain alive and take your orders from Mr. Paull. You can still serve your country. Your job is to—wait."

" 'And why not you, sir?' whispers Nordin." Preece's voice again.

"I am going to join my crew as soon as I have made my report," was Oram's quiet answer.

He wrote out the report and signed it. He had the bodies placed in an end compartment. Then he called the shore station.

At that flat, unemotional voice: "I have arranged that Lieutenant Paull, Engineers Nordin and Jenvey, Torpedoman Preece and Coxswain Speer will survive, by arranging the death of the fifteen others—" there was a horrified squawk from the earphones. He went on: "None of the others had the least idea of what I intended doing. I arranged that the men with families should survive. The entire responsibility is mine . . . No, sir, you won't be able to court-martial me. I could condemn my whole crew to death or sacrifice fifteen and save five, and am going to join the others. Good-bye, sir."

"Then six days later they reached us, sirs. God, we was glad."

"That is all," said the president of the court. He turned to the officers: "Gentlemen, it is for you to decide, guilty or not guilty."

*Michael Bruce, born in Alberta, was a gunner in the Canadian Army during the Second World War. He spent three years overseas in the artillery and in a note to* MACLEAN'S, *which published his 'Gentlemen, Your Verdict' (Jan. 1, 1947), he said that the idea for his story "grew out of a barrack room argument—whether a commander was justified in sacrificing some of his men to save others".*

"The old man was right beside her. All he had to do was reach over the side and pull her in. It would be easy."

Easy for him? A sick man cannot save a little girl from drowning, but in the presence of death *everything changes.*

# a few notes for orpheus

Don Bailey

i was sitting in my room when the phone rang.

"Hello."

"It's me," she said. Mother. I was almost glad to hear her. But something must be wrong. She never phoned me.

"Is something wrong?"

"Your father," she said. "The doctor called yesterday and told me."

"What! What did he tell you?" Why did she have to turn everything into one of those serial mysteries? Each episode yanked from her between commercials.

"I've been telling him for years," she said.

"Never mind that. What did the doctor say?"

"Cancer. It's in his lungs. I've been telling him for years but he'd never listen. Stubborn. Smoking his damn cigarettes like a train. I told him . . . ."

Her voice broke. She was crying. It made me angry to hear her crying for herself. She never once mentioned cigarettes that I could remember.

"Will you come up to the cottage this weekend?"

"Why? What's the point?"

"He's going to die!" she said, back to her favourite soap opera. "He's your father, Jake. You're his only son."

And you're his wife, I felt like saying; his only wife, but what was the point; it would be like taking away her bingo card with one number to go.

"Come," she said.

"All right. Tomorrow. I'll drive up in the afternoon."

"In the morning," she said. "Or tonight, Jake. Come up tonight. I'm scared. When I'm alone with him I don't know what to say."

"I'll be up tomorrow."

"Early," she said.

"Yeah." And I hung up. It was crazy, her being scared after all these years of being alone with him. But it scared me too in a way. It was like suddenly now that he was going to die we had to face the fact that he was alive.

I sat staring at the telephone for a long time and thought about statues. I hated them. Statues were the way other people made you stand still. Like dying. People loved you, made you their hero and killed you so they could build a monument to their feelings. Statues. And now in my mother's mind I could see the old man turning to stone. She would buy the biggest and best headstone. Bingo! A perfect card. A prize.

I picked up the phone and called my wife.

"It's me," I said. My mother's son.

"You sound like the ghost of somebody I used to know . . . ."

The father, the son, the holy ghost. Yes the holy ghost was the rattling skeleton in my closet.

"I haven't got this month's cheque yet," she said.

"It's in the mail," I lied. I'd drunk it the weekend before with some girl from Baltimore who was in Toronto for a hairdressers' convention. You might say she clipped me, but I didn't mind, I needed a trim.

I like to make jokes to myself. It's a good cover for all the laughing I do.

"So how are things," she said. "Selling lots of cars?"

"Great, but I'm thinking of going into another field. Selling head-stones."

"You make money at that?"

"People keep dying."

"I suppose . . . ."

I could see her, face pulled in like an accordion to squeeze her thoughts into a recognizable tune. Everything has to be familiar to her before she can accept it. I guess I never became familiar enough. And when I left she kept expecting me to come back. Like Eurydice waiting and I didn't even look back.

"Is this a social call or what?" she said. "I haven't heard anything from you for months."

"Sort of business," I said. "How's the kid?"

"Great. She even mentioned you a couple of days ago; the man that used to live with us."

"I was wondering if it'd be okay for me to take her away for the week-end."

"Where?"

"Up to my parents' cottage."

"Since when did you get chummy with them?"

"Look Edith, it's just a thing. The old lady asked me up, the old man's sick and I said I'd come. I thought it'd be nice for the kid. Fresh air, swimming, the whole thing."

"What about me? I'm supposed to sit in this lousy sweat box while you and her go gallivanting off."

If she'd been in my room I would have punched her. It made me sick, the petty talk that led to this kind of thought. It was a way of chiselling at you, a re-forming. My wife, the reformer.

"She hasn't even met your father," she continued. "I can't understand why you'd want her to get involved with them now. You never did before. You hardly saw them yourself."

"Forget it then," I said. "I just thought she might enjoy the outing."

"I don't want to forget it, I want to know why all of a sudden you want to be nice to everybody. You know how often I've asked you to take her for the weekend so I could get away by myself, but you were always too busy. Now all of a sudden you're the good samaritan."

"Edith, my old man's sick. I want the kid to meet him at least once before he dies. At least once."

I was tired of this and sorry I had called. It had been a stupid idea and only proved how scared I was too. Frightened to go up there alone.

"Is he that bad?"

"Yeah."

"I never met him either," she said and began to cry. I began to wish that the hairdressers' convention hadn't been the week before and that it would happen this weekend. Or that my phone was disconnected. I felt the same way from the calls being made to me and the ones I made too.

"I'm sorry," I said. And I was. I was sorry that that was all I could be. There was nothing I could change or would if I could, except may-be to never have had a phone installed.

"What time did you want her?" she asked.

"Whatever time's best for you."

"I'll send her over about ten," she said. "She can ride the streetcar by herself now."

She sounded proud. "That's great," I said. "I'll have her back Sunday after supper. Okay?"

"Take care of her."

"I will. Goodbye."

"Goodbye Jake."

I hung up and spent another long time staring at the phone. It was black like the night was becoming outside my windows. The phone could brighten up the night; one call to someone. A name somewhere in a directory.

I walked out to the balcony. The stars were like tiny animals' eyes. A coldness out there. "This is the winter of the world; and here we die." Did Shelley mean that? I'd have liked to have been on the moon with an endless supply of light bulbs; wire the moon to shine away the night.

I dreamed a while. Night dream of people I'd lost long ago in a daylight somewhere.

The old man was dying and I preferred to be seen in the dark. It was as though I was preparing myself for a sudden departure. Cutting myself off except for the phone. And telling myself I liked my privacy.

I went to bed early without even one drink.

A knock woke me. The room was full of light. A beam of dust particles formed a moving mural in one corner. In a way it was more of a picture than the posters I had pasted on the walls. Art should always be elusive. Somebody said that, I'm sure.

"Come in," I said. "It's not locked." I never lock the door. Locking anything defeats its own purpose.

"It's me," she said and stood in the doorway with a brown shopping bag and a brown face split like a potato with a jagged grin.

"Com'on in," I said again. "Close the door."

She closed it and discreetly held her back to me while I fumbled around for my pants. They were on the floor and in a minute I was up and jamming the blankets from the studio couch into the closet.

"You look great," I said. "How's school?" Standard question.

"It's holidays," she said.

"Oh yeah. I forgot."

"You always forget," she said softly so I almost didn't hear her.

"You're starting to sound like your mother."

"I'm sorry. I didn't mean that. But you do forget. All the time when I see you, you always say you forgot this or you forgot that. All the time you say that."

It's true. And it's strange because I really want to be remembered. But not as a statue. I want to be remembered in an unclear way. Like a stranger that you see some night on the subway and never forget.

"Let's forget it," I said.

She laughed. "See!"

I laughed too. "I'm just lazy," I said.

She continued to laugh in the nervous way my wife has. An unnatural sound from a ten-year-old. But maybe not. I don't know any other ten-year-olds. Maybe they all end up sounding like that.

I shaved and came back to find her asleep. It frightened me.

"Hey, com'on sleepy-head, time to go. Didn't you get any sleep last night?"

"I couldn't," she said. "I was too excited."

At least she's still honest enough to admit what she feels.

"Let's go then. You got all your stuff?"

"Right here. I put my bathing-suit in too."

Because my living is made selling cars I always have a road-worthy vehicle at my disposal. My boss believes that as I zoom along the highway in one of his red convertibles, people will flag me down and make wild offers to buy the thing from me. So far the only person who's flagged me down was a hitch-hiker headed for the east coast. Another dreamer. But still it's pleasant to have a nice car waiting for you at the curb. And the kid liked it.

"Can you put the top down?" she asked.

"Sure," I said.

The drive took less than two hours. Just over a hundred miles from Toronto. The old man had bought the cottage years back when I was still a kid and prices were on a level that only demanded a man's right arm stopping at the first joint. Now they wanted the shoulder and both legs.

With the top down it was difficult to talk and after a few distorted questions to each other that the wind blew around we gave up. When I pulled off the highway onto the dirt road that led to the lake she asked me something she seemed to have been saving for a long time.

"Do you have any girl friends?"

It startled me. Was she a spy? My wife liked to know things like that, but the kid had never sought information to take back with her before. Not that I could remember. Maybe I hadn't noticed. I didn't want to have to be cautious with her.

"Sometimes," I said.

"What do you mean?"

"I mean sometimes women are my friends but sometimes they won't leave me alone. You know what I mean?"

"Like mommy when she calls you?"

"Yeah, like that." But you're my friend, I wanted to say, but perhaps that wasn't true either. An infiltrator.

The old lady was sitting in a lawn chair when I pulled in the lane. Waiting. She got up slowly as though unwilling to admit we had arrived.

"I thought you'd be coming up on your own," she said when we got out.

"Thought I'd surprise you," I said. "You remember Bernice."

"I should say, my only grandchild. And how you've grown."

She didn't touch the kid. Standard policy. She hadn't seen her for over two years, since the separation, and she still didn't even put a hand out. Some families grow like trees, each separate but the branches touching from one to another and intertwining. Our family was like a series of telephone poles strung along a highway without even the wires to link us up. We were not a close family. I mean that as a kind of joke.

"What a lovely outfit," my mother said. "I'll bet your father got you that."

"My mother."

"Oh, wasn't that nice? And yellow too. You look so nice in yellow."

"Thank you," the kid said. I could tell it was killing her, this crap, and I was glad. All she had to do was one of those curtseys and the old lady would have been all over her, but the kid held back. No fancy dog tricks to get a bone and a pat on the head.

"Could you run along and play, Bernice? I want to talk to your daddy for a minute."

The kid fluttered around and took off into the trees behind the cottage; her yellow skirt like a wind-borne kite.

"What was the idea of bringing her up?"

"It was just an idea. You don't like it we can leave."

"You don't think I've got enough to worry about with him in that condition? And what's he going to think? He hasn't even met the girl."

"That's not my fault," I said. "And he can think what he wants. I figured it was time he met her. Where is he anyway?"

"Down at the dock," she said, and began to smile her secret scorn.

"What's he doing down there?"

The dirty pool look was there now. She was out to get him. She would have her revenge before she bought the statue. Her rule.

"When I told him you were coming, he decided you'd like to go fishing. He's down at the dock now getting the boat ready."

"That sounds like a hell of an idea. I haven't been fishing for years. We can take the kid too. She's never been."

"Crazy foolishness, in his condition." She was disappointed. She wanted me to join her in lashing out at the crazy old bastard. She was right, he probably wasn't in any condition to fish, but maybe he was looking for revenge too. It was hard to say and I wondered where I'd fit in, if I did, and the kid too.

"He even took a case of beer down too," she said, as if this were some final proof of his unbalanced state.

"I'll go down and see him," I said. "Has he got the rods and stuff with him?"

"Everything. It's all gone down. He carried it all. If he'd've died on the path it's me that would've had to drag him back. He doesn't care. It's just too bad."

"Stop it, will you? Just leave the guy alone. We'll be back later."

She muttered something at my back that I didn't hear, but I'd heard it all before.

I found the kid sitting on a stump along the path to the lake. She faced the trail as though she'd been waiting. Sure I'd come. That felt nice for some reason.

"Is he really my grandfather?" she asked.

"Sure. My father, your grandfather."

She took my hand and hers was warm and wet and I moulded its gentle roughness like an autumn apple. She knew the gestures that lead me to standing still. For statue making. To become a hero. But it was only for today, I thought. I could afford it for one day at least.

"Mommy's father is dead," she said. "He was my grandfather too."

"I know."

"How come your father never came to see us. Mommy's did sometimes."

"He's pretty busy," I said. "I hardly ever see him myself."

"Like you," she said. "Always busy too."

"Not like that. I mean . . ." I couldn't assemble the words to build the picture the way it really was. Maybe someday.

"He's been sick a lot," I said.

"Oh." It was a wounded sound. A moan. Orpheus looking back and regretting it in his throat.

We passed out of the trees and could see the water now. The sight, sheared from our full view by more trees, left the shape of an orchestra pit. It shone in the sun like a bluefuzz blanket. And the old man was there in front of us loading something in the boat.

"That's him," I said.

"I see. He's smaller than you."

She was right. I had always thought of him as being bigger, but he was tiny and shrivelled in an old-dog kind of way. I hadn't seen him in over two years and it was like I had forgotten what he looked like.

"This is a surprise," he said. "Who've we got here?"

"This is my daughter Bernice. This is my father, Bernice, your grandfather."

"Well," he said, and took her hand smoothly. They walked away, he holding her hand and talking. "I was just gettin' the boat ready to do a bit of fishin'. You ever been fishin'?"

She shook her head. The long brown strands of hair reflecting gold in the sharply focussed sun. Her mother's hair. It had reflected like that two summers ago in this very spot. Nothing changes.

"It okay to bring her along Jake?"

His tone was polite but we all knew the question had been settled. He was already helping her into the boat.

"Sure," I said. "You got an extra rod?"

"She can use mine."

He'd done it again. I stood there feeling awkward, the way I had so often in the past. Like I was a kid again and didn't know what to do with my hands or feet, or the words in my mouth.

"You comin' Jake?" He was behind the motor tugging at the cord, as thin as the cord himself and looking frail in a tough way with an old raggedy wine-coloured sweater dropping from his shoulders. So often in the past when he had offered things in that tone I'd refused. Now I jumped into the boat before he left without me.

He had the kid sitting across from him helping steer the boat as it plowed through the water making miniature rainbows in the spray. He was talking to her but I couldn't make out the words above the sound of the engine.

Once he had taken me to a baseball game at Maple Leaf Stadium. In the eighth inning I had to go to the bathroom, and he didn't want to miss any of the game so he let me go by myself. I was seven or eight. I got lost and he didn't find me until an hour after the place was cleared out. He wasn't angry. Disappointed maybe. And I was ashamed. Always when I was around him I did things to make me ashamed.

The motor slowed, gurgled, stopped. He dropped the paint can full of stones he used for an anchor.

"Is this the place where you catch the fish?" the kid asked. She was excited now, on the brink of some new discovery. Animated face like her mother.

"This is it," he said, "but don't forget what I said, fish can hear, so you've gotta be real quiet."

She put her hand to her mouth and ssshed.

"Right," he said.

So easy for her to get his approval. Was it easier now than it had been for me? He baited the hook for her as she watched intently. He plunked the line in the water and looked up to see me watching him.

"I was just remembering the first time you showed me how to put a worm on a hook," I said. "You remember?"

He laughed drowsily and coughed quietly. He was a quiet man, I thought. A quiet, polite man. He was sitting four feet away dying the same way he had lived.

"You were worse than a girl," he said.

"Yeah," and I tried to smile politely too, but I had always resented that about him; his attitude to my . . . what did the old lady call it? My frailness.

"Sssh daddy, the fish'll hear," Bernice cautioned, her face serious.

The old man smiled. He had a way. Maybe I was jealous. I was a
sickly kid, lousy at sports, anything physical, but he had a way of
making it harder for me. Just stand there politely smiling at my attempts. He never laughed. Just that damn polite smile. And sometimes,
now that I remembered, not even that. He wasn't always around when
I tried my stunts; the day I finally made the hockey team and actually
scored a goal. The second-place medal for swimming. He was busy
playing golf, a game he was so good at different people encouraged
him to turn pro. That made me proud when I heard that. I had day-
dreams of caddying for him in the big tournaments, but he just smiled
his polite smile and said no.

I watched him put together a cigarette. He rolled his own and his
hands moved quickly like a woman knitting.

"Nothin' bitin'," he said.

"No, not today by the look of it. Could be too hot. Maybe we should
go in. The kid's got no hat, she might get sun-stroke."

"I'm okay daddy. This is fun."

She kept standing up when she thought she had a bite. It made me
nervous but the old man was right beside her. She was okay. Just my
nerves.

"A beer?" he said.

"Yeah. Okay." He handed me a bottle and it was warm in the clammy
way of a fish. I drank it quickly. I like beer, it reminds me of my
mother: from hand to mouth, that's the way she describes the way I
live, from hand to mouth. The beer being lifted, sucked at, the liquid
measuring out my life. Like Hemingway, I thought with a sudden
fright. From hand to mouth; his hand taking the gun to his mouth
because he had nothing left to say and no reason to go on living. His
statue moulded and waiting for his death.

My trouble is I want to be remembered so much and yet I spend my
time trying to forget. That's what my life is about these days; trying
to forget. My wife. The kid. Mother. Everyone including the old man,
and I never wanted to be spending this weekend with him in a boat
supposedly fishing. I've dreaded the thought of such a weekend all my
life.

"Surprised you're up this way," he said.

"Mom invited me."

"Probably told you about the business," he said.

So like him; business, his death.

"Yeah, she mentioned you weren't well."

"She gets excited."

Not like you with your polite smile.

"Daddy, you guys are gonna scare all the fish."

The old man puffed on his cigarette and grinned, his mouth unsealing like a steamed envelope. What was behind the flap? What songs had found their way out, or had any? Had the old man ever made music somewhere with someone? I'd have liked to have known. Somehow I felt it would make me feel better if he had. More hopeful. Something.

And suddenly the kid was standing, jerking forward like a Buddhist monk in prayer falling to his knees.

"There's something . . ." she yelled and splashed into the water.

It was a short distance to fall from her position at the back of the boat and I watched the bright yellow dress congeal into a dish rag. It was all so strange: once I had fallen off the end of the dock when I was five. I may even have done it on purpose and I kept my eyes open in the water as I sank and I saw the eerie arm of my father reach down and grab me. He used a fish gaff to hook me. I still have the scars on my shoulder. The proof. Of something.

The old man was right beside her. All he had to do was reach over the side and pull her in. It would be easy for him.

He yelled at me. Something was wrong. He never yelled. A quiet polite man.

"Get her Jake! Move, you stupid bugger!"

Me.

I plunged in. The water turned my clothes into a smothering blanket. It was cold. I couldn't see her. I had to go up. I couldn't breathe. I didn't want to drown. I didn't want to die. I really didn't.

Oh God! Everything was ending. God. God. God. Damn. And then I saw her. She was upside down, her dress over her head. She seemed to be spinning slowly and I grabbed a leg. I pawed upward with my hand, not knowing any longer that there was anything beyond. The surface was a spot in my mind that had receded to a soft blur. Like a memory of a long-ago pain.

But it was there waiting. I punched into the air, my arm clawing for something to hold but the boat was several yards away. I saw the old man still seated. He spotted me and leaned forward, yelling something and I was under again. I fought to turn the girl around. She was like a shot deer. Stiff feeling. Her head was up and I cupped her under the chin and swam back to the boat just the way I'd been taught in the Red Cross life-saving course. The old man hadn't been around when I got that certificate either.

He was waiting and held her arms while I crawled in the boat. Everything was clear now. Pull her aboard, put her on the bottom of the boat with his sweater under her head. Check her mouth for obstructions. Head to one side. Arms in position. Pushing down gently. Pulling back. Counting. And repeating the whole thing over and over again.

The old man watched. He rolled a cigarette and coughed politely several times. He didn't smile and I saw he was sweating.

She began to cough. And then she was sick. That was good. It was okay. She began to cry. And then louder, screaming. Shock. The old man handed me his sweater and I wrapped her in it. Soon it was reduced to a sob.

"Daddy, the fish tried to take me away."

"It's okay baby. Everything's okay. I've got you now."

And as suddenly as the tears had come, she fell asleep in my arms.

We sat there for a few minutes and then the old man spoke.

"I'm sorry Jake. I just didn't have the strength. She was right there but I didn't have the strength to get her. She could've drowned."

"She didn't," I said. "That's the main thing. Everything's all right now."

"We'd better go back," he said.

He turned and started the motor. The girl slept huddled against me, and I thought of the phone in my room, the receiver in its cradle. And I thought of all the nights when I had almost called so many people like the girl I was holding. After today I would have to begin to make some of those calls or have the phone removed. I wasn't sure why, but something had changed and I'd have to face it.

At the dock he helped me lift her out of the boat.

"Careful," I said.

"I'm fine now," he said. "Just sometimes my strength goes all out of me."

"You shouldn't've gone to all this trouble with the boat," I said.

He smiled. Polite again. We began walking back to the cottage, the girl asleep still in my arms.

"See Jake," he said, when he reached the trees, "I'm a selfish man."
"We all are," I said.

"Yeah, but with me it was different in some way. Sometimes I feel like
I missed something. I always figured the most important thing to a
man was his privacy. A man's got to have his privacy. I always lived
that way Jake."

It may have been an explanation or even an apology but whatever it
was, it was enough. He'd had his polite smile all his life and I had my
telephone. You could hide behind either one or use it to reach out. I
could learn a lot from the old man. If only he'd tell me. Maybe, though
I had to ask. And maybe privacy was another way of saying lonely.

The old lady was waiting for us on the path. He walked straight
toward her voice. I felt the pinch of her words and fell behind. The man
walked straight ahead and didn't look back.

*A relative newcomer to the Canadian short story scene, Don Bailey is a fine
young writer who will undoubtedly be heard from many times in the future.
His story, ' A Few Notes for Orpheus', appeared as one of the best stories of
1971. We chose this story, not because it was recent, but simply because we
thought it was one of the finest stories we had read. Bailey is a native of
Toronto.*

Paper dolls!
Theodore,
King of Upalia
Zikla,
Duke of Anders
The evil Emperor Kang
The fearless Duke Lani
All the battles
All the armies
All—paper dolls!

# the fall of a city

Alden Nowlan

Outside, rain fell with such violence that great, pulsating sheets of water seemed to hang suspended between earth and sky. Squatting in the attic, Teddy watched raindrops roll like beads of quicksilver down the glass of the high, diamond-shaped window, and listened to the muted banjo twanging on the roof.

Blinking, he shifted his position and transferred his attention to the things that lay around him on the floor. In the centre of the room stood a fort and a palace, painstakingly constructed from corrugated cardboard cartons. These were surrounded by humbler dwellings made from matchboxes and the covers of exercise books. The streets and alleys were full of nobles, peasants and soldiers, their two-dimensional bodies scissored from paper, their faces and clothing drawn in crayon and lead pencil. From the turreted roof of the palace, hung a green, white and gold tricolour, the flag of the Kingdom of Upalia . . .

Sombre gray eyes glinted in Teddy's pale, triangular face. He shoved his hands deeper in the pockets of his worn khaki shorts. He decided that what he heard was not the rattle of rain on the roof and window, but the muffled roar of distant cannon. The armies of the Emperor Kang of Danova were attacking the fortifications on the Upalian frontier!

Teddy inhaled deeply and held his breath, his thin chest pressing against his sweat shirt. His Majesty King Theodore I, resplendent in the red and black uniform of a generalissimo, emerged on the balcony of his winter palace in Theodoresburg, capital of the Kingdom of Upalia. Through the square below rode squadrons of lancers, dragoons and hussars, batteries of horse artillery; behind them marched regiments of infantry. Grasping the diamond-studded hilt of his sword, King Theodore watched his army march out to give battle to the enemy.

This would be the third war between Danova and Upalia. The first had been fought in the year 2032 and had ended in the defeat of the Emperor Kang and his imprisonment on the Isle of Hawks. But he had escaped through the treachery of Zikla, Duke of Anders, a general in the Upalian army, and in 2043 the Danovans had invaded Upalia a second time, aided by a renegade force under the command of Zikla. This time, they conquered Theodoresburg and massacred the populace before being routed by King Theodore. On the day of victory, the Duke of Anders was brought to Theodoresburg in chains and hanged in the city square.

The Emperor Kang was as evil and cunning as the Fu Manchu about whom Teddy had read in books. Now, astride a black war-horse, he directed his troops as they besieged Fort Lion on the Carian River. Hopelessly outnumbered, the defenders rallied behind their commander, Duke Lani of Caria, and prayed for the coming of King Theodore . . .

"Teddy!"

He sighed. This was his aunt, shouting from the foot of the stairs. "Teddy!"

He opened the door. "Yeah?" he called sulkily.

"Come down here this minute and get ready for supper! How many times do I have to call you?"

"Okay, okay, I'm comin'!"

"—And be quick about it!"

"I'm comin', I told yuh!"

His sneakers whacked the carpeted stairs.

She stood in the hall, a tall, stooped woman with tired, suspicious eyes.

"Seems to me that you're spending a lot of time in that attic." She wiped red, swollen hands on her apron. "You been into some mischief up there?"

He shrugged impatiently. "I ain't been doin' nothin'—just playin'," he told her sullenly.

"Well, young man, you better wipe that scowl off your face and march to the bathroom and get ready for supper."

"Yes, ma'am," he enunciated carefully.

During supper, he was scarcely aware of what he ate; he was so deep in thought that his pork chop tasted no different from his whipped cream and jello. Mechanically, he obeyed his aunt when she told him to take smaller bites and to take his elbows off the table. He was pondering on the tactics that would have to be used by King Theodore in relieving the siege of the fort by the river.

If the Upalian army crossed the Tabelian marshes, they might succeed in encircling the Danovans, but there was the risk that their cannon would founder in the morass. On the other hand, if they scaled the Theodoran mountains . . .

"Look what you're doing, for heaven's sake!"

"Huh?"

His aunt glared at him. "Don't say 'huh' when you answer me. Look what you've done! You've spilled cream all over yourself."

Blushing, he rubbed at his sweat shirt with a paper napkin.

"He's got his head in the clouds again." His uncle laughed mirthlessly. "Half the time, he doesn't know whether he's living on earth or on Mars." Out of the corner of his eye, Teddy looked at his uncle's round, florid face and reflected on his resemblance to Zikla, Duke of Anders.

"Well, he'd better smarten up if he knows what's good for him," his aunt grated.

"If he doesn't, I know something that *will* smarten him," his uncle said. He laughed again and reached for another helping of potatoes. Behind him, cloudy white marbles of rain slid down the window.

Suddenly, a cold shiver ran down Teddy's spine. What if the Danovans attacked Theodoresburg while the king and his army were in the mountains? Old Kang was as cunning as a serpent. If . . .

"He spent most of the afternoon in the attic," his aunt said.

His uncle gave him a disdainful look. "He just about lives up there, doesn't he?"

"Yes. I think it's about time that one of us went up there and found out what he's been doing."

"No!" Teddy cried sharply.

His uncle laid down his knife and fork. "Look here, mister, I don't like your tone of voice. Have you been up to some of your monkey-shines up there?"

Teddy stared at his plate. "No," he said.

"Look at me when I speak to you. Have you been playing with matches up there?"

Teddy looked up. "No," he repeated. "I ain't been doin' nothin'."

"You better not be, not if you want to be able to sit down the rest of the week." The man resumed eating. "After supper, I'll take a look and see just what you *have* been doing," he said.

As his aunt gathered up the dishes, his uncle went into the living room and sat down in his easy chair to read his newspaper. Teddy sat by the window and looked out at the rain. The sodden grass of the lawn had turned a darker green and foaming rivers of rainwater ran down the street. He shut his eyes. Here in the kitchen, he could not hear the strumming of the rain on the roof. There was no rumble of Danovan cannon. He frowned and rested his chin in an upturned palm. Anyhow, the cannon were only playthings: scraps of cardboard held together with cellophane tape. What did it matter if his uncle saw them, or even, destroyed them? But it did matter. Theodoresburg had been growing for a year and, often, it seemed more real than the town, the street and the home in which he lived with his uncle and aunt.

"You'd better get at your homework. You won't get it done by sitting there mooning out the window," his aunt told him.

"Yeah." He fetched exercise books and spread them on the table. His aunt and uncle did not mean to be cruel, he knew. From time to time, by their acts and words, they showed that they were fond of him. Twice that summer, his uncle had taken him trout fishing and on both occasions there had been something subtly warm between them. And sometimes he detected a hint of affection in his aunt's voice even as she nagged him. But . . .

His uncle stood in the doorway between kitchen and living room, his shoulders shaking with laughter.

"You'd never guess what that kid has been doing up there!" He shook his head in wonder and amusement.

Teddy flushed and stiffened. His aunt turned from the sink where she was drying the last of the supper dishes.

"What's he been up to, now?"

"You'd never believe it, but that great big lummox has been playing with paper dolls!"

"Paper dolls!" his aunt laughed dubiously.

"They ain't paper dolls," Teddy mumbled. He pushed his chair back from the table and stood up.

"They looked pretty much like paper dolls to me. Paper dolls and doll houses. An eleven-year-old boy!" The man choked, trying to restrain his laughter. "The next thing we know, you'll be wanting us to put skirts on you!"

"I never heard of such a thing. Paper dolls!"

"They ain't dolls, I told you!" Teddy's fists were clenched, his arms stiff by his sides, his voice shaking.

His uncle pointed a warning finger. "Don't get saucy now, mister. I know paper dolls when I see 'em." Once again he burst into laughter. His cheeks were the colour of a tomato.

"Sit down and finish your homework, Teddy," his aunt said. To his surprise, her voice was not harsh: it contained a suggestion of weary sympathy. He resumed his seat and tried to focus on the blue lines in his exercise book. His uncle, still chuckling, returned to the living room and picked up his newspaper.

Paper dolls! His uncle had said that he should be dressed in skirts and hair ribbons. And he could never explain; they would never let him explain. Theodore, King of Upalia, and all his armies—paper dolls! He slumped, doodling on the paper before him so that his aunt would think he was working. Yes, they *were* paper dolls. There was no King Theodore, no Emperor Kang, no Theodoresburg, no Upalia, no Danova. There was only an attic full of preposterous cardboard buildings and ridiculous paper people.

It was still daylight when he finished his homework. The rain had stopped, but water still poured from the elms along the street. When Teddy went through the living room, his uncle did not speak, but he glanced up from his newspaper and grinned slyly. The boy was blushing to the roots of his hair as he opened the hall door and started up the stairs.

The city was as he had left it. Yet everything had changed. Always before when he had come here, his flesh had tingled, his eyes had shone with excitement. Now there was only a taste like that of a spoilt nutmeat.

He bent and seized the cardboard palace. Gritting his teeth and grunting, he tore at its walls. The corrugated board was sturdy: he was crying by the time he finished tearing it to shreds.


*Alden Nowlan is probably best known to most Canadians as the New Bruns-wick poet who has published many fine volumes of poetry. However, Now-lan's stories also exhibit the poet's sensitivity to human feelings and concerns. Nowlan submitted 'The Fall of a City' to us; it appeared in* THE ATLANTIC ADVOCATE (*Sept. 1962*). *A collection of Alden Nowlan's stories,* MIRACLE AT INDIAN RIVER, *was published in 1968. Nowlan lives in Fredericton.*

'He shouldn't have gone', she whispered silently. 'He saw the double wheel—he knew. He shouldn't have left me here alone.'

# the painted door

Sinclair Ross

Take a terrifying prairie blizzard,
   a lonely farm wife,
   an absent husband,
   a handsome young neighbour,
   and one snow-swirled farm house . . .
Bring these elements together
   under the touch
   of a sensitive writer . . .

and you have a Canadian short story masterpiece.

Straight across the hills it was five miles from John's farm to his father's. But in winter, with the roads impassable, a team had to make a wide detour and skirt the hills, so that from five the distance was more than trebled to seventeen.

'I think I'll walk,' John said at breakfast to his wife. 'The drifts in the hills wouldn't hold a horse, but they'll carry me all right. If I leave early I can spend a few hours helping him with his chores, and still be back by suppertime.'

Moodily she went to the window, and thawing a clear place in the frost with her breath, stood looking across the snowswept farmyard to the huddle of stables and sheds. 'There was a double wheel around the moon last night,' she countered presently. 'You said yourself we could expect a storm. It isn't right to leave me here alone. Surely I'm as important as your father.'

He glanced up uneasily, then drinking off his coffee tried to reassure her. 'But there's nothing to be afraid of—even if it does start to storm. You won't need to go near the stable. Everything's fed and watered now to last till night. I'll be back at the latest by seven or eight.'

She went on blowing against the frosted pane, carefully elongating

the clear place until it was oval-shaped and symmetrical. He watched
her a moment or two longer, then more insistently repeated, 'I say you
won't need to go near the stable. Everything's fed and watered, and I'll
see that there's plenty of wood in. That will be all right, won't it?'

'Yes—of course—I heard you—' It was a curiously cold voice now,
as if the words were chilled by their contact with the frosted pane.
'Plenty to eat—plenty of wood to keep me warm—what more could a
woman ask for?'

'But he's an old man—living there all alone. What is it, Ann? You're
not like yourself this morning.'

She shook her head without turning. 'Pay no attention to me. Seven
years a farmer's wife—it's time I was used to staying alone.'

Slowly the clear place on the glass enlarged: oval, then round, then
oval again. The sun was risen above the frost mists now, so keen and
hard a glitter on the snow that instead of warmth its rays seemed shed-
ding cold. One of the two-year-old colts that had cantered away when
John turned the horses out for water stood covered with rime at the
stable door again, head down and body hunched, each breath a little
plume of steam against the frosty air. She shivered, but did not turn. In
the clear, bitter light the long white miles of prairie landscape seemed
a region strangely alien to life. Even the distant farmsteads she could
see served only to intensify a sense of isolation. Scattered across the
face of so vast and bleak a wilderness it was difficult to conceive them
as a testimony of human hardihood and endurance. Rather they
seemed futile, lost. Rather they seemed to cower before the implacability of snow-swept earth and clear pale sun-chilled sky.

And when at last she turned from the window there was a brooding
stillness in her face as if she had recognized this mastery of snow and
cold. It troubled John. 'If you're really afraid,' he yielded, 'I won't go
today. Lately it's been so cold, that's all. I just wanted to make sure
he's all right in case we do have a storm.'

'I know—I'm not really afraid.' She was putting in a fire now, and he
could no longer see her face. 'Pay no attention to me. It's ten miles
there and back, so you'd better get started.'

'You ought to know by now I wouldn't stay away,' he tried to
brighten her. 'No matter how it stormed. Twice a week before we were
married I never missed—and there were bad blizzards that winter too.'

He was a slow, unambitious man, content with his farm and cattle,

naively proud of Ann. He had been bewildered by it once, her caring
for a dull-witted fellow like him: then assured at last of her affection he
had relaxed against it gratefully, unsuspecting it might ever be less
constant than his own. Even now, listening to the restless brooding in
her voice, he felt only a quick, unformulated kind of pride that after
seven years his absence for a day should still concern her. While she,
his trust and earnestness controlling her again:

'I know. It's just that sometimes when you're away I get lonely . . .
There's a long cold tramp in front of you. You'll let me fix a scarf
around your face.'

He nodded. 'And on my way I'll drop in at Steven's place. Maybe
he'll come over tonight for a game of cards. You haven't seen anybody
but me for the last two weeks.'

She glanced up sharply, then busied herself clearing the table. 'It will
mean another two miles if you do. You're going to be cold and tired
enough as it is. When you're gone I think I'll paint the kitchen wood-
work. White this time—you remember we got the paint last fall. It's
going to make the room a lot lighter. I'll be too busy to find the day
long.'

'I will though,' he insisted, 'and if a storm gets up you'll feel safer,
knowing that he's coming. That's what you need, Ann—someone to
talk to besides me.'

She stood at the stove motionless a moment, then turned to him
uneasily. 'Will you shave then, John—now—before you go?'

He glanced at her questioningly, and avoiding his eyes she tried to
explain, 'I mean—he may be here before you're back—and you won't
have a chance then.'

'But it's only Steven—he's seen me like this—'

'He'll be shaved, though—that's what I mean—and I'd like you too
to spend a little time on yourself.'

He stood up, stroking the heavy stubble on his chin. 'Maybe I
should all right, but it makes the skin too tender. Especially when I've
got to face the wind.'

She nodded and began to help him dress, bringing heavy socks and
a big woollen sweater from the bedroom, wrapping a scarf around his
face and forehead. 'I'll tell Steven to come early,' he said, as he went
out. 'In time for supper. Likely there'll be chores for me to do, so if I'm
not back by six don't wait.'

From the bedroom window she watched him nearly a mile along the road. The fire had gone down when at last she turned away, and already through the house there was an encroaching chill. A blaze sprang up again when the drafts were opened, but as she went on clearing the table her movements were furtive and constrained. It was the silence weighing upon her—the frozen silence of the bitter fields, and sun-chilled sky —lurking outside as if alive, relentlessly in wait, mile-deep between her now and John. She listened to it, suddenly tense, motionless. The fire crackled and the clock ticked. Always it was there. 'I'm a fool,' she whispered hoarsely, rattling the dishes in defiance, going back to the stove to put in another fire. 'Warm and safe—I'm a fool. It's a good chance when he's away to paint. The day will go quickly. I won't have time to brood.'

Since November now the paint had been waiting warmer weather. The frost in the walls on a day like this would crack and peel it as it dried, but she needed something to keep her hands occupied, some- thing to stave off the gathering cold and loneliness. 'First of all,' she said aloud, opening the paint and mixing it with a little turpentine, 'I must get the house warmer. Fill up the stove and open the oven door so that all the heat comes out. Wad something along the window sills to keep out the drafts. Then I'll feel brighter. It's the cold that depresses.'

She moved briskly, performing each little task with careful and exag- gerated absorption, binding her thoughts to it, making it a screen between herself and the surrounding snow and silence. But when the stove was filled and the windows sealed it was more difficult again. Above the quiet, steady swishing of her brush against the bedroom door the clock began to tick. Suddenly her movements became precise, deliberate, her posture self-conscious, as if someone had entered the room and were watching her. It was the silence again, aggresive, hover- ing. The fire spit and crackled at it. Still it was there. 'I'm a fool,' she repeated. 'All farmers' wives have to stay alone. I mustn't give in this way. I mustn't brood. A few hours now and they'll be here.'

The sound of her voice reassured her. She went on: 'I'll get them a good supper—and for coffee tonight after cards bake some of the little cakes with raisins that he likes . . . Just three of us, so I'll watch, and let John play. It's better with four, but at least we can talk. That's all I need—someone to talk to. John never talks. He's stronger—he doesn't understand. But he likes Steven—no matter what the neighbours say.

Maybe he'll have him come again, and some other young people too.
It's what we need, both of us, to help keep young ourselves . . . And
then before we know it we'll be into March. It's cold still in March
sometimes, but you never mind the same. At least you're beginning to
think about spring.'

She began to think about it now. Thoughts that outstripped her
words, that left her alone again with herself and the ever-lurking silence.
Eager and hopeful first; then clenched, rebellious, lonely. Windows
open, sun and thawing earth again, the urge of growing, living things.
Then the days that began in the morning at half-past four and lasted till
ten at night; the meals at which John gulped his food and scarcely
spoke a word; the brute-tired stupid eyes he turned on her if ever she
mentioned town or visiting.

For spring was drudgery again. John never hired a man to help him.
He wanted a mortgage-free farm; then a new house and pretty clothes
for her. Sometimes, because with the best of crops it was going to take
so long to pay off anyway, she wondered whether they mightn't better
let the mortgage wait a little. Before they were worn out, before their
best years were gone. It was something of life she wanted, not just a
house and furniture; something of John, not pretty clothes when she
would be too old to wear them. But John of course couldn't understand. To him it seemed only right that she should have the clothes—
only right that he, fit for nothing else, should slave away fifteen hours a
day to give them to her. There was in his devotion a baffling, insur-
mountable humility that made him feel the need of sacrifice. And when
his muscles ached, when his feet dragged stolidly with weariness, then
it seemed that in some measure at least he was making amends for his
big hulking body and simple mind. That by his sacrifice he succeeded
only in the extinction of his personality never occurred to him. Year
after year their lives went on in the same little groove. He drove his
horses in the field; she milked the cows and hoed potatoes. By dint of
his drudgery he saved a few months' wages, added a few dollars more
each fall to his payments on the mortgage; but the only real difference
that it all made was to deprive her of his companionship, to make him
a little duller, older, uglier than he might otherwise have been. He never
saw their lives objectively. To him it was not what he actually accomplished by means of the sacrifice that mattered, but the sacrifice itself,
the gesture—something done for her sake.

And she, understanding, kept her silence. In such a gesture, however futile, there was a graciousness not to be shattered lightly. 'John,'
she would begin sometimes, 'you're doing too much. Get a man to
help you—just for a month—' but smiling down at her he would
answer simply, 'I don't mind. Look at the hands on me. They're made
for work.' While in his voice there would be a stalwart ring to tell her
that by her thoughtfulness she had made him only the more resolved to
serve her, to prove his devotion and fidelity.

They were useless, such thoughts. She knew. It was his very devotion that made them useless, that forbade her to rebel. Yet over and
over, sometimes hunched still before their bleakness, sometimes her
brush making swift sharp strokes to pace the chafe and rancour that
they brought, she persisted in them.

This now, the winter, was their slack season. She could sleep sometimes till eight, and John till seven. They could linger over their meals
a little, read, play cards, go visiting the neighbours. It was the time to
relax, to indulge and enjoy themselves; but instead, fretful and impatient, they kept on waiting for the spring. They were compelled now,
not by labour, but by the spirit of labour. A spirit that pervaded their
lives and brought with idleness a sense of guilt. Sometimes they did
sleep late, sometimes they did play cards, but always uneasily, always
reproached by the thought of more important things that might be
done. When John got up at five to attend to the fire he wanted to stay
up and go out to the stable. When he sat down to a meal he hurried his
food and pushed his chair away again, from habit, from sheer work-
instinct, even though it was only to put more wood in the stove, or go
down cellar to cut up beets and turnips for the cows.

And anyway, sometimes she asked herself, why sit trying to talk with
a man who never talked? Why talk when there was nothing to talk
about but crops and cattle, the weather and the neighbours? The
neighbours, too—why go visiting them when still it was the same—
crops and cattle, the weather and the other neighbours? Why go to the
dances in the schoolhouse to sit among the older women, one of them
now, married seven years, or to waltz with the work-bent, tired old
farmers to a squeaky fiddle-tune? Once she had danced with Steven six
or seven times in the evening, and they had talked about it for as many
months. It was easier to stay at home. John never danced or enjoyed
himself. He was always uncomfortable in his good suit and shoes. He

didn't like shaving in the cold weather oftener than once or twice a week. It was easier to stay at home, to stand at the window staring out across the bitter fields, to count the days and look forward to another spring.

But now, alone with herself in the winter silence, she saw the spring for what it really was. This spring—next spring—all the springs and summers still to come. While they grew old, while their bodies warped, while their minds kept shrivelling dry and empty like their lives. 'I mustn't,' she said aloud again. 'I married him—and he's a good man. I mustn't keep on this way. It will be noon before long, and then time to think about supper . . . . Maybe he'll come early—and as soon as John is finished at the stable we can all play cards.'

It was getting cold again, and she left her painting to put in more wood. But this time the warmth spread slowly. She pushed a mat up to the outside door, and went back to the window to pat down the woollen shirt that was wadded along the sill. Then she paced a few times round the room, then poked the fire and rattled the stove lids, then paced again. The fire crackled, the clock ticked. The silence now seemed more intense than ever, seemed to have reached a pitch where it faintly moaned. She began to pace on tiptoe, listening, her shoulders drawn together, not realizing for a while that it was the wind she heard, thin-strained and whimpering through the eaves.

Then she wheeled to the window, and with quick short breaths thawed the frost to see again. The glitter was gone. Across the drifts sped swift and snakelike little tongues of snow. She could not follow them, where they sprang from, or where they disappeared. It was as if all across the yard the snow were shivering awake—roused by the warnings of the wind to hold itself in readiness for the impending storm. The sky had become a sombre, whitish grey. It too, as if in readiness, had shifted and lay close to earth. Before her as she watched a mane of powdery snow reared up breast-high against the darker background of the stable, tossed for a moment angrily, and then subsided again as if whipped down to obedience and restraint. But another followed, more reckless and impatient than the first. Another reeled and dashed itself against the window where she watched. Then ominously for a while there were only the angry little snakes of snow. The wind rose, creaking the troughs that were wired beneath the eaves. In the distance, sky and prairie now were merged into one another linelessly.

All round her it was gathering; already in its press and whimpering there strummed a boding of eventual fury. Again she saw a mane of snow spring up, so dense and high this time that all the sheds and stables were obscured. Then others followed, whirling fiercely out of hand; and, when at last they cleared, the stables seemed in dimmer outline than before. It was the snow beginning, long lancet shafts of it, straight from the north, borne almost level by the straining wind. 'He'll be there soon,' she whispered, 'and coming home it will be in his back. He'll leave again right away. He saw the double wheel—he knows the kind of storm there'll be.'

She went back to her painting. For a while it was easier, all her thoughts half-anxious ones of John in the blizzard, struggling his way across the hills; but petulantly again she soon began, 'I knew we were going to have a storm—I told him so—but it doesn't matter what I say. Big stubborn fool—he goes his own way anyway. It doesn't matter what becomes of me. In a storm like this he'll never get home. He won't even try. And while he sits keeping his father company I can look after his stable for him, go ploughing through snowdrifts up to my knees—nearly frozen—'

Not that she meant or believed her words. It was just an effort to convince herself that she did have a grievance, to justify her rebellious thoughts, to prove John responsible for her unhappiness. She was young still, eager for excitement and distractions; and John's stead-fastness rebuked her vanity, made her complaints seem weak and tri-vial. Fretfully she went on, 'If he'd listen to me sometimes and not be so stubborn we wouldn't be living still in a house like this. Seven years in two rooms—seven years and never a new stick of furniture . . . . There—as if another coat of paint could make it different anyway.'

She cleaned her brush, filled up the stove again, and went back to the window. There was a void white moment that she thought must be frost formed on the window pane; then, like a fitful shadow through the whirling snow, she recognized the stable roof. It was incredible. The sudden, maniac raging of the storm struck from her face all its pettishness. Her eyes glazed with fear a little; her lips blanched. 'If he starts for home now,' she whispered silently—'But he won't—he knows I'm safe—he knows Steven's coming. Across the hills he would never dare.'

She turned to the stove, holding out her hands to the warmth.

Around her now there seemed a constant sway and tremor, as if the air were vibrating with the violent shudderings of the walls. She stood quite still, listening. Sometimes the wind struck with sharp, savage blows. Sometimes it bore down in a sustained, minute-long blast, silent with effort and intensity; then with a foiled shriek of threat wheeled away to gather and assault again. Always the eavetroughs creaked and sawed. She started towards the window again, then detecting the morbid trend of her thoughts, prepared fresh coffee and forced herself to drink a few mouthfuls. 'He would never dare,' she whispered again. 'He wouldn't leave the old man anyway in such a storm. Safe in here—there's nothing for me to keep worrying about. It's after one already. I'll do my baking now, and then it will be time to get supper ready for Steven.'

Soon, however, she began to doubt whether Steven would come. In such a storm even a mile was enough to make a man hesitate. Especially Steven, who, for all his attractive qualities, was hardly the one to face a blizzard for the sake of someone else's chores. He had a stable of his own to look after anyway. It would be only natural for him to think that when the storm rose John had turned again for home. Another man would have—would have put his wife first.

But she felt little dread or uneasiness at the prospect of spending the night alone. It was the first time she had been left like this on her own resources, and her reaction, now that she could face and appraise her situation calmly, was gradually to feel it a kind of adventure and responsibility. It stimulated her. Before nightfall she must go to the stable and feed everything. Wrap up in some of John's clothes—take a ball of string in her hand, one end tied to the door, so that no matter how blinding the storm she could at least find her way back to the house. She had heard of people having to do that. It appealed to her now because suddenly it made life dramatic. She had not felt the storm yet, only watched it for a minute through the window.

It took nearly an hour to find enough string, to choose the right socks and sweaters. Long before it was time to start out she tried on John's clothes, changing and rechanging, striding around the room to make sure there would be play enough for pitching hay and struggling over snowdrifts; then she took them off again, and for a while busied herself baking the little cakes with raisins that he liked.

Night came early. Just for a moment on the doorstep she shrank

back, uncertain. The slow dimming of the light clutched her with an
illogical sense of abandonment. It was like the covert withdrawal of an
ally, leaving the alien miles unleashed and unrestrained. Watching the
hurricane of writhing snow rage past the little house she forced herself,
'They'll never stand the night unless I get them fed. It's nearly dark
already, and I've work to last an hour.'

Timidly, unwinding a little of the string, she crept out from the
shelter of the doorway. A gust of wind spun her forward a few yards,
then plunged her headlong against a drift that in the the dense white
whirl lay invisible across her path. For nearly a minute she huddled still,
breathless and dazed. The snow was in her mouth and nostrils, inside
her scarf and up her sleeves. As she tried to straighten a smothering
scud flung itself against her face, cutting off her breath a second time.
The wind struck from all sides, blustering and furious. It was as if the
storm had discovered her, as if all its forces were concentrated upon her
extinction. Seized with panic suddenly she threshed out a moment with
her arms, then stumbled back and sprawled her length across the drift.

But this time she regained her feet quickly, roused by the whip and
batter of the storm to retaliative anger. For a moment her impulse was
to face the wind and strike back blow for blow; then, as suddenly as it
had come, her frantic strength gave way to limpness and exhaustion.
Suddenly, a comprehension so clear and terrifying that it struck all
thoughts of the stable from her mind, she realized in such a storm her
puny insignificance. And the realization gave her new strength, stilled
this time to a desperate persistence. Just for a moment the wind held
her, numb and swaying in its vise; then slowly, buckled far forward,
she groped her way again towards the house.

Inside, leaning against the door, she stood tense and still a while. It
was almost dark now. The top of the stove glowed a deep, dull red.
Heedless of the storm, self-absorbed and self-satisfied, the clock ticked
on like a glib little idiot. 'He shouldn't have gone,' she whispered
silently. 'He saw the double wheel—he knew. He shouldn't have left
me here alone.'

For so fierce now, so insane and dominant did the blizzard seem, that
she could not credit the safety of the house. The warmth and lull
around her was not real yet, not to be relied upon. She was still at the
mercy of the storm. Only her body pressing hard like this against the
door was staving it off. She didn't dare move. She didn't dare ease the

ache and strain. 'He shouldn't have gone,' she repeated, thinking of
the stable again, reproached by her helplessness. 'They'll freeze in their
stalls—and I can't reach them. He'll say it's all my fault. He won't
believe I tried.'

Then Steven came. Quickly, startled to quietness and control, she
let him in and lit the lamp. He stared at her a moment, then flinging off
his cap crossed to where she stood by the table and seized her arms.
'You're so white—what's wrong? Look at me—' It was like him in
such little situations to be masterful. 'You should have known better
than to go out on a day like this. For a while I thought I wasn't going
to make it here myself—'

'I was afraid you wouldn't come—John left early, and there was the
stable—'

But the storm had unnerved her, and suddenly at the assurance of
his touch and voice the fear that had been gripping her gave way to an
hysteria of relief. Scarcely aware of herself she seized his arm and
sobbed against it. He remained still a moment, unyielding, then slipped
his other arm around her shoulder. It was comforting and she relaxed
against it, hushed by a sudden sense of lull and safety. Her shoulders
trembled with the easing of the strain, then fell limp and still. 'You're
shivering,'—he drew her gently towards the stove. 'There's nothing to
be afraid of now, though. I'm going to do the chores for you.'

It was a quiet, sympathetic voice, yet with an undertone of insolence,
a kind of mockery even, that made her draw away quickly and busy
herself putting in a fire. With his lips drawn in a little smile he watched
her till she looked at him again. The smile too was insolent, but at the
same time companionable; Steven's smile, and therefore difficult to
reprove. It lit up his lean, still-boyish face with a peculiar kind of
arrogance: features and smile that were different from John's, from
other men's—wilful and derisive, yet naively so—as if it were less the
difference itself he was conscious of, than the long-accustomed privi-
lege that thereby fell his due. He was erect, tall, square-shouldered.
His hair was dark and trim, his young lips curved soft and full. While
John, she made the comparison swiftly, was thickset, heavy-jowled,
and stooped. He always stood before her helpless, a kind of humility
and wonderment in his attitude. And Steven now smiled on her apprais-
ingly with the worldly-wise assurance of one for whom a woman holds
neither mystery nor illusion.

'It was good of you to come, Steven,' she responded, the words
running into a sudden, empty laugh. 'Such a storm to face—I suppose
I should feel flattered.'

For his presumption, his misunderstanding of what had been only a
momentary weakness, instead of angering quickened her, roused from
latency and long disuse all the instincts and resources of her femininity.
She felt eager, challenged. Something was at hand that hitherto had
always eluded her, even in the early days with John, something vital,
beckoning, meaningful. She didn't understand, but she knew. The
texture of the moment was satisfyingly dreamlike: an incredibility
perceived as such, yet acquiesced in. She was John's wife—she knew—
but also she knew that Steven standing here was different from John.
There was no thought or motive, no understanding of herself as the
knowledge persisted. Wary and poised round a sudden little core of
blind excitement she evaded him, 'But it's nearly dark—hadn't you
better hurry if you're going to do the chores? Don't trouble—I can get
them off myself—'

An hour later when he returned from the stable she was in another
dress, hair rearranged, a little flush of colour in her face. Pouring warm
water for him from the kettle into the basin she said evenly, 'By the
time you're washed supper will be ready. John said we weren't to wait
for him.'

He looked at her a moment, 'But in a storm like this you're not
expecting John?'

'Of course.' As she spoke she could feel the colour deepening in her
face. 'We're going to play cards. He was the one that suggested it.'

He went on washing, and then as they took their places at the table,
resumed, 'So John's coming. When are you expecting him?'

'He said it might be seven o'clock—or a little later.' Conversation
with Steven at other times had always been brisk and natural, but now
suddenly she found it strained. 'He may have work to do for his father.
That's what he said when he left. Why do you ask, Steven?'

'I was just wondering—it's a rough night.'

'He always comes. There couldn't be a storm bad enough. It's easier
to do the chores in daylight, and I knew he'd be tired—that's why I
started out for the stable.'

She glanced up again and he was smiling at her. The same insolence,
the same little twist of mockery and appraisal. It made her flinch sud-

denly, and ask herself why she was pretending to expect John—why
there should be this instinct of defence to force her. This time, instead
of poise and excitement, it brought a reminder that she had changed her
dress and rearranged her hair. It crushed in a sudden silence, through
which she heard the whistling wind again, and the creaking saw of the
eaves. Neither spoke now. There was something strange, almost
terrifying, about this Steven and his quiet, unrelenting smile; but
strangest of all was the familiarity: the Steven she had never seen or
encountered, and yet had always known, always expected, always
waited for. It was less Steven himself that she felt than his inevitability.
Just as she had felt the snow, the silence and the storm. She kept her
eyes lowered, on the window past his shoulder, on the stove, but his
smile now seemed to exist apart from him, to merge and hover with the
silence. She clinked a cup—listened to the whistle of the storm—
always it was there. He began to speak, but her mind missed the meaning of his words. Swiftly she was making comparisons again; his face
so different to John's, so handsome and young and clean-shaven.
Swiftly, helplessly, feeling the imperceptible and relentless ascendancy
that thereby he was gaining over her, sensing sudden menace in this
new more vital life, even as she felt drawn towards it.

The lamp between them flickered as an onslaught of the storm sent
shudderings through the room. She rose to build up the fire again and
he followed her. For a long time they stood close to the stove, their
arms almost touching. Once as the blizzard creaked the house she spun
around sharply, fancying it was John at the door; but quietly he inter-
cepted her. 'Not tonight—you might as well make up your mind to it.
Across the hills in a storm like this—it would be suicide to try.'

Her lips trembled suddenly in an effort to answer, to parry the
certainty in his voice, then set thin and bloodless. She was afraid now.
Afraid of his face so different from John's—of his smile, of her own
helplessness to rebuke it. Afraid of the storm, isolating her here alone
with him in its impenetrable fastness. They tried to play cards, but she
kept starting up at every creak and shiver of the walls. 'It's too rough a
night,' he repeated. 'Even for John. Just relax a few minutes—stop
worrying and pay a little attention to me.'

But in his tone there was a contradiction to his words. For it implied
that she was not worrying—that her only concern was lest it really
might be John at the door.

And the implication persisted. He filled up the stove for her, shuffled the cards—won—shuffled—still it was there. She tried to respond to his conversation, to think of the game, but helplessly into her cards instead she began to ask, Was he right? Was that why he smiled? Why he seemed to wait, expectant and assured?

The clock ticked, the fire crackled. Always it was there. Furtively for a moment she watched him as he deliberated over his hand. John, even in the days before they were married, had never looked like that. Only this morning she had asked him to shave. Because Steven was coming —because she had been afraid to see them side by side—because deep within herself she had known even then. The same knowledge, furtive and forbidden, that was flaunted now in Steven's smile. 'You look cold,' he said at last, dropping his cards and rising from the table. 'We're not playing, anyway. Come over to the stove for a few minutes and get warm.'

'But first I think we'll hang blankets over the door. When there's a blizzard like this we always do.' It seemed that in sane, commonplace activity there might be release, a moment or two in which to recover herself. 'John has nails in to put them on. They keep out a little of the draft.'

He stood on a chair for her, and hung the blankets that she carried from the bedroom. Then for a moment they stood silent, watching the blankets sway and tremble before the blade of wind that spurted around the jamb. 'I forgot,' she said at last, 'that I painted the bedroom door. At the top there, see—I've smeared the blankets coming through.'

He glanced at her curiously, and went back to the stove. She followed him, trying to imagine the hills in such a storm, wondering whether John would come. 'A man couldn't live in it,' suddenly he answered her thoughts, lowering the oven door and drawing up the chairs one on each side of it. 'He knows you're safe. It isn't likely that he'd leave his father, anyway.'

'The wind will be in his back,' she persisted. 'The winter before we were married—all the blizzards that we had that year—and he never missed—'

'Blizzards like this one? Up in the hills he wouldn't be able to keep his direction for a hundred yards. Listen to it a minute and ask yourself.'

His voice seemed softer, kindlier now. She met his smile a moment, its assured little twist of appraisal, then for a long time sat silent, tense, careful again to avoid his eyes.

Everything now seemed to depend on this. It was the same as a few hours ago when she braced the door against the storm. He was watching her, smiling. She dared not move, unclench her hands, or raise her eyes. The flames crackled, the clock ticked. The storm wrenched the walls as if to make them buckle in. So rigid and desperate were all her muscles set, withstanding, that the room around her seemed to swim and reel. So rigid and strained that for relief at last, despite herself, she raised her head and met his eyes again.

Intending that it should be for only an instant, just to breathe again, to ease the tension that had grown unbearable—but in his smile now, instead of the insolent appraisal that she feared, there seemed a kind of warmth and sympathy. An understanding that quickened and encouraged her—that made her wonder why but a moment ago she had been afraid. It was as if the storm had lulled, as if she had suddenly found calm and shelter.

Or perhaps, the thought seized her, perhaps instead of his smile it was she that had changed. She who, in the long, wind-creaked silence, had emerged from the increment of codes and loyalties to her real, unfettered self. She who now felt suddenly an air of appraisal as nothing more than an understanding of the unfulfilled woman that until this moment had lain within her brooding and unadmitted, reproved out of consciousness by the insistence of an outgrown, routine fidelity.

For there had always been Steven. She understood now. Seven years —almost as long as John—ever since the night they first danced together.

The lamp was burning dry, and through the dimming light, isolated in the fastness of silence and storm, they watched each other. Her face was white and struggling still. His was handsome, clean-shaven, young. Her eyes were fanatic, believing desperately, fixed upon him as if to exclude all else, as if to find justification. His were cool, bland, drooped a little with expectancy. The light kept dimming, gathering the shadows round them, hushed, conspiratorial. He was smiling still. Her hands again were clenched up white and hard.

'But he always came,' she persisted. 'The wildest, coldest nights— even such a night as this. There was never a storm—'

'Never a storm like this one.' There was a quietness in his smile now,

a kind of simplicity almost, as if to reassure her. 'You were out in it
yourself for a few minutes. He would have five miles, across the hills
.... I'd think twice myself, on such a night, before risking even one.'

Long after he was asleep she lay listening to the storm. As a check on
the draft up the chimney they had left one of the stovelids partly off,
and through the open bedroom door she could see the flickerings of
flame and shadow on the kitchen wall. They leaped and sank fan-
tastically. The longer she watched the more alive they seemed to be.
There was one great shadow that struggled towards her threateningly,
massive and black and engulfing all the room. Again and again it
advanced, about to spring, but each time a little whip of light subdued
it to its place among the others on the wall. Yet though it never reached
her still she cowered, feeling that gathered there was all the frozen
wilderness, its heart of terror and invincibility.

Then she dozed a while, and the shadow was John. Interminably he
advanced. The whips of light still flicked and coiled, but now suddenly
they were the swift little snakes that this afternoon she had watched
twist and shiver across the snow. And they too were advancing. They
writhed and vanished and came again. She lay still, paralyzed. He was
over her now, so close that she could have touched him. Already it
seemed that a deadly tightening hand was on her throat. She tried to
scream but her lips were locked. Steven beside her slept on heedlessly.

Until suddenly as she lay staring up at him a gleam of light revealed
his face. And in it was not a trace of threat or anger—only calm, and
stonelike hopelessness.

That was like John. He began to withdraw, and frantically she tried
to call him back. 'It isn't true—not really true—listen, John—' but the
words clung frozen to her lips. Already there was only the shriek of
wind again, the sawing eaves, the leap and twist of shadow on the wall.

She sat up, startled now and awake. And so real had he seemed
there, standing close to her, so vivid the sudden age and sorrow in his
face, that at first she could not make herself understand she had been
only dreaming. Against the conviction of his presence in the room it
was necessary to insist over and over that he must still be with his father
on the other side of the hills. Watching the shadows she had fallen
asleep. It was only her mind, her imagination, distorted to a nightmare
by the illogical and unadmitted dread of his return. But he wouldn't

come. Steven was right. In such a storm he would never try. They were
safe, alone. No one would ever know. It was only fear, morbid and
irrational; only the sense of guilt that even her new-found and challenged womanhood could not entirely quell.

She knew now. She had not let herself understand or acknowledge it
as guilt before, but gradually through the wind-torn silence of the
night his face compelled her. The face that had watched her from the
darkness with its stonelike sorrow—the face that was really John—
John more than his features of mere flesh and bone could ever be.

She wept silently. The fitful gleam of light began to sink. On the
ceiling and wall at last there was only a faint dull flickering glow. The
little house shuddered and quailed, and a chill crept in again. Without
wakening Steven she slipped out to build up the fire. It was burned to
a few spent embers now, and the wood she put on seemed a long time
catching light. The wind swirled through the blankets they had hung
around the door, and struck her flesh like laps of molten ice. Then
hollow and moaning it roared up the chimney again, as if against its
will drawn back to serve still longer with the onrush of the storm.

For a long time she crouched over the stove, listening. Earlier in the
evening, with the lamp lit and the fire crackling, the house had seemed
a stand against the wilderness, against its frozen, blizzard-breathed
implacability, a refuge of feeble walls wherein persisted the elements of
human meaning and survival. Now, in the cold, creaking darkness, it
was strangely extinct, looted by the storm and abandoned again. She
lifted the stove lid and fanned the embers till at last a swift little tongue
of flame began to lick around the wood. Then she replaced the lid,
extended her hands, and as if frozen in that attitude stood waiting.

It was not long now. After a few minutes she closed the drafts, and
as the flames whirled back upon each other, beating against the top of
the stove and sending out flickers of light again, a warmth surged up
to relax her stiffened limbs. But shivering and numb it had been easier.
The bodily well-being that the warmth induced gave play again to an
ever more insistent mental suffering. She remembered the shadow that
was John. She saw him bent towards her, then retreating, his features
pale and overcast with unaccusing grief. She re-lived their seven years
together and, in retrospect, found them to be years of worth and
dignity. Until crushed by it all at last, seized by a sudden need to suffer
and atone, she crossed to where the draft was bitter, and for a long

time stood unflinching on the icy floor.

The storm was close here. Even through the blankets she could feel
a sift of snow against her face. The eaves sawed, the walls creaked.
Above it all, like a wolf in howling flight, the wind shrilled lone and
desolate.

And yet, suddenly she asked herself, hadn't there been other storms,
other blizzards? And through the worst of them hadn't he always
reached her?

Clutched by the thought she stood rooted a minute. It was hard
now to understand how she could have so deceived herself—how a
moment of passion could have quieted within her not only conscience,
but reason and discretion too. John always came. There could never be
a storm to stop him. He was strong, inured to the cold. He had crossed
the hills since his boyhood, knew every creek-bed and gully. It was
madness to go on like this—to wait. While there was still time she
must waken Steven, and hurry him away.

But in the bedroom again, standing at Steven's side, she hesitated.
In his detachment from it all, in his quiet, even breathing, there was
such sanity, such realism. For him nothing had happened; nothing
would. If she wakened him he would only laugh and tell her to listen
to the storm. Already it was long past midnight; either John had lost
his way or not set out at all. And she knew that in his devotion there
was nothing foolhardy. He would never risk a storm beyond his endurance, never permit himself a sacrifice likely to endanger her lot or
future. They were both safe. No one would ever know. She must
control herself—be sane like Steven.

For comfort she let her hand rest a while on Steven's shoulder. It
would be easier were he awake now, with her, sharing her guilt; but
gradually as she watched his handsome face in the glimmering light
she came to understand that for him no guilt existed. Just as there had
been no passion, no conflict. Nothing but the sane appraisal of their
situation, nothing but the expectant little smile, and the arrogance of
features that were different from John's. She winced deeply, remembering how she had fixed her eyes on those features, how she had tried
to believe that so handsome and young, so different from John's, they
must in themselves be her justification.

In the flickering light they were still young, still handsome.
No longer her justification—she knew now—John was the man—but

wistfully still, wondering sharply at their power and tyranny, she touched them a moment with her fingertips again.

She could not blame him. There had been no passion, no guilt; therefore there could be no responsibility. Suddenly looking down at him as he slept, half-smiling still, his lips relaxed in the conscienceless complacency of his achievement, she understood that thus he was revealed in his entirety—all there ever was or ever could be. John was the man. With him lay all the future. For tonight, slowly and contritely through the day and years to come, she would try to make amends.

Then she stole back to the kitchen, and without thought, impelled by overwhelming need again, returned to the door where the draft was bitter still. Gradually towards morning the storm began to spend itself. Its terror blast became a feeble, worn-out moan. The leap of light and shadow sank, and a chill crept in again. Always the eaves creaked, tortured with wordless prophecy. Heedless of it all the clock ticked on in idiot content.

They found him the next day, less than a mile from home. Drifting with the storm he had run against his own pasture fence and overcome had frozen there, erect still, both hands clasping fast the wire.

'He was south of here,' they said wonderingly when she told them how he had come across the hills. 'Straight south—you'd wonder how he could have missed the buildings. It was the wind last night, coming every way at once. He shouldn't have tried. There was a double wheel around the moon.'

She looked past them a moment, then as if to herself said simply, 'If you knew him, though—John would try.'

It was later, when they had left her a while to be alone with him, that she knelt and touched his hand. Her eyes dimmed, still it was such a strong and patient hand; then, transfixed, they suddenly grew wide and clear. On the palm, white even against its frozen whiteness, was a little smear of paint.

*Probably no writer has been more successful in capturing the tragic drama of the prairie people during the Great Depression. Ross was born in Saskatchewan and worked in small prairie banks as a young man. Though not a prolific writer, Sinclair Ross has earned a permanent place in Canadian literature. 'The Painted Door' is, in our opinion, a masterpiece.*

'Why, what was he doing that was so awful? He was simply commanding a firing squad to execute a soldier who had committed a murder. That's all—he was commanding a firing squad; he was, he was—an executioner!'

Captain John Adam has just come to a terrible realization. To refuse to carry out this order will be regarded as an act of cowardice and Adam cannot afford to be branded a coward *again* . . . .

# the firing squad

Colin McDougall

He was the first Canadian soldier sentenced to death, and rear headquarters in Italy seethed with the prospect of carrying it out. At his marble-topped desk in Rome Major-General Paul Vincent read the instructions from London with distaste. The findings of the court martial had been confirmed by Ottawa—that meant by a special session of the cabinet, the General supposed—and it was now the direct responsibility of the Area Commander that the execution of Private Sydney Jones should be proceeded with "as expeditiously as possible."

The hum of voices and the quick beat of teletypes in the outer office marked the measure of Rome's agitation. No one had expected this confirmation of sentence. Not even the officers who had sentenced Private Jones to death. For them, indeed, there had been little choice; Jones had even wanted to plead guilty, but the court had automatically changed his plea, and gone on to record its inevitable finding and sentence.

The salient facts of the case filed quickly through the neat corridors of General Vincent's mind. This Jones, a young soldier of twenty-two, had deserted his unit, had joined with a group of deserter-gangsters who operated in Rome and Naples, and had been present when his companions shot and killed a U.S. military policeman.

All this Jones admitted, and the court could pass no other sentence. The execution of a Canadian soldier, however, was more than a military matter: it touched on public policy; and higher authorities had never before confirmed a sentence of death. But now the confirming order was in his hands and the train of events must be set in motion.

General Vincent sighed. He preferred to think of himself as the business executive he happened to be rather than a general officer whose duty it was to order a man's death. An execution was something alien and infinitely distasteful. Well, if this thing had to be done under his command at least it need not take place under his personal orders. From the beginning he had known just the man for the job. Already the teletype had clicked off its command to Volpone, the reinforcement base where Private Jones was imprisoned, and a staff car would now be rushing the commander of that base, Brigadier Benny Hatfield, to Rome. The General sighed again and turned to some more congenial correspondence on his desk.

A dirt track spiraled out of Volpone and mounted in white gashes upon the forested mountain side. Fifty infantry reinforcements, fresh from Canada, were spaced along the first two miles of zigzag road. They carried all the paraphernalia of their fledgling trade: rifles, machine guns, and light mortars. Some were trying to run, lurching ahead with painful steps; others stopped to stand panting in their own small lakes of sweat. One or two lay at the roadside, faces turned from the sun, awaiting the stabbing scorn of their sergeant with spent indifference. But they all spat out the clogging dust, and cursed the officer who led them.

Farther up the hillside this man ran with the gait of an athlete pushing himself to the limit of endurance. Head down he ran doggedly through the dust and the heat; he ran as though trying to outdistance some merciless pursuer. His eyes were shut tight and he was inhaling from an almost empty reservoir of breath. Captain John Adam was going to run up that mountainside until he could run no more. He was running from last night, and all the nights which still lay ahead. He was running from his own sick self.

Then, almost at the halfway mark, he aimed himself at a patch of bush underneath the cliff and smashed into it headlong. He lay quite still; he had achieved exhaustion: the closest condition to forgetfulness he could ever find.

For Captain John Adam found it unbearable to live with himself and with his future. He had lost his manhood. As an infantry company commander he had drawn daily strength and sustenance from the respect of his fellow fighting men. They knew him as a brave leader, a compassionate man. He had been granted the trust and friendship of men when it is all they have left to give, and this he knew to be the ultimate gift, the highest good. And then, one sun-filled morning, he had forfeited these things for ever. He had cracked wide open; he had cried his fear and panic to the world; he had run screaming from the battle, through the ranks of his white-faced men. He had been sent back here to Volpone in unexpressed disgrace while the authorities decided what to do with him.

Now Captain John Adam rolled over. There was always some supremely unimportant next matter which had to be decided. He lighted a cigarette and gave his whole attention to the small column of climbing smoke. Well, he would sit here until Sergeant Konzuk whipped this miserable, straggling pack up to him, and then he would reveal their next phase of training.

He stood up, a tall young man, looking brisk and competent. His sun-browned face, his blue eyes, the power of his easy movements, even the cigarette dangling negligently from his lips, all seemed to proclaim that here was the ideal young infantry officer.

"Sergeant Konzuk," Captain Adam called now. "Get these men the hell back to barracks, and leave me alone here!"

The sergeant did not look surprised. He was used to such things by now, and this was no officer to argue with. Sure, he'd take them back to barracks, and let Adam do his own explaining. "All right, you guys —on your feet!" said Konzuk. It was no skin to him.

It was late afternoon by the time he had smoked the last of his cigarettes and Adam came down from the mountain. Striding through the camp he frowned with displeasure when he saw the hulking form of Padre Dixon planted squarely in his path. Normally, he knew, he would have liked this big chaplain. There was a sense of inner calm, of repose and reliability about Padre Dixon. Although in his early fifties he had served with devoted competence as chaplain to an infantry battalion. But Adam considered himself to be an outcast, no longer holding any claims upon the men who did the fighting: the men who still owned their self-respect. He made a point of refusing the friendliness which this big man was trying to offer.

"Mind if I walk along with you, son?" Adam was forced to stop while the Padre knocked his pipe against his boot.

The two men walked on together through the dusk, picking their way between the huts and the barrack blocks. As they neared the officers' mess the Padre stopped and his fingers gripped Adam's arm. He pointed to a small grey hut just within the barbed wire of the camp entrance.

"That's where poor Jones is waiting out his time," the Padre said.

"Well?"

The Padre shrugged and seemed busy with his pipe. "No matter what he's done he's a brave boy, and he's in a dreadful position now."

"He won't be shot." Adam repeated the general feeling of the camp without real interest. "They'll never confirm the sentence."

The Padre looked him directly in the face. "Adam," he said. "It *has* been confirmed. He is going to be executed!"

"No!" Adam breathed his disbelief aloud. He was truly shocked, and for this instant his own sick plight was forgotten. This other thing seemed so—improper. That a group of Canadians could come together in this alien land for the purpose of destroying one of their own kind . . . And every day, up at the battle, every effort was being made to *save* life; there were so few of them in Italy, and so pitifully many were being killed every day. This thing was simply—not right.

His eyes sought for the Padre's. "But why?" he asked, with a kind of hurt in his voice. "Tell me—why?"

"The boy's guilty, after all."

"Technically—he was only a witness. And even if he is guilty, do you think this thing is right?"

The Padre could not ignore the urgency in Adam's voice. He spoke at last with unaccustomed sharpness. "No," he said. "It may be something that has to be done—but it will never be right."

The two men looked at one another in the gathering Italian night. For a moment their thoughts seemed to merge and flow together down the same pulsing stream. But then a new idea came to Adam. "Padre," he said. "Why are you telling *me* about this?"

Then they both saw the figure running toward them from the officers' mess. It was Ramsay, the ever-flurried, ever-flustered Camp Adjutant. He panted to a stop in front of them. "Adam," he gasped out. "The Brigadier wants you at once!"

Brigadier Benny Hatfield waited patiently in his office. He liked to feed any new or disturbing thoughts through the mill of his mind until the gloss of familiarity made them less troublesome. Early in his career he had discovered that the calibre of his mind was not sufficiently large for the rank he aspired to and so deliberately he had cultivated other qualities which would achieve the same end. He emphasized an air of outspoken bluntness, his physical toughness, a presumed knowledge of the way the "troops" thought, and his ability to work like a horse. Indeed the impression he sometimes conveyed was that of a grizzled war horse, fanatic about good soldiering, but with it all intensely loyal, and a very good fellow. His appearance served to support this role: there was something horselike in the wide grin that lifted his straggling mustache, a grin that proved how affable and immensely approachable he really was.

Now he sat and considered his interview with General Vincent. He understood his superior's unexpressed motives perfectly well: it was a straight question of passing the buck and he intended staying up all night looking after his own interests. This execution was a simple matter of military discipline, after all, and he would ensure that it was carried out in such a way that no possible discredit could reflect on himself. The General, he believed, had made an intelligent choice, and he had an equally good selection of his own in mind. The file of Captain John Adam lay open on his desk.

The Brigadier sat up straight. Ramsay was ushering Captain Adam into his presence.

This was the interview Adam had dreaded since his arrival at the reinforcement base. But he showed no sign now of the sickness and fear that gnawed inside him. He stood at attention while the Brigadier leafed through the file before him.

The Brigadier looked up at last. "Well," he stated. "Captain John Adam." His eyes bored steadily at Adam's face and he waited in silence. He knew that in a moment his unwavering stare would force some betrayal of guilt or inferiority. He waited and at last he was rewarded: the sweat swelled on Adam's forehead, and the man before him felt it essential to break the intolerable silence. "Yes, sir," Adam had to say.

The Brigadier stood up then. "Well," he said again. "It can't be as bad as all that, can it, boy?" His mouth lifted the straggling mustache in a grimace of affability, and despite himself Adam felt a small rush of gratitude.

But then the smile died. "It does not please me," the Brigadier said coldly, "to receive the worst possible reports about you." He consulted the notes on his desk. "You have been AWL twice; there is some question of a jeep you took without permission; and my officers say that you act with no sense of responsibility."

The Brigadier was frowning, his lips pursed. His glance bored steadily at Adam. But then there was a sudden transformation. His smile was reborn in new and fuller glory. "Sit down, boy," he urged. He clapped Adam on the shoulder and guided him into the chair beside his desk.

The Brigadier hitched forward in his seat. Now there was a warmth of friendly concern in his voice. "Adam, boy," he said. "*We* know none of that piddling stuff matters. However—you have read this report from Colonel Dodd?"

It was a needless question. Adam knew the report by memory. It was an "adverse" report: it was the reason why he was back here at Volpone. That piece of paper was his doom. "Not fit to command men in action," it read; "not suitable material for the field." And Colonel Dodd had phrased it as gently as possible; in his own presence he had written it down with pity on his face.

With ungoverned ease his mind slipped back to that sun-filled morning on the Hitler Line. They were walking through a meadow—slowly, for there were Schu mines in the grass—and they moved toward a hidden place of horror: a line of dug-in tank turrets, and mine-strewn belts of wire. And then the earth suddenly erupted with shell and mortar bursts; they floundered in a beaten zone of observed machine-gun fire. A few men got as far as the wire, but none of them lived. There was a regrouping close to the start line, and Adam was ordered to attack again.

The first symptom he noticed was that his body responded to his mind's orders several seconds too late. He became worried at this time lag, the fact that his mind and body seemed about to divide, to assume their own separate identities. Then the air bursts shook the world; no hole in the ground was shelter from the rain of deafening black explosions in the sky above them. Then he remembered the terrible instant that the separation became complete, that he got up and shouted his shame to the world. He got up from his ditch, and he ran blubbering

like a baby through his white-faced men. And some of his men followed him, back into the arms of Colonel Dodd.

"Yes," Adam said now, his face white. "I've read the report."

Brigadier Hatfield spoke softly. "If that report goes forward from
here you'll be in a bad way—at least returned to Canada for Adjutant
General's disposal, some second-rate kind of discharge, the reputation
always clinging to you . . ." The Brigadier shook his head. "That would
be a pity."

*If* the report goes forward . . . A pulse of excitement beat in Adam's
throat. What did he mean—was there any possibility that the report
could be stopped here, that in the eyes of the world he could retain
some shreds of self-respect? Adam's breath came faster; he sat up
straight.

"Adam!" The Brigadier pounded a fist upon his desk. "*I* have confidence in you. Of all the officers under my command I have selected
*you* for a mission of the highest importance."

Adam blinked his disbelief, but the hope swelled strong inside him.

"Yes," the Brigadier said steadily. "*You* are to command the firing
squad for the execution of Private Jones!"

Adam blinked again and he turned his head away. For a moment he
was weak with nausea the flood of shame was so sour inside him. "No,"
he heard his voice saying. "I can't do it."

The Brigadier's smile grew broader, and he spoke with soft assurance. "But you can, my boy. But you can." And the Brigadier told him
how.

It was all very neatly contrived. Adam had his choice, of course. On
the one hand he could choose routine disposal of his case by higher
authorities. Colonel Dodd's report, together with Brigadier Hatfield's
own statement, would ensure an outcome which, as the Bridgadier
described it, would cause "deep shame to his family and friends," and
Adam was sure of that. On the other hand if he performed this necessary act of duty, this simple military function, then Colonel Dodd's
report would be destroyed. He could return to Canada as soon as he
desired, bearing Brigadier Hatfield's highest recommendations.

The Brigadier went on to say that the man Jones was a convicted
murderer—that Adam should have no scruples on that score; that he
relied on his known ability to handle men under difficult circum-
stances . . .

Adam listened and each soft word seemed to add to his degradation. This was where the Hitler Line had brought him; this was the inevitable consequence of his lost manhood.

The Brigadier's voice was kindly; his words flowed endlessly like a soft stream of liquid. Then the voice paused. "Of course," the Brigadier said, "it is a task for a determined and courageous man." His glance darted over Adam's bent head and flickered around the room.

Adam broke the silence at last. He spoke without looking up. "All right," he said, "I'll do it."

The Brigadier's response was quick and warm. "Good," he said. "Good *fellow!*" His smile was almost caressing. But to Adam that smile seemed to spread across the horselike face like a stain. The small office and the space between the two men was suddenly close and unbearably warm.

"One more thing, Adam." The Brigadier spoke with soft emphasis. "The members of the firing sqaud can be detailed later, but your sergeant must be a first-rate man, and—it is most desirable that he be a volunteer. Do you understand?"

Adam forced himself to nod.

The Brigadier stared directly in Adam's face. His voice now rang with the steel of command. "All right," he said. "Bring me the sergeant's name and a draft of your parade orders by 1100 hours tomorrow. Any questions?"

"No, sir." Adam stood up.

"Good boy. Get to it, and remember—I'm relying on you."

"Yes, sir."

The Brigadier leaned back and allowed the smile to possess his face. He had selected exactly the right man for this delicate job: a man of competence who was *bound* to carry the thing through to its final conclusion.

By next morning the news had raced to every Canadian in Italy. At the battle up north men heard about this execution with a dull kind of wonder. Advancing into the attack it was brought to them like bad news in a letter from home; they looked at each other uneasily, or they laughed and turned away. It was not the death of one man back in a place called Volpone that mattered. It was simply that up here they measured and counted their own existence so dear that an unnecessary death, a *planned* death of one of their own fellows seemed somehow shameful. It made them sour and restless as they checked their weapon and ammunition loads.

In the camp at Volpone it was the sole topic of conversation. All officers had been instructed by Brigadier Hatfield to explain to the men that the prisoner, Jones, had been convicted of murder, and therefore had to pay the penalty that the law demanded. But the law was not clear to these men: from their own close knowledge of sudden death they did not understand how a man could commit a murder without lifting a weapon. And those who had seen Private Sydney Jones could not picture that harmless boy as a murderer. Still, the officers went to great pains to explain the legal point involved.

It was soon known that the news had reached the prisoner also, although, to be sure, it did not seem to have changed his routine in the least. All his waking hours were busied with an intense display of military activity. The guard sergeant reported that he made and remade his bed several times a day, working earnestly to achieve the neatest possible tuck of his blanket. The floor was swept five times a day and scrubbed at least once. His battle-dress was ironed to knife-edge exactitude, and his regimental flashes resewn to his tunic as though the smartest possible fit at the shoulder was always just eluding him. At times he would glance at the stack of magazines the Padre brought him, but these were thrown aside as soon as a visitor entered his room. Private Jones would spring to a quiveringly erect position of attention; he would respond to questions with a quick, cheerful smile. He was the embodiment of the keen, alert, and well turned-out private soldier.

The truth was, of course, that Private Jones was a somewhat pliable young man who was desperately anxious to please. He was intent on proving himself such a good soldier that the generals would take note and approve, and never do anything very bad to him. The idea that some of his fellow soldiers might take him out and shoot him was a terrible abstraction, quite beyond his imagination. Consequently Private Jones did not believe in the possibility of his own execution. Even when the Padre came and tried to prepare him Private Jones simply jumped eagerly to attention, polished boots glittering, and rattled off, head high: "Yes, sir. Very good, sir."

A surprising amount of administrative detail is required to arrange an execution. The Brigadier was drawing up an elaborate operation order, with each phase to be checked and double-checked. There were

the official witness, the medical officers, the chaplain, the guards, the
firing squad, of course; and the conveyance and placing of all these to
the proper spot at the right time.

But Captain Adam's first problem was more serious than any of this:
his first attempts to recruit the sergeant for his firing squad met with
utter failure. After conferring with the Brigadier he decided upon a new
approach, and he went in search of Sergeant Konzuk.

The sergeant was lying at ease on his bed reading a magazine. When
Adam came in Konzuk scowled. He swung his boots over the side of
the bed and he crossed his thick arms over his chest.

Adam wasted no time. "Konzuk," he said. "I want you as sergeant
of the firing squad."

The sergeant laughed rudely.

"Never mind that," Adam said. "Wait till you hear about this deal."

"Look," Sergeant Konzuk said. He stood up and his eyes were angry
on Adam's face. "I done my share of killing. Those that like it can do
this job."

Adam's tone did not change. "You're married, Konzuk. You've a
wife and two kids. Well, you can be back in Winnipeg within the
month."

Konzuk's mouth opened; his eyes were wide. His face showed all the
wild thoughts thronging through his mind. The sergeant had left
Canada in 1940; his wife wrote him one laborious letter a month. But
his frown returned and his fists were clenched.

"Look," Konzuk said, fumbling with his words. "This kid's one of
us—see. It ain't right!"

"Winnipeg—within the month."

Konzuk's eyes shifted and at last his glance settled on the floor.
"All right," he said, after a moment. "All right, I'll do it."

"Good." Adam sought for and held the sergeant's eyes. "And remember this, Konzuk—that 'kid' is a murderer!"

"Yes, sir."

Then they sat down together. Adam found no satisfaction in his
victory, in the full obedience he now commanded. Sitting on the iron
bed in Konzuk's room they spoke in lowered voices, and Adam felt as
though they were conspiring together to commit some obscene act.

The ten members of the firing squad were detailed the same day.
Adam and Konzuk prepared the list of names and brought the group to

be interviewed by Brigadier Hatfield in his office. And after that Sergeant Konzuk had a quiet talk with each man. Adam did not ask what the sergeant said; he was satisfied that none of the men came to him to protest.

Adam found his time fully occupied. He had installed his ten men in a separate hut of their own; there were some drill movements to be practised; and Sergeant Konzuk was drawing new uniforms from the quartermaster's stores. Ten new rifles had also been issued.

Crossing the parade square that night he encountered Padre Dixon, and he realized that this man had been avoiding him during the past two days. "Padre," he called out. "I want to talk to you."

The Padre waited. His big face showed no expression.

"Padre—will you give me your advice?"

The Padre's glance was cold. "Why?" he asked. "It won't change anything."

And looking into that set face Adam saw that the Padre was regarding him with a dislike he made no attempt to conceal. He flushed. He had not expected this. Only days ago this man had been trying to help him.

His anger slipped forward. "What's the matter, Padre—you feeling sorry for the boy-murderer?"

Adam regretted his words at once; indeed he was shocked that he could have said them. The Padre turned his back and started away.

Adam caught at his arm. "Ah, no," he said. "I didn't mean that. Padre—is what I'm doing so awful, after all?"

"You've made your choice. Let it go at that."

"But—my duty . . ." Adam felt shame as he used the word.

The Padre stood with folded arms. "Listen," he said. "I told you before: no matter how necessary this thing is it will never be right!"

Adam was silent. Then he reached out his hand again. "Padre," he said in a low voice. "Is there no way it can be stopped?"

The Padre sighed. "The train has been set in motion," he said. "Once it could have been stopped—in Ottawa—but now . . ." He shrugged. He looked at Adam searchingly and he seemed to reflect. "There *might* be one way—." After a moment he blinked and looked away. "But no—that will never come to pass. I suppose I should wish you good luck," he said. "Good night, Adam."

That meeting made Adam wonder how his fellow officers regarded him. In the officers' mess that night he looked about him and found out. Silence descended when he approached a group and slowly its members would drift away; there was a cleared circle around whichever chair he sat in. Even the barman seemed to avoid his glance.

All right, Adam decided then, and from the bar he looked murderously around the room. All right, *he* would stick by Benny Hatfield— the two of them, at least, knew what duty and soldiering was! Why, what was he doing that was so awful? He was simply commanding a firing squad to execute a soldier who had committed a murder. That's all—he was commanding a firing squad; he was, he was—an executioner!

His glass crashed to the floor. Through all the soft words exchanged with Brigadier Hatfield, all the concealing echelons of military speech, the pitiless truth now leaped out at him. He was an executioner. Captain John Adam made a noise in his throat, and the faces of the other men in the room went white.

When he left the mess some instinct led him toward the small grey hut standing at the camp entrance. Through the board walls of that hut he could see his victim, Jones, living out his allotted time, while he, Adam the executioner, walked implacably close by. The new concept of victim and executioner seized and threatened to suffocate him.

His eyes strained at the Italian stars in their dark-blue heaven. How had it happened? Only days ago he had regarded the possibility of this execution with horror, as something vile. But now he stood in the front rank of those who were pushing it forward with all vigour. For an instant his mind flamed with the thought of asking Brigadier Hatfield to release him, but at once the fire flickered out, hopelessly. That night John Adam stayed in his room with the light burning. He tried to pray.

Brigadier Hatfield had the most brilliant inspiration of his career: The place of execution would be changed to Rome! There was ample justification, of course, since the effect on the troops' morale at Volpone would be bad to say the least. No one could dispute this, and all the while the Brigadier relished in imagination the face of General Vincent when he found the affair brought back to his own doorstep. It only showed that a regular soldier could still teach these civilian generals a thing or two!

The Brigadier was in high good humor as he presided at the conference to discuss this change. All the participants were present, including

one newcomer, an officer from the Provost Corps, introduced as
Colonel McGuire. This colonel said nothing, but nodded his head in
agreement with the Brigadier's points. His eyes roamed restlessly from
face to face and his cold glance seemed to strip bare the abilities of
every person in the room.

Colonel McGuire, the Brigadier announced, had been instrumental in
finding the ideal place for the affair. It was a former Fascist barracks on
the outskirts of Rome, and all the—ah, facilities— were readily available. Everyone taking part, and he trusted that each officer was now
thoroughly familiar with his duties, would move by convoy to Rome
that very afternoon. The execution—here he paused for a solemn moment—the execution would take place at 0800 hours tomorrow morning. Any questions? No? Thank you, gentlemen.

Adam was moving away when the Brigadier stopped him. "John,"
he called. He had slipped into the habit of using his first name now. "I
want you to meet Colonel McGuire."

They shook hands and Adam flushed under the chill exposure of
those probing eyes. After a moment the Colonel's glance dropped; he
had seen sufficient. As Adam moved off to warn his men for the move
he felt those cold eyes following him to the door, and beyond.

Adam kept his eyes closed while Sergeant Konzuk drove. In the
back of the jeep Padre Dixon had not spoken since the convoy was
marshaled; it was clear that these were not the traveling companions of
his choice.

Although Adam would not look all his awareness was centred on a
closed three-ton truck which lumbered along in the middle of the convoy. The condemned man and his guards rode inside that vehicle.

The concept of victim and executioner filled Adam's mind to the
exclusion of all else. He had tried throwing the blame back to the
comfortable politicians sitting at their polished table in Ottawa, but it
was no use. He knew that it was *his* voice that would issue the last command. *He* was the executioner . . . Then another thought came to torment him without mercy: How did his victim, Jones, *feel* now?

They stopped for ten minutes outside a hilltop town, where pink
villas glinted among the green of olive trees. Adam followed Padre
Dixon to the place where he sat in an orchard. The Padre looked up at
him wearily.

"How is he taking it?" Adam demanded at once.

The Padre scrambled to his feet. His eyes flashed with anger. "Who? The boy-murderer?"

"Please, Padre—I've *got* to know!"

The Padre stared at Adam's drawn face. Then he passed a hand across his eyes. "Adam—forgive me. I know it's a terrible thing for you. If it makes it any easier . . . well, Jones is brave; he's smiling and polite, and that's all. But Adam—the boy still doesn't understand. He doesn't believe that it's really going to happen!" The Padre's voice shook with his agitation.

Adam nodded his head. "That other time, Padre—you said there might be a way of stopping it—."

"No, forget that—it's too late." The spluttering cough of motorcycles roared between them. "Come. It is time to go." And the Padre laid his hand on Adam's arm.

Adam and Konzuk stood on the hard tarmac and surveyed the site gloomily. The place they had come to inspect was a U-shaped space cut out of the forest. The base of the U was a red-brick wall, and down each side marched a precise green line of cypresses. The wall was bullet-pocked because this place had been used as a firing range, although imagination balked at what some of the targets must have been. On the right wing of the U a small wooden grandstand was set in front of the cypresses. Adam looked around at all this, and then his gaze moved over the trees and up to the pitilessly blue sky above. "All right, Konzuk," he said. "You check things over." And he went away to be alone.

Adam was lying on his bed in the darkness. His eyes were wide open but he made no move when he saw the Padre's big form stumble into his room. Then the Padre stood over his bed, eyes groping for him. He was breathing loudly.

"Adam—he wants to see you!"

"No!"

"You must!"

"I couldn't!" Now Adam sat up in bed. His battle-dress tunic was crumpled. His face was protected by the dark, but his voice was naked. "No, Padre," he pleaded. "I couldn't."

"Look son—it's your job. You've no choice. Do you understand?"

There was silence. Adam made a noise in the darkness which seemed to take all the breath from his body.

"Yes, I understand." He was fumbling for his belt and cap in the dark.
"Padre—what time is it?"

"Twelve o'clock."

"Eight hours."

"Yes."

"Well. Good-by, Padre."

"Good-by, son."

The Provost Sergeant came to attention and saluted. His face was
stiff but he could not keep the flicker of curiosity from his eyes. Adam
saw that this was a real prison: concrete flooring, steel doors, and iron
bars. They stood in what seemed to be a large brightly lit guardroom.
A card game had been taking place, and there were coffee mugs, but
the guards stood now at respectful attention.

"Where is he?" Adam turned to the Sergeant.

A dark-haired young man stepped from among the group of guards.
A smartly dressed soldier, clean and good-looking in his freshly
pressed battle-dress. "Here I am, sir," the young man said.

Adam took a step back; he flashed a glance at the door.

The Sergeant spoke then, apologetically. "He wanted company, sir.
I thought it would be all right."

"It was good of you to come, sir." This was Private Jones speaking
for his attention.

Adam forced himself to return the glance. "Yes," he said. "I mean—
it's no trouble. I—I was glad to."

The two men looked one another in the face, perhaps surprised to
find how close they were in years. Jones' smile was friendly. He was like
a host easing the embarrassment of his guest. "Would you like to sit
down, sir?"

"Yes. Oh, yes."

They sat in Jones' cell, on opposite sides of a small table. Because he
had to Adam held his eyes on the prisoner's face and now he could see
the thin lines of tension spreading from the eyes and at the mouth.
It was certain that Jones *now* believed in the truth of his own death, and
he carried this fact with quiet dignity. Adam was gripped by a passion
of adoration for this boy; he would have done anything for him—he
who was his executioner.

"It was good of you to come," Private Jones said again. "I have a
request."

Surely, Adam thought, it took more courage to act as Jones did now than to advance through that meadow to the Hitler Line . . .

"Well, sir," Jones went on, his face set. "I'm ready to take—tomorrow morning. But one thing worries me: I don't want you and the other boys to feel bad about this. I thought it might help if I shook hands with all the boys before—before it happens."

Adam looked down at the concrete floor. This was worse than a thousand Hitler Lines; *he knew now he would be able to go back there anytime.* A dim electric-light bulb hung from the ceiling and swayed hypnotically between them. Well, he had to say something. The thing was impossible, of course: he'd never get his men to fire if they shook hands first.

But Jones read the working of his face. "Never mind, sir—maybe you'd just give them that message for me—."

"I will, Jones. I *will!*"

He stood up; he could not stay here another moment.

Jones said, "Maybe—*you* would shake hands with me?"

Adam stood utterly still. His voice came out as a whisper in that small space. "Jones," he said, "I was going to ask you if I could."

When he came back to the guard-room Adam looked ill. The Provost Sergeant took his arm and walked him back to his quarters.

It was a softly fragrant Italian morning. The dew was still fresh on the grass and a light ground mist rolled away before the heat of the climbing sun. In the forest clearing the neat groups of soldiers looked clean and compact in their khaki battle-dress with the bright regimental flashes gleaming at their shoulders.

The firing squad stood "at ease," but with not the least stir or motion. Sergeant Konzuk was on their right; Captain Adam stood several paces apart at the left, aligned at right angles to his ten-man rank. The grandstand was filled with a small group of official witnesses. A cordon of military policemen stayed at rigid attention along the top and down each side of the U.

In front of the grandstand stood Brigadier Benny Hatfield, an erect military figure, his stern eye ranging with satisfaction around the precise groupings and arrangements he had ordered. A step behind the Brigadier was Ramsay, his adjutant; then Padre Dixon, and the chief medical officer. The assembly was complete—except for one man.

Somewhere in the background a steel door clanged, a noise which no one affected to hear. Then there came the sound of rapid marching. Three military figures came into view and halted smartly in front of Brigadier Hatfield. Private Jones, hatless, stood in the centre, a provost sergeant on each side. The boy's lips were white, his cheeks lacked color, but he held his head high, his hands were pressed tight against the seams of his battle-dress trousers. It was impossible not to notice the brilliant shine of his polished boots as they glittered in the morning sun.

Brigadier Hatfield took a paper from Ramsay's extended hand. He read some words from it but his voice came as an indistinct mumble in the morning air. The Brigadier was in a hurry. Everyone was in a hurry; every person there suffered an agony of haste. Each body strained and each mind willed: Go! Go! Have this thing over and done with!

The Brigadier handed the paper back to Ramsay with a little gesture of finality. But the three men remained standing in front of him as though locked in their attitudes of attention. Seconds of silence ticked by. The Brigadier's hand sped up to his collar and he cleared his throat with violence. "*Well*, sergeant?" his voice rasped. "Carry on, man!"

"Yessir. Left turn—quick march!"

The three men held the same brisk pace, marching in perfect step. The only sound was the thud of their heavy boots upon the tarmac. They passed the firing squad and halted at the red-brick wall. Then the escorting NCOs seemed to disappear and Private Jones stood alone against the wall. A nervous little smile was fixed at the corners of his mouth.

Again there was silence. Adam had not looked at the marching men, nor did he now look at the wall. Head lowered, he frowned as he seemed to study the alignment of his ten men in a row. More seconds ticked by.

"Captain Adam!"

It was a bellow from Brigadier Hatfield and it brought Adam's head up. Then his lips moved soundlessly, as though rehearsing what he had to say. "Squad," Captain Adam ordered, "Load!" Ten left feet banged forward on the tarmac, ten rifles hit in the left hand, ten bolts smashed open and shut in unison. Ten rounds were positioned in their chambers.

There were just two remaining orders: "Aim!" and "Fire!" and these should be issued immediately, almost as one. But at that moment a late rooster crowed somewhere and the call came clear and sweet through the morning air, full of rich promise for the summer's day which lay ahead.

Adam took his first glance at the condemned man. Jones' mouth still held hard to its smile, but his knees looked loose. His position of attention was faltering.

"Squad!" Adam ordered in a ringing voice, "Unload! Rest!" Ten rifles obeyed in perfect unison.

Adam turned half right so that he faced Brigadier Hatfield. "Sir," he called clearly. "I refuse to carry out this order!"

Every voice in that place joined in the sound which muttered across the tarmac.

The Brigadier's face was deathly white. He peered at Private Jones, still in position against the wall, knees getting looser. He had a split second to carry the thing through. "Colonel McGuire!" he shouted.

"Yes, sir!" McGuire came running toward the firing squad. He knew what had to be done, and quickly. The Brigadier's face had turned purple now; he appeared to be choking with the force of his rage. "Colonel McGuire," he shouted. "Place that officer under close arrest!"

"Sir?" McGuire stopped where he was and his mouth dropped open. Private Jones began to fall slowly against the wall. Then a rifle clattered loudly on the tarmac. Sergeant Konzuk was racing toward the wall and in an instant he had his big arms tight around Jones' body.

"McGuire!" The Brigadier's voice was a hoarse shriek now. "March the prisoner away!"

Padre Dixon stood rooted to the ground. His lips were moving and he stared blindly at Adam's stiffly erect figure. "He found the way!" he cried then in a ringing voice, and he moved about in triumph, although no one paid him attention. At his side Ramsay was spluttering out his own ecstasy of excitement: "Jones will get a reprieve after this! It will have to be referred to London and then to Ottawa. And they'll never dare to put him through this again—."

Ramsay looked up as he felt the Padre's fingers bite into his shoulder.

He laughed nervously. "Yes," he chattered on. "Jones may get a reprieve, but Adam's the one for sentencing now." He peered across the tarmac where Adam still stood alone, his face slightly lifted to the warmth of the morning sun. He looked at Adam's lone figure with fear and admiration. "Yes," he said, suddenly sobered. "God help Adam now."

"Don't worry about that, son," said the Padre, starting to stride across the tarmac. "He already has."

*Colin McDougall's 'The Firing Squad' first appeared in* MACLEAN'S; *it became the most widely known Canadian story to emerge from the Second World War and it has been anthologized many times. McDougall later expanded this material into the novel,* EXECUTION. *McDougall is an Ontario native.*

Visualize two fishermen—*any* two fishermen. What do you see? Two affable people sharing a common interest which draws them close together? Two happy men swapping stories, experiences, the usual fishing yarns . . . yes, and even confidences?

Here are two men—fishing partners for the first time, sharing the kinship of rod and reel.

But one man is drawn into this relationship by a morbid fascination—
*For his fishing partner is the hangman!*

# two fishermen

Morley Callaghan

**t**he only reporter on the town paper, the *Examiner*, was Michael Foster, a tall, long-legged, eager young fellow, who wanted to go to the city some day and work on an important newspaper.

The morning he went into Bagley's Hotel, he wasn't at all sure of himself. He went over to the desk and whispered to the proprietor, Ted Bagley, 'Did he come here, Mr. Bagley?'

Bagley said slowly, 'Two men came here from this morning's train. They're registered.' He put his spatulate forefinger on the open book and said, 'Two men. One of them's a drummer. This one here, T. Woodley. I know because he was through this way last year and just a minute ago he walked across the road to Molson's hardware store. The other one . . . here's his name, K. Smith.'

'Who's K. Smith?' Michael asked.

'I don't know. A mild, harmless-looking little guy.'

'Did he look like the hangman, Mr. Bagley?'

'I couldn't say that, seeing as I never saw one. He was awfully polite

and asked where he could get a boat so he could go fishing on the lake
this evening, so I said likely down at Smollet's place by the power-
house.'

'Well, thanks. I guess if he was the hangman, he'd go over to the jail
first,' Michael said.

He went along the street, past the Baptist church to the old jail with
the high fence around it. Two tall maple trees, with branches drooping
low over the sidewalk, shaded one of the walls from the morning sunlight. Last night, behind those walls, three carpenters, working by
lamplight, had nailed the timbers for the scaffold. In the morning,
young Thomas Delaney, who had grown up in the town, was being
hanged: he had killed old Mathew Rhinehart whom he had caught
molesting his wife when she had been berry-picking in the hills behind
the town. There had been a struggle and Thomas Delaney had taken a
bad beating before he had killed Rhinehart. Last night a crowd had
gathered on the sidewalk by the lamp-post, and while moths and smaller insects swarmed around the high blue carbon light, the crowd had
thrown sticks and bottles and small stones at the out-of-town work-
men in the jail yard. Billy Hilton, the town constable, had stood under
the light with his head down, pretending not to notice anything.
Thomas Delaney was only three years older than Michael Foster.

Michael went straight to the jail office, where Henry Steadman, the
sheriff, a squat, heavy man, was sitting on the desk idly wetting his
long moustaches with his tongue. 'Hello, Michael, what do you want?'
he asked.

'Hello, Mr. Steadman, the *Examiner* would like to know if the hangman arrived yet.'

'Why ask me?'

'I thought he'd come here to test the gallows. Won't he?'

'My, you're a smart young fellow, Michael, thinking of that.'

'Is he in there now, Mr. Steadman?'

'Don't ask me. I'm saying nothing. Say, Michael, do you think
there's going to be trouble? You ought to know. Does anybody seem
sore at me? I can't do nothing. You can see that.'

'I don't think anybody blames you, Mr. Steadman. Look here, can't
I see the hangman? Is his name K. Smith?'

'What does it matter to you, Michael? Be a sport, go on away and
don't bother us any more.'

'All right, Mr. Steadman,' Michael said very competently, 'just leave it to me.'

Early that evening, when the sun was setting, Michael Foster walked south of the town on the dusty road leading to the power-house and Smollet's fishing pier. He knew that if Mr. K. Smith wanted to get a boat he would go down to the pier. Fine powdered road dust whitened Michael's shoes. Ahead of him he saw the power-plant, square and low, and the smooth lake water. Behind him the sun was hanging over the blue hills beyond the town and shining brilliantly on square patches of farm land. The air around the power-house smelt of steam.

Out of the jutting, tumbledown pier of rock and logs, Michael saw a little fellow without a hat, sitting down with his knees hunched up to his chin, a very small man with little gray baby curls on the back of his neck, who stared steadily far out over the water. In his hand he was holding a stick with a heavy fishing line twined around it and a gleaming copper spoon bait, the hooks brightened with bits of feathers such as they used in the neighbourhood when trolling for lake trout. Apprehensively Michael walked out over the rocks toward the stranger and called, 'Were you thinking of going fishing, mister?' Standing up, the man smiled. He had a large head, tapering down to a small chin, a birdlike neck and a very wistful smile. Puckering his mouth up, he said shyly to Michael, 'Did you intend to go fishing?'

'That's what I came down here for. I was going to get a boat back at the boat-house there. How would you like if we went together?'

'I'd like it first rate,' the shy little man said eagerly. 'We could take turns rowing. Does that appeal to you?'

'Fine, fine. You wait here and I'll go back to Smollet's place and ask for a row-boat and I'll row around here and get you.'

'Thanks. Thanks very much,' the mild little man said as he began to untie his line. He seemed very enthusiastic.

When Michael brought the boat around to the end of the old pier and invited the stranger to make himself comfortable so he could handle the line, the stranger protested comically that he ought to be allowed to row.

Pulling strongly at the oars, Michael was soon out in the deep water and the little man was letting his line out slowly. In one furtive glance, he had noticed that the man's hair, gray at the temples, was inclined to curl to his ears. The line was out full length. It was twisted around the

little man's forefinger, which he let drag in the water. And then
Michael looked full at him and smiled because he thought he seemed
so meek and quizzical. 'He's a nice little guy,' Michael assured himself
and he said, 'I work on the town paper, the *Examiner*.'

'Is it a good paper? Do you like the work?'

'Yes. But it's nothing like a first-class city paper and I don't expect
to be working on it long. I want to get a reporter's job on a city paper.
My name's Michael Foster.'

'Mine's Smith. Just call me Smitty.'

'I was wondering if you'd been over to the jail yet.'

Up to this time the little man had been smiling with the charming
ease of a small boy who finds himself free, but now he became furtive
and disappointed. Hesitating, he said, 'Yes, I was over there first thing
this morning.'

'Oh, I just knew you'd go there,' Michael said. They were a bit
afraid of each other. By this time they were far out on the water which
had a mill-pond smoothness. The town seemed to get smaller, with
white houses in rows and streets forming geometric patterns, just as
the blue hills behind the town seemed to get larger at sundown.

Finally Michael said, 'Do you know this Thomas Delaney that's
dying in the morning?' He knew his voice was slow and resentful.

'No. I don't know anything about him. I never read about them.
Aren't there any fish at all in this old lake? I'd like to catch some fish,'
he said rapidly. 'I told my wife I'd bring her home some fish.' Glancing
at Michael, he was appealing, without speaking, that they should do
nothing to spoil an evening's fishing.

The little man began to talk eagerly about fishing as he pulled out a
small flask from his hip pocket. 'Scotch,' he said, chuckling with
delight. 'Here, take a swig.' Michael drank from the flask and passed it
back. Tilting his head back and saying, 'Here's to you, Michael,' the
little man took a long pull at the flask. 'The only time I take a drink,'
he said chuckling, 'is when I go on a fishing trip by myself. I usually
go by myself,' he added apologetically as if he wanted the young fellow
to see how much he appreciated his company.

They had gone far out on the water but they had caught nothing. It
began to get dark. 'No fish tonight, I guess, Smitty,' Michael said.

'It's a crying shame,' Smitty said. 'I looked forward to coming up
here when I found out the place was on the lake. I wanted to get some

fishing in. I promised my wife I'd bring her back some fish. She'd often
like to go fishing with me, but of course, she can't because she can't
travel around from place to place like I do. Whenever I get a call to go
some place, I always look at the map to see if it's by a lake or on a river,
then I take my lines and hooks along.'

'If you took another job, you and your wife could probably go
fishing together,' Michael suggested.

'I don't know about that. We sometimes go fishing together anyway.'
He looked away, waiting for Michael to be repelled and insist that he
ought to give up the job. And he wasn't ashamed as he looked down at
the water, but he knew that Michael thought he ought to be ashamed.

'Somebody's got to do my job. There's got to be a hangman,' he said.

'I just meant that if it was such disagreeable work, Smitty.'

The little man did not answer for a long time. Michael rowed steadily
with sweeping, tireless strokes. Huddled at the end of the boat, Smitty
suddenly looked up with a kind of melancholy hopelessness and said
mildly, 'The job hasn't been so disagreeable.'

'Good God, man, you don't mean you like it?'

'Oh no,' he said, to be obliging, as if he knew what Michael expected
him to say. 'I mean you get used to it, that's all.' But he looked down
again at the water, knowing he ought to be ashamed of himself.

'Have you got any children?'

'I sure have. Five. The oldest boy is fourteen. It's funny, but they're
all a lot bigger and taller than I am. Isn't that funny?'

They started a conversation about fishing rivers that ran into the lake
farther north. They felt friendly again. The little man, who had an extra-
ordinary gift for story-telling, made many quaint faces, puckered up
his lips, screwed up his eyes and moved around restlessly as if he
wanted to get up in the boat and stride around for the sake of more
expression. Again he brought out the whiskey flask and Michael
stopped rowing. Grinning, they toasted each other and said together,
'Happy days.' The boat remained motionless on the placid water. Far
out, the sun's last rays gleamed on the water-line. And then it got dark
and they could only see the town lights. It was time to turn around and
pull for the shore. The little man tried to take the oars from Michael,
who shook his head resolutely and insisted that he would prefer to have
his friend catch a fish on the way back to the shore.

'It's too late now, and we may have scared all the fish away,' Smitty laughed happily. 'But we're having a grand time, aren't we?'

When they reached the old pier by the power-house, it was full night, and they hadn't caught a single fish. As the boat bumped against the rocks Michael said, 'You can get out here. I'll take the boat around to Smollet's.'

'Won't you be coming my way?'

'Not just now. I'll probably talk with Smollet a while.'

The little man got out of the boat and stood on the pier looking down at Michael. 'I was thinking dawn would be the best time to catch some fish,' he said. 'At about five o'clock. I'll have an hour and a half to spare anyway. How would you like that?' He was speaking with so much eagerness that Michael found himself saying, 'I could try. But if I'm not here at dawn, you go on without me.'

'All right. I'll walk back to the hotel now.'

'Good night, Smitty.'

'Good night, Michael. We had a fine neighbourly time, didn't we?'

As Michael rowed the boat around to the boat-house, he hoped that Smitty wouldn't realize he didn't want to be seen walking back to town with him. And later, when he was going slowly along the dusty road in the dark and hearing all the crickets chirping in the ditches, he couldn't figure out why he felt so ashamed of himself.

At seven o'clock next morning Thomas Delaney was hanged in the town jail yard. There was hardly a breeze on that leaden gray morning and there were no small whitecaps out over the lake. It would have been a fine morning for fishing. Michael went down to the jail, for he thought it his duty as a newspaperman to have all the facts, but he was afraid he might get sick. He hardly spoke to all the men and women who were crowded under the maple trees by the jail wall. Everybody he knew was staring at the wall and muttering angrily. Two of Thomas Delaney's brothers, big, strapping fellows with bearded faces, were there on the sidewalk. Three automobiles were at the front of the jail.

Michael, the town newspaperman, was admitted into the courtyard by old Willie Mathews, one of the guards, who said that two news-papermen from the city were at the gallows on the other side of the building. 'I guess you can go around there, too, if you want to,' Mathews said, as he sat down slowly on the step. White-faced, and afraid, Michael sat down on the step with Mathews and they waited and said nothing.

At last the old fellow said, 'Those people outside there are pretty sore, ain't they?'

'They're pretty sullen, all right. I saw two of Delaney's brothers there.'

'I wish they'd go,' Mathews said. 'I don't want to see anything. I didn't even look at Delaney. I don't want to hear anything. I'm sick.' He put his head back against the wall and closed his eyes.

The old fellow and Michael sat close together till a small procession came around the corner from the other side of the yard. First came Mr. Steadman, the sheriff, with his head down as though he were crying, then Dr. Parker, the physician, then two hard-looking young newspapermen from the city, walking with their hats on the backs of their heads, and behind them came the little hangman, erect, stepping out with military precision and carrying himself with a strange cocky dignity. He was dressed in a long black cutaway coat with gray striped trousers, a gates-ajar collar and a narrow red tie, as if he alone felt the formal importance of the occasion. He walked with brusque precision till he saw Michael, who was standing up, staring at him with his mouth open.

The little hangman grinned and as soon as the procession reached the doorstep, he shook hands with Michael. They were all looking at Michael. As though his work were over now, the hangman said eagerly to Michael, 'I thought I'd see you here. You didn't get down to the pier at dawn?'

'No. I couldn't make it.'

'That was tough, Michael. I looked for you,' he said. 'But never mind. I've got something for you.' As they all went into the jail, Dr. Parker glanced angrily at Michael, then turned his back on him. In the office, where the doctor prepared to sign a certificate, Smitty was bending down over his fishing-basket which was in the corner. Then he pulled out two good-sized salmon-bellied trout, folded in a newspaper, and said, 'I was saving these for you, Michael. I got four in an hour's fishing.' Then he said, 'I'll talk about that later, if you'll wait. We'll be busy here, and I've got to change my clothes.'

Michael went out to the street with Dr. Parker and the two city newspapermen. Under his arm he was carrying the fish, folded in the newspaper. Outside, at the jail door, Michael thought that the doctor and the two newspapermen were standing a little apart from him. Then the small crowd, with their clothes all dust-soiled from the road, surged forward, and the doctor said to them, 'You might as well go home, boys. It's all over.'

'Where's old Steadman?' somebody demanded.

'We'll wait for the hangman,' somebody else shouted.

The doctor walked away by himself. For a while Michael stood beside the two city newspapermen, and tried to look as nonchalant as they were looking, but he lost confidence in them when he smelled whiskey. They only talked to each other. Then they mingled with the crowd, and Michael stood alone. At last he could stand there no longer looking at all those people he knew so well, so he, too, moved out and joined the crowd.

When the sheriff came out with the hangman and two of the guards, they got half-way down to one of the automobiles before someone threw an old boot. Steadman ducked into one of the cars, as the boot hit him on the shoulder, and the two guards followed him. The hangman, dismayed, stood alone on the sidewalk. Those in the car must have thought at first that the hangman was with them for the car suddenly shot forward, leaving him alone on the sidewalk. The crowd threw small rocks and sticks, hooting at him as the automobile backed up slowly towards him. One small stone hit him on the head. Blood trickled from the side of his head as he looked around helplessly at all the angry people. He had the same expression on his face, Michael thought, as he had had last night when he had seemed ashamed and had looked down steadily at the water. Only now, he looked around wildly, looking for someone to help him as the crowd kept pelting him. Farther and farther Michael backed into the crowd and all the time he felt dreadfully ashamed as though he were betraying Smitty, who last night had had such a good neighbourly time with him. 'It's different now, it's different,' he kept thinking, as he held the fish in the newspaper tight under his arm. Smitty started to run toward the automobile, but James Mortimer, a big fisherman, shot out his foot and tripped him and sent him sprawling on his face.

Mortimer, the big fisherman, looking for something to throw, said to Michael, 'Sock him, sock him.'

Michael shook his head and felt sick.

'What's the matter with you, Michael?'

'Nothing, I got nothing against him.'

The big fisherman started pounding his fists up and down in the air. 'He just doesn't mean anything to me at all,' Michael said quickly. The fisherman, bending down, kicked a small rock loose from the road bed and heaved it at the hangman. Then he said, 'What are you holding there, Michael, what's under your arm? Fish. Pitch them at him. Here, give them to me.' Still in a fury, he snatched the fish, and threw them one at a time at the little man just as he was getting up from the road. The fish fell in the thick dust in front of him, sending up a little cloud. Smitty seemed to stare at the fish with his mouth hanging open, then he didn't even look at the crowd. That expression on Smitty's face as he saw the fish on the road made Michael hot with shame and he tried to get out of the crowd.

Smitty had his hands over his head, to shield his face as the crowd pelted him, yelling, 'Sock the little rat. Throw the runt in the lake.' The sheriff pulled him into the automobile. The car shot forward in a cloud of dust.

*Probably Canada's most widely known short story writer, Morley Callaghan was a contemporary of Ernest Hemingway and Scott Fitzgerald in Paris during the 1920's. Callaghan's stories have been universally recognized in anthologies of the world's finest short stories. His story 'Two Fisherman' was included as Callaghan's choice in a collection called* THIS IS MY BEST (*Dial Press, 1942*). *In a letter to the editors of this anthology he wrote, "The reasons I gave for that story selection are perfectly valid, when I look at that story. At different times I look at different stories. Ultimately there's never any 'best story'. Just one you like at the time you read it."*
*Callaghan lives in Toronto.*

The fishing fleet goes out in the early morning; it returns in the early evening. And so it has gone since men fished the sea. And all fishermen leave as one man, return as one man.
But one man is late. And each day sees him later.
Another man wonders why.
And *he must find the answer.*

# the late man

Andreas Schroeder

**O**n the morning after the storm, the fishermen got up earlier than usual to survey the damage and repair what could be saved. Unusually strong winds and rain had scattered the nets and flattened gardens, bushes, even trees. Fishing boats lay strewn about the beach like broken teeth. Everywhere an exhausted silence hung limply; even the occasional seagull screech seemed blunted and uncertain. Across the mud-flats the faint rush of breakers seemed to fade, though the tide was coming in, slowly and without apparent conviction.

At this time in the morning the fishermen rarely spoke. They arranged their lines, oiled pulleys, checked over their engines and wordlessly pushed out to sea. To break the fragile silence of the first few hours would have been like bursting a delicate membrane without preparation; it was tacitly understood that a man needed more time to clear away in his mind the rubble and destruction of the preceding night than was available to him between his getting up and the launching of his boat. Even after they had cleared the beach and set their course for the large fishing-grounds farther north, the fishermen rarely raised their voices—as if in instinctive respect for the precariousness of the human mind launched before sunrise on an uncertain sea.

But someone broke the silence that morning; as the last remaining boats poled into deeper water to lower their engines, a young bearded fisherman pointed to a single unattended boat lying on its side on the beach and asked in a low voice: "Where's he?"

The man being addressed looked startled, puzzled, then shrugged
his shoulders.

The bearded fisherman risked a further offence. "Could he be sick,
d'you think?"

There was no response. The other man slid his oar into the water and
pushed them off.

A man opens his cabin door and steps into view. He is the late man,
the man whose boat still lies untouched on the beach below his cabin.
There is nothing particularly unusual about this man except perhaps a
certain slight hesitation in his manner; the hesitation of a man for
whom the world became at some point intensely suspect, for whom, at
that point, a glass on a table became less and less a glass on a table
and more and more a thing too strange and amazing to grasp by name.
As he stands in his doorway, his hand rests gingerly on the frame, as if
constantly ready in case of attack.

About fifteen minutes have passed since the last boat was launched
and the late man stepped from his cabin. Now, his boat ready and his
outboard spluttering half-submerged, he pushes off and follows the
fleet toward the fishing-grounds.

A few hours later the fishing village begins to yawn, stretch and get
up; children and fishwives clutter the streets and tangle the air with
punctuation marks.

When they return in the early evening and pull their boats out of the
water above the high-tide markers, the late man is not with them.
During the interval of time between the last fisherman's ascent from
his stranded boat to his waiting dinner and the late man's arrival at the
launching site fifteen minutes later, silence holds the beach like an
indrawn breath. The sound of his prow on the pebbles, therefore grates
in an unusually harsh way on the nerves of the woman waiting for him
above the high-tide markers. He has caught fewer fish than the other
fishermen.

The next morning the late man appears at his cabin door half an hour
after the fishermen have left the beach.

Their boats are already vague in the distance when he finally manages
to haul his boat to the water-line, which has by this time fallen far
below his landing place with the receding tide. He seems somehow

weakened, older, leaning wearily against the wheel of his boat. When
the fishermen return that night he is an uncertain speck on the horizon,
half an hour behind the last of the fishing fleet, and when the catch is
scored, he has caught fewer fish than the day before.

Around noon the following day the boats were anchored in clusters to
share both lunch and small-talk on the fishing-grounds, and the conversation turned to the late man. "Can't figure 'im out," one fisherman
mused, pulling thoughtfully at his beard. "Won't tell nobody what's
wrong." "Ain't sayin' a thing," another agreed. "Asked him yesterday
what the problem was, but I'll be damned if he didn't seem like he
wasn't even listening." There was a pause as if to let the spoken words
disperse. Then: "Sea can do that to a man. Catches up with him, it
does." The speaker slowly shook his head, threw an orange peel over-
board, then absently ignored a deck-hand who had asked him what he
meant. The deck-hand finally turned away, assuming his question was
naive; he was new in the fleet and often found himself being un-
answered. As it was, he was already on the other side of the boat when
the old man muttered his answer to no-one in particular: "I don't know
what happens; I just know it does. Ain't no man can whirl the world
by hand."
    The next morning the late man launched his boat some forty-five
minutes after the fleet had left the beach.

Little is known of the late man's history, though this isn't realized
until he first begins to attract attention by his mystifying dislocation
of schedule; suddenly everyone rummages about in their memory for
initial impressions, former opinions, latent suspicions, old predictions.
Little in the way of substantial information is collected. It is generally
agreed that he is a relatively young man, hard-working and "well-
disciplined." Some feel him to be a little too much given to reflection,
but one suspects this is said chiefly in reaction to his if not exactly
anti-social, at least fairly reticent manner. He cares little for other
people, though he has been known to go to the aid of a complete
stranger for no reason. A slightly more observant villager notes his
peculiar tendency to touch (with a curiously disbelieving air) whatever
happens to be around him; the remark is received in uncertain silence.
Many frankly admit they have no idea what to make of the whole busi-

ness, and that the man is probably simply under the attack of some un-
settling virus. This fails to explain, however (as someone points out),
his consistent, almost plan-like deceleration of pace in relation to the
normal fishing schedule of the village—by this time he is reported
leaving the beach a full three hours after the last of the other boats has
been launched.

By the time the late man pulls his boat from the water, the sun is little
more than an almost-submerged leer on a mindless horizon and the
waves have jelled to heavy, slowly swirling jibes. Night winds begin to
cover the eastern part of the sky with a thick, cumulous ceiling of
ridicule. Sardonic chuckles ripple along the waterline where the undertow pursues an endless foreplay with beach gravel. The late man stands
motionless, looking strangely as if he belongs neither to the water nor
the land; his face is a ploughed field but his eyes dart about the beach
like frightened piranhas. His boat is a crazily tilted sneer lying on its
side in the pebbles, with rope dangling from the prow like corded
spittle. Wave upon wave of curling laughter lampoons the beach. Everywhere, everything grins. The late man no longer defends himself. He
has committed the blunder of allowing himself and the universe to
discover his detective activities, his secret investigations into the nature
and composition of himself and whatever he finds it possible to appre-
hend. But he has allowed this discovery prematurely, before he has had
time to properly anaesthetize his specimens, and now, suddenly aware
of a spy in their midst, they have disintegrated into countless labyrinth-
ine possibilities and traps and the late man is cut off without the possibility of retreat. He has long since given up trying to sledge-hammer
his brain to sleep.
     But a violated universe will not be satisfied with the simple deflection
of an inquisitive mind, and as if to make certain that such a trespassing
will never again be possible, it has turned glaring spotlights against the
late man's brain, blinding and overwhelming it with confusion and
derision. Stiffly aligned principles and corollaries suddenly go limp
and begin to collapse; endless qualifications overrun simple premises
and leave behind a shambles of tattered and useless shreds of belief.
Above all, the horror is set creeping up the back stairs of the late man's
mind that all this is beyond his control, and that like a retaining pin
pulled from a spring-loaded wheel, this destruction will continue

relentlessly until it has unrolled the tension from the spring.

There appears to be little he can do but to hold on until all is done, and to hope that he doesn't become so weakened in the process as to fall prey to a useless madness.

In a matter of months the departures and arrivals of the late man and the fishing fleet have diverged to such an extent that the returning fishermen see the late man's boat heading toward them at dusk, on its way north toward open water. He stands huddled over his wheel, eyes staring unseeing at the darkening horizon as if in purposeful blindness. The fishing fleet parts to let him pass; though no one appears to understand, everyone sees the desperate undertow in his eyes and says nothing. When all the boats are secured and the gear locked away, the late man is a dissolving blotch against black evening. A few moments later he is gone.

The late man had returned the previous morning with no fish at all.

As he sat down to dinner, the young fisherman who had asked about the late man early one morning suddenly spoke of him to his wife. "Nobody knows anything, or they won't say anything. Everybody pretends to ignore him. I've got to find out."

His wife said nothing. He looked at her curiously, then threw down his knife. "Well damn it, here's a man digging his own grave in plain view of the whole village, and nobody has the guts to look into the matter." His wife remained silent but a worried look began to unsettle her face. The young fisherman stood up abruptly. "I'm going to find out," he said, reaching for his squall-jacket and opening the door. "Even if for no other reason than a simple matter of self-defence!" he added as the door slammed shut. Footsteps receded from the cabin. Within minutes the sound of his outboard began to move across the bay toward the fishing grounds and the open sea.

For a time the young fisherman directs his boat through thick total darkness; a bulging cloud cover muffles the moon and the night sways and sidesteps in ponderous movements that are blind but everywhere. The occasional clear splash falls short among the sluggish gurgle and sagging cough of deep-water waves beneath the keel. The young fisherman peers at the bleakness but steers his boat by instinct.

As he moves farther and farther into deeper water the night begins to thin out; his eyes detect edges, outlines, occasional glimpses of phosphoric glitter—eventually the moon disentangles from the clouds and trudges higher into the sky, spraying a fine shower of thin light over the fishing grounds. By this time the young fisherman can make out the dark shape of the late man's boat, lying at anchor on his starboard side. The young fisherman shuts off his engine and drifts closer. The booms on the boat before him are out, trailing thin glistening lines into the water. The late man is fishing.

The young fisherman sits unmoving at his wheel, uncertain as to what should follow. Possibilities dart in and out of his mind, unwilling to bite. He waits, his brain idling slowly, his thoughts loose.

A creak from a rusty tackle interrupts the silence. A glass float dips and scrambles; the late man comes alive and begins to reel it in. A strike.

The young fisherman straightens up and strains to see. The glass float tugs and splashes at the end of a stiff line; the late man's figure curves against the mast, his arms taut like two rigid claws shaking with exertion. The young fisherman feels an instinctive excitement thrill through his body as if the strike were his own. Something huge is on the end of that line.

The glass float is almost at boat's-edge, momentarily calmer. The late man reaches for his fish-net and plunges it over the side, scooping carefully. His back is turned to the young fisherman, obscuring the float as he brings it to the boat's side. The fish-net rises from the water, then stops.

Surprised, the young fisherman leans forward but sees only the hunched back of the late man leaning over his net. A fierce rippling movement shakes the arm holding the handle as something twists and writhes in the meshes, but the late man makes no move to pull it into the boat. Ten minutes pass; the late man still stands bent over his net, gazing at his catch. The young fisherman is unable to see his face.

Finally, in a slow but deliberate movement, the late man empties his net into the sea and straightens up.

The young fisherman watches, still dumbfounded, as the late man repeats the same procedure moments later when another line snaps alive. This time his demeanour seems to indicate recognition or less interest; a short look suffices to make him empty the net again. After a short pause a third float begins to bob and the late man reels it in. Half

an hour later he is still engrossed in the net's contents ignoring all the
other lines which are jerking at the boom. Bent over the gunwale, his
hair blowing about his head like spray in the wind, the late man stares
at his catch in silence, then throws it back into the sea.

As a faint paleness begins to tinge the outermost edges of the dark,
the young fisherman stands up stiffly, a nervous flutter in his stomach,
strangely excited yet uncertain why. He detects traces of the intoxica-
tion of discovery in his feelings, though he has no idea what he has
discovered or realized.

Carefully pulling out his oars, he mounts them in the oarlocks and
prepares to slip away. By the time the sun appears he will be back in the
bay and in his cabin. Then there will be time to think.

A small sound from the other boat stops his raised oars short. The
late man has emptied his net and stepped back toward the mast. As he
half-turns to re-apply bait to one of the lines the young fisherman
catches a glimpse of the late man's face. He almost drops his oars.

The late man's face is totally disfigured. Crumbled skin, twitching lips
and bleached white hair, he is suddenly old—an uncertain fool barely
able to hold his balance in the rocking boat. The young fisherman is
stunned. The late man was of the same generation as the others in the
fishing fleet—chronologically about thirty years old. Now he looks
three times that age.

But there is no time to lose; the horizon is becoming a thin pencil-
line of light across the dark and he will be discovered. Stealthily moving
his oars, the young fisherman pulls away toward the south and the
fishing village.

As his boat moves into the bay, he sees the first cabin doors opening
and the fishermen walking down the beach toward their boats. Several
of them look up, surprised to see his incoming boat at such an odd
time. Obviously his wife has said nothing. He steers toward an unused
part of the beach and runs his boat aground.

There, his boat bouncing slightly to the rhythm of his fading wash,
he sat on the bow and twisted a piece of rope between his fingers;
uncertain, almost nervous, uncertain again. The spreading sun warmed
his back as he sat, but his stomach remained cold and unsettled; he
felt the desperate urge to run, to commit a violence, tear something to
shreds, but somehow he was numbed or simply unable to move. For

no apparent reason something seemed to have snapped; his senses
coiled and bunched up in twisting knots, thoughts whirled in ever-
tightening circles about his head and a steadily mounting pressure
threatened to explode inside him like a surfacing deep-water fish.

Then the faint growl from a distant engine punctured the silence and
the tension drained away with an almost audible hiss. The young
fisherman looked over his shoulder and watched the late man's boat
increase toward the bay. Several of the other fishermen paused and
shaded their eyes. For a short while everything hung in suspension . . .

Suddenly the late man's boat is in the bay, its engine silent, drifting toward the beach. As its prow gouges into the sand the late man
struggles feebly to climb off the deck onto the gravel, half-falling
several times in the process. Then, hoisting the bow rope over his
shoulder, he attempts to pull his boat higher up onto the beach.

Later, after the late man had been buried and the fishermen had
returned to their boats, the young fisherman was heard to say that in a
totally paralyzed landscape, the only moving thing had been the late
man trying to beach his boat. They had watched him for an incredibly
long time, trying to raise the bow above the gravel, and when he finally
collapsed, still no-one had moved. When they eventually began to climb
down toward the fallen figure, the landscape seemed to stretch and
expand in every direction and they walked for hours before reaching
him. They found him lying on his back, his face contorted with a
mixture of agony and amazement; it was the oldest face they had ever
seen. So they had buried him, quietly and without looking at each
other, and the young fisherman had beached the boat. The next morning, due possibly to the tiring events of the preceding night and day,
the young fisherman slept a little longer, and eventually launched his
boat some fifteen minutes after the last of the fishing boats had cleared
the bay.

*German-born Andreas Schroeder, one of Canada's fine young writers, now
makes his home in British Columbia. He has published both poetry and prose.
'The Late Man' was picked by Helwig and Marshall as one of the best
Canadian stories of 1971 (*FOURTEEN STORIES HIGH, *Oberon Press, 1971).
Schroeder is associated with the west coast magazine,* CANADIAN FICTION
MAGAZINE. *'The Late Man' indicates that we might expect fine stories from
Andreas Schroeder in coming years.*

Joe Manetti says he is innocent
—but who will believe him when
he has
such a strong motive
*for kidnapping?*

# always a motive

Dan Ross

**h**e hesitated under the blue
glow of the mercury streetlight. Carefully, he gathered the sleeping
youngster tighter in his arms and looked down at the innocent baby
face and wispy yellow hair of the boy with a glance of infinite sadness.

He stood a moment longer in the deserted street as if not quite sure
what he should do. He was young and shabbily dressed. It was a warm
summer night and he wore no hat. His hair was jet black and curly and
his face was pale and wore a haunted look.

Suddenly he made up his mind and walked down the street to a
brick apartment building. He stepped inside the open vestibule door,
and hurriedly scanned the many white name cards over the mail boxes.
He saw that the Millers lived on the second floor and at once started on
his way upstairs.

There was a moment of waiting after he pressed the Miller doorbell.
He stood with the still-sleeping child in the hallway's dim light. Then
the door opened and a blond, tanned young man in trousers and white
undershirt appeared, a questioning look in his sleepy tormented eyes.

He held out the little boy. "Here's your kid," he said quietly, "he's
all right." His eyes searched the startled face of the young father.

Miller took the boy in his arms with something like a sob, then he
gave a quick frightened glance at the man and ran back into the apartment with his precious bundle.

By that time the young man was hurrying back down the stairs in a
confused state of emotions. He stepped out of the apartment and
started off down the street when everything suddenly happened. Figures came out of the shadows, bright lights blinded his eyes, hands
gripped him cruelly.

"Don't try to resist," a hard voice warned him. "It's the police."

The trip to headquarters took only a few minutes. Reporters crowded around the car as the two detectives elbowed their way across the sidewalk and into the big, gloomy building.

At last he found himself in a big office with three men. And the one who'd warned him first addressed him across the wide desk in the same hard tones. "I'm Inspector Winters. You'd better begin to talk. It'll make it easier for all of us. Especially you."

The young man with the curly, black hair licked his lips. "You think that I kidnapped that boy. But you're making a mistake."

The Inspector had a broad face, a slash mouth. Now he smiled. "That isn't even original." He pulled out a form and poised a pen. "Name and address?"

"Joe Manetti, 284 West 79th Street." His tone was flat and hopeless.

The Inspector nodded. "Occupation?"

"Musician. But I'm not working at it now."

"Married?"

Joe nodded. "Yes. But my wife left me. She's somewhere on the West Coast."

The Inspector took it all down. Then he cocked his head at him and said, "What was your motive? I mean, first taking the child, and then bringing him back that way."

Joe took a deep breath. "I didn't kidnap the boy. I just brought him back."

The Inspector regarded his two associates, who had taken stands on either side of the dark young man. Then he stared at the prisoner with a not-unkind expression. "Let's not talk in riddles. What's your story?"

Joe made a simple gesture. "I was out driving. I drive a lot. I like to get away from my apartment. I parked in a supermarket lot to get some groceries. When I came back, I found the kid on the front seat of the car. And there was a note saying that it was the Miller boy."

The Inspector shook his head in sad disbelief. "What did you do with the note?"

"I unpinned it from his shirt," Joe said. "The kid was restless and crying. So I gave him some milk. Later I tore up the note."

"Just to make sure this isn't all imagination," the Inspector said, reaching for another sheet, "we'll want the store name, location, and what time you were there."

Joe gave him the details, finishing with, "After that I drove back to my place and took the kid with me."

"We'll go into that in due time," the Inspector told him and handing the sheet of information to one of his assistants ordered him, "Make a check on this." He gave his attention to Joe again. "Of course you knew right away that the Miller baby had been kidnapped?"

The dark young man nodded. "I heard it on my car radio while I was driving earlier in the afternoon."

The Inspector clasped his hands before him on the desk and leaned forward, his voice full of accusation. "And yet you made no effort to turn the child over to the authorities but held on to him for hours. Do you expect me to swallow this story?"

Joe shrugged. "I'm telling the truth," he said resignedly.

"I think you kidnapped the Miller child yourself and then you lost your nerve," the Inspector snapped. "And that's why you brought him back to his parents."

The telephone on the Inspector's desk rang and he answered it and listened for a few minutes, interrupting now and then with suitable grunts of acknowledgement. When at last he put it down he stared at Joe Manetti with a different light in his eyes. A glint that was close to one of understanding.

"Joe," he said, "that call came from your apartment. One of our men has been there finding out some things about you. Is it true that you lost your six-year-old son a few months ago?"

Joe Manetti reacted strangely to the question. His face became even more pale and he sat up very straight, and there was no revealing expression on his face. He answered in a monotone. "He was killed by a truck. A street accident when I was out of town on a job."

The Inspector's heavy face took on a chastened look. He glanced down at his desk top and his tone was low when he spoke. "I want you to know, Joe, that I try to be human on this job. It's not always easy, but I do. I can see that this must have been hard for you, alone, trying to bring up your kid. But it's also pretty damning evidence against you. In a lot of these cases when they don't follow the beaten track there's usually someone like you involved. Most times it's a mother who's lost her own baby. Do you follow me?"

Joe met his glance with tormented eyes. "I didn't do it, Inspector," he repeated softly.

"Okay," the Inspector said wearily. "Now we've got to establish where you were at the time the kid was taken. Where were you at approximately eleven-thirty this morning?"

Joe bowed his head. "I don't know. Out driving somewhere."

"That's not much help, is it?" Sarcasm was edging its way back into the Inspector's tone. "The boy was picked up from in front of the apartment building between eleven-twenty and eleven-thirty-five. Unless you can prove you were somewhere else then, I think you're in bad trouble."

The young man looked up again. "I don't see how I'll be able to prove anything," he said. "I get spells when I can't stand it in my place. I take the car and I drive. Anywhere! I just drive until I feel better."

"Where did you go today?"

"Out toward the north. I drove quite a distance into the country and then I came back again."

"I see," the Inspector said. "And there was no one with you? You didn't meet anyone you knew? Or stop at any gas station or restaurant?"

"I had plenty of gas and I don't eat much these days." His tone was dejected.

The questions continued and the answers were just as hopeless as in the beginning. After a long time the Inspector took him by the arm, and led him to the door. In the corridor a uniformed officer took him in charge and led him to a regular cell.

At ten the next morning he was back in the Inspector's office sitting across the desk from the man with the big face again.

The Inspector leaned forward. "I'd like you to go over your story once more, Manetti. Everything from when you got up yesterday morning."

The dark-haired young man slumped wearily in his chair and recited the same story over in a weary, agonized voice so low that the Inspector strained to hear what was being said.

"I've told you the truth," he said at the end.

The Inspector lit a cigarette. "Maybe you have. But it looks to me as if you're going to have to face trial for kidnapping."

Just then there was a knock on the office door and a policeman entered along with another man in a different, gray uniform.

The policeman addressed the Inspector. "This party has something he wants to tell you, sir."

"Is it important?" The Inspector showed irritation.

The small man in the gray uniform stepped forward and spoke for himself. "I think it is, sir." He glanced at Joe Manetti with a friendly smile. "This young man didn't kidnap the Miller boy."

The sentence caused a second of pin-dropping silence in the room.

The Inspector showed astonishment. "What's that you say?"

"I read the story in the morning papers and saw Mr. Manetti's picture and I knew it was him right away," the little man in gray said proudly.

"Knew it was who?" the Inspector demanded with fading patience.

"The young fellow who didn't wait for his change at the expressway toll station where I was on duty. He gave me a dollar and before I could hand him his change he'd driven off. Seemed to be in some sort of daze. I yelled after him, but that didn't work. But that's him, all right, and it was eleven-thirty. I know because my relief is due then and I was waiting for him. So he couldn't have been way out there and here in the city picking up that kid at the same time."

The Inspector frowned. "Why didn't you report all these things before?"

The little man shrugged. "Until I saw the paper I didn't know it was so important."

The Inspector looked at Joe Manetti and a smile of encouragement crossed the big face. "Looks like you're in the clear, young man."

The young man with the pale face and black, curly hair showed no special sign of relief. "I told you I was telling the truth," he said.

Some time later the Inspector saw him to the door of the headquarters building. It was an unusual gesture for the big man and he carried it out with a shade of awkwardness. But when he held out his hand and took Joe Manetti's in it, his grip was firm and the handshake a very friendly one.

"There was one thing I couldn't understand," he said, studying the young man with concerned eyes. "In fact I still can't see it. Why didn't you bring the kid directly to us?"

Joe Manetti hesitated to answer. He looked away from the Inspector, his gaze settling on the busy street where youngsters played amid the traffic. "I doubt if you'd be able to follow my thinking, Inspector," he said quietly.

The Inspector said, "Give me a chance."

"Okay," the young man said with a deep sigh. "I wanted to see the face of a father who had lost his kid and then got it back." And he walked slowly down the steps without looking back and lost himself in the crowded street.


*Dan Ross is one of the world's most prolific writers of popular fiction. This native of Saint John, N.B., under a host of pseudonyms, has written well over a hundred novels and over five hundred stories. We asked Dan Ross to submit from his voluminous files a favorite story of his. 'Always a Motive' was the result, a story which, according to the writer, "has been widely printed and reprinted over the world'.*

# man in community

She never really knew the shapes
of their souls or the range of their
emotions, and only had rare
glimpses of the mines and
orchards, weavers and goldbeaters,
that produced what she used and
ate. Sometimes she thought she
had glimpses of city spires beyond
the forests, and though she knew
that the Colonies often shifted
with the seasons, there was no
change as long as she was with
them, and she never found out
what they traded for with coins or
feathers, or if they sacrificed the
living on stone altars, nor the
names of their strange gods.

from *A Grain of Manhood*
by Phyllis Gotlieb

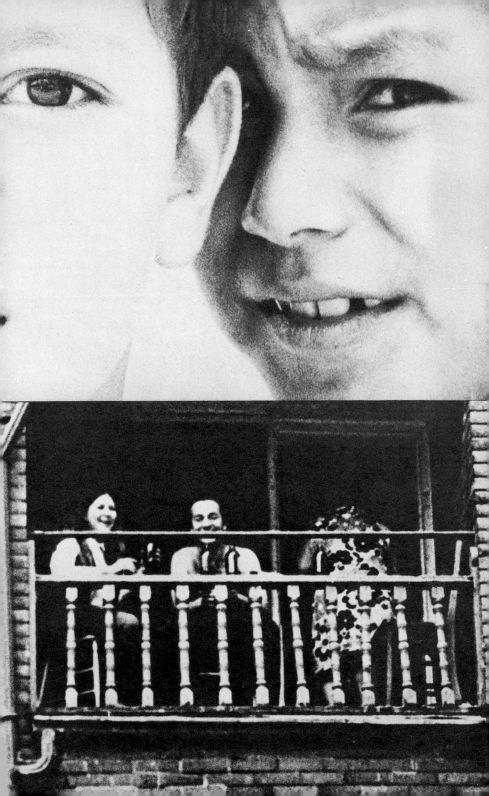

When the Devil encounters a powerful adversary in head-to-head conflict the sparks are bound to fly. The resulting struggle makes for exciting reading.

But when the Devil is pitted against a fearless young preacher in a remote prairie settlement, the clash is highly unique and totally engrossing.

The weapons: fiddles in a lonely shack.

The prize: control of a prairie town—with the Devil's beautiful daughter as an added bonus.

# dance for the devil

Edward McCourt

Coyote Gully isn't a place you'd notice twice, because it's like so many other districts in the Canadian West—flat, windy, dry—but thirty years ago, when the Reverend Dugald Cameron first came among the people, things were different. Coyote Gully was a name then that you might hear in parts far off; for nearly everybody who went there stayed only a little while and likely said hard things afterward about the place and its inhabitants. It wasn't a soil where you'd figure the Word would ever take root, and maybe it wouldn't have but for one thing, a thing the like of which isn't often heard in a new country. For the Reverend Dugald Cameron met the devil face to face in old Raftery's hut on the top of Dead Man's Butte and sent him packing. After that people did what he told them, not wishing to argue with a man who had faced up to the devil; and today you won't find a more respectable God-fearing community the length and breadth of the land.

In those days settlers were few and far apart—small ranchmen mostly, living along the foothills, for on the plain itself the soil was light and sandy and rain hardly ever fell. A queer and ill-assorted lot

they were too. Blond restless Swedes from the Dakotas; a scattering of
Englishmen, younger sons mostly, their veins flowing blue blood and
alcohol; black-haired Slavs from Central Europe who wrested a living
somehow from the sandy soil of the prairie itself; a settlement of Scots
—not the dour industrious kind you mostly get on the Western farm-
lands, but dark wild men who were the riffraff of the Glengarry
counties back East; and a family of slow-spoken loose-jointed Southerners who'd come up a year or two before from the hills of Georgia or
maybe Tennessee. There were hardly any women; it wasn't a woman's
country then, though of course things are different now.

There was no town to speak of in the district—just a general store at
the crossroads run by Olaf Svenson, a big Swede who'd left the States
for reasons you didn't ask about, and a stock corral alongside the rail-
road tracks where the ranch men loaded their cattle. The Mounted
Police were forty miles away; the settlers pretty well made their own
laws and ran their lives without interference from the outside. Sometimes, though, a policeman would come snooping round for a day or
two, trying to figure out where the citizens got their liquor from; for
those were prohibition days, and Saturday night and most nights in
between, Coyote Gully flowed raw alcohol. Some of the liquor got as
far as the Indian reserve up north, and that was bad, but the police
never found anything. After a while they always got discouraged and
went away, and everyone would celebrate by getting drunk again. That
was the way things were when the preacher came.

He held his first service in the crossroads store. Nearly everyone
turned out, for there wasn't much doing in Coyote Gully Sundays, the
Scots having strong convictions about getting drunk on the Sabbath.
Even the Graingers were there—the Southerners who'd moved in a
couple of years before. They kept to themselves mostly, and nobody
knew much about them, for they raised no grain and kept no stock
except a string of saddle horses, Kentucky bred, that they rode a lot at
nights. Old Man Grainger looked like one of the patriarchs you read
about in the Bible, if you could overlook the trickle of tobacco juice
that ran out the corner of his mouth and stained his long gray beard.
Six-feet-four, he must have been when he straightened up, pale-eyed,
hawk-nosed, a mane of white hair hanging near to his shoulders. He
sat up front at the end of a bench by an open window, and every minute
or so, regular as clockwork, he'd turn his head and let fly. There wasn't

a mark on the sill you could see afterward. His three sons slouched on the bench beside him. It was easy telling they'd be like their old man in thirty years, if they lived that long. Kitsy was different.

Kitsy was worth looking at twice. Often, if you were a man. She was small—maybe she favored her dead mother—with a waist you could buckle a hatband round. Her face was a golden oval studded with the bluest eyes you ever saw, under a shock of hair that looked like sunlight when she let it flow over her shoulders the way she mostly did. Today, though, she had it done up top in braids. She wore a gingham dress that was tight in places, the skirt crisped out so you could see a lot of white lace underneath. Not the kind of girl you'd find it easy to stand up in front of and talk about things of the spirit. Not when she kept her blue eyes fixed all the time on your face.

Maybe the Reverend Dugald Cameron didn't make much of a hit his first time up, but the odds were all against him. Nobody wanted him in Coyote Gully, not even the Scots. It's a wonder he didn't quit the minute he saw the manse where he was supposed to live—a two-room tumble-down shack half a mile from the crossroads, full of holes and mice and dirt. Standing up front he looked tired and rumpled, like he'd slept in his clothes. He was pretty young, and women maybe thought him handsome; only too thin, all joints and angles, his face lean and gaunt. You could see he needed a woman to feed him up.

The hymn singing wasn't much, for there were no hymnbooks. The preacher had a fine bass voice, and a few of the Scots strung along with him for a line or two, but they petered out pretty quick and he had to finish all by himself. By preaching time he was looking pretty discouraged. But after a while the fire in his eyes got fanned up and you could tell he was getting a grip on himself. He had nerve anyway. He told those people what he or any other God-fearing man thought of them. He talked about the way they scorned to make provision for their minister, having the manse in mind and forgetting that no one had invited him—he'd been sent by the church back East to reopen a mission that had been closed for twenty years. But it was liquor he had most in his mind. For a Scotsman he attacked it in a manner unexpected and violent. He told the people that their drunken carousals were the shame of the whole nation. He told them about what happened to Sodom and Gomorrah, and though he didn't go so far as to complete the comparison, you could see what he was driving at. He made it seem like a straight fight between himself and the Little Brown Jug, and long before he was through you had a feeling the jug was going to get smashed.

Even Old Man Grainger rested his cud and listened. Especially when the preacher got to talking about the devil. For he talked about him in an intimate, personal sort of way, as if he'd known him all his life. Near the end, the sweat was running down his face and he'd taken to pounding the counter so hard you could see Olaf Svenson was concerned about the tinned goods piled on top of it.

"Brethren," the preacher said—and how he could call that congregation "brethren" with a straight face was hard to figure—"the devil is here, among us! He lives and thrives in Coyote Gully! He must be driven out, wholly and forever! That is my task! There is nowhere room for the devil and the Word! I am the bearer of the Word! I shall not go hence while the devil dwells among us!"

He didn't call for a hymn to wind up with. He said the benediction in a subdued sort of way and stood there up front looking tired and white, the fire all gone out of him. Maybe he figured that what he said hadn't made an impression on anyone. He was wrong. Old Lauchlan Fraser, who all through service had been out of sight behind the flour barrel, got slowly to his feet.

"Mr. Cameron," he said, "if you're lookin' for the de'il, we all ken fine where you'll find him."

The fire came back into the preacher's eye. "I have found him," he said. "In this room."

"I'm no speakin' o' the de'il in ony metaphysical sense," Lauchlan said. He had studied philosophy in Edinburgh before his brain went queer on him. "But perhaps ye dinna believe in him as a visible reality in the form o' the flesh?"

"Old man," the preacher said, "I am a Presbyterian."

The answer seemed to satisfy Lauchlan. "Verra weel, then," he said. "You'll find him nights in the old cabin at the top o' Dead Man's Butte."

A kind of shiver ran through the congregation then, and people looked at one another sideways. Old Lauchlan had spoken of things best kept quiet. For there was no denying something queer about the tumble-down log cabin on the summit of Dead Man's Butte. An old man had lived there till two years before—an Irishman named Raftery

who claimed to be a descendant of the fiddler of Dooney; and it was
true he played the fiddle the way that made you think he couldn't have
learned it just by practice like ordinary folk.

" 'Tis the devil's gift," he used to say when he was drunk, which
toward the end was nearly all the time. "He gave it to the family a long
time back, a reward for faithful service. But it's myself is the last of the
Rafterys, and when I'm gone there's none will fiddle like me, except
the devil himself. For he'll take back his gift, you see. It's a way he has
with men."

The night old Raftery died people heard music coming from the
cabin, wilder than they'd ever heard before, and when they went to the
cabin next morning they found Raftery stiff and cold in his chair, his
fiddle across his knee, bow broken on the floor beside him. And the
strange thing was, so people whispered, that though they buried
Raftery, his music played on. Clear, still nights they could hear the
sound a long way off, and nobody ever went near the cabin any more.
For the devil had come to Coyote Gully—it was then that the liquor
started to flow the way it hadn't done before—and set himself up in
Raftery's hut.

Not that there was much talk about such things, for they weren't
supposed to happen in a new country. That was why, when Lauchlan
brought the devil's music out in the open before a stranger, people
looked at one another from the corners of their eyes, furtive and half
ashamed.

Old Man Grainger unbent himself and stood up. His face was dark
and his thin lips twitched. "I ain't got time fer listenin' to loony talk,"
he said. "Hants don't skeer me none." And he stumped down the
room and outside, his tribe at his heels.

All except Kitsy. She stood up before the Reverend Dugald Cameron
and looked him over slow, from head to foot. All the time his face got
redder and redder, till it looked like any minute it would catch fire.

"Preacher," Kitsy said, in that soft drawl of hers that always made
men's blood run faster, no matter what they thought of her, "why don't
you go home? Coyote Gully is no place for a man of God."

Maybe what she said was kindly meant, but the preacher didn't take
it that way. The fire left his face and shot out from his eyes. "Child," he
said, "on your lips the name of God is blasphemy."

For just a second Kitsy looked as if she'd been slapped hard across

the face. Then she put her hands on her hips, thrust out her bosom.
" 'Child,' did you say?" She was smiling now in a way that didn't look
natural. "I'm a woman, preacher. And there's no man here knows it
better than yourself."

She went out then, chin up, petticoats aswirl, and for a minute the
preacher just stood there up front, staring after her. Then he faced the
congregation.

"Mr. Fraser," he said, "I will count it a great favor to be shown the
way to Dead Man's Butte." And he went out without shaking hands
with anyone.

Old Lauchlan came to the manse one night when the air was so still you
could hear the smallest sound five miles away, and the moon shone
now and then between great banks of cloud that hung low in the sky.

"The de'il's makin' music on the hilltop," was all he said.

The preacher answered never a word. He saddled the spavined old
gray nag one of the Scots had sold him for a lively four-year-old, and
followed Lauchlan across the prairie toward the foothills, till after an
hour's riding they could see the queer humped outline of Dead Man's
Butte rising from the level plain. At the foot of the hill Lauchlan drew
rein.

" 'Tis a dark business ye may be engaged upon, sir," he said. "A dark
and evil business. And since a layman would be no help at all in exor-
cisin' the de'il, I'll be leavin' ye here. But perhaps this wee token may be
a bit comfort to ye, gin the de'il is vulgarly no supposed to be suscept-
ible to lead."

He shoved a Colt revolver into the preacher's hand. The preacher
considered it in silence.

"Thank you, Mr. Fraser," he said after a while. "But I share the
vulgar opinion." And he gave back the gun.

He tied his horse to a nearby sapling and started up the overgrown
path leading to the top of the hill. What he thought about on the way
up, there's no telling. Maybe, in spite of his calling, he was afraid; for
the wind had risen across the foothills and made strange noises in the
trees, and the moon shone through ragged edges of cloud and the light
it cast was wild and beautiful and sad. He couldn't see the cabin, but
he saw a dull glow up top, like a dying fire far off; and wind or no, he
heard always the thin wail of a fiddle, an eerie outland sound full of

queer trills and shivers like you'd expect to hear when the devil made music in the cabin of a sinful old man who had died.

The preacher reached the top and walked easier. He could see the cabin ahead, and the dull glow coming through a windowpane covered over with paper or maybe dirt. For a minute he stood still. The music was louder now—shrill, high-pitched, the kind of music you'd figure a bow held by man couldn't drag out of any fiddle ever made.

Then the moon shone clear and the music stopped and the preacher went on. There was a clearing on the far side of the cabin, and a wide track running away from it down the side of the Butte facing the foothills, but the preacher didn't stop to wonder why. He walked right up to the cabin door, pulled it open and stepped inside.

His legs carried him clear to the middle of the room before he was able to stop them. And by the time he'd stopped he knew it wasn't any use turning back. There were figures between him and the door, and they closed the door and for a minute there was no sound at all in the cabin except the preacher's heavy breathing and the sputter of embers on the stone hearth that had been Raftery's pride.

The preacher drew a deep breath right into the bottom of his lungs and straightened his shoulders. He faced the figure sitting quiet in a broken-backed chair beside the dying fire.

"They told me," he said, "that in this cabin I would meet the devil face to face."

Old Man Grainger got up off the chair, moving slow and quiet, and stretched himself to his full height. "They told true," he said. He shoved his hawk nose close to the preacher's face. "Why have ye come here?" His voice had a rasp in it.

The preacher never turned a hair. "To drive you out of Coyote Gully," he said. "You and your spawn."

The shadowy figures behind the preacher moved away from the door and drew around him. They spoke no words, but looked at Old Man Grainger as if expectant of the sign that would move them to violence and blood.

"And destroy your works," the preacher said. He waved his hand toward the row of puncheons standing along the cabin wall.

The old man laughed, low and short, as if he didn't think what the preacher had said was funny. "Watch him close, boys," he said. "We'll settle him when the time comes."

They flushed the preacher for concealed weapons, dragged him to a chair in the corner and sat him down, a guard on either side. The preacher didn't say anything at all, but his lips moved all the time. Maybe he was praying; you couldn't tell from his face.

Old Man Grainger went back to his chair. He dipped a tin mug in the puncheon beside him and drank deep. Then he picked up the fiddle lying by the chair and drew a bow across it. The fiddle let out a melancholy screech. He tucked it under his chin and began to play.

He played a long time. But he played only one tune, over and over again; a wild haunting melody, plaintive and sad at first, but getting faster and faster till near the end you could hardly see the flash of the bow or the twinkle of the old man's fingers on the strings. But sometimes, when he played the trills and quavers that had lifted the preacher's hair when he heard them far off, the music broke for a split second and a false note would jar a man who had an ear for such things. And whenever that happened, the preacher's head would come up and he looked at Old Man Grainger with a gleam in his eyes that hadn't been there before.

The music snapped off clean in the middle of a bar. Old Man Grainger shot out of his chair as if a tack had stuck into him, and the words that came out of his mouth were the kind you'd figure the devil would say when he was upset. For the door had burst open with a bang that could be heard a mile off, and Kitsy stood in the middle of the cabin floor. Her hair was wild over her shoulders, her clothes wind-tossed and disheveled, but her smile was as gay as the morning. She stood right in front of the preacher, hands on her hips, and looked at him the way she did in church.

"So you've come, preacher," she said. "Lauchlan told me. I didn't believe him."

The preacher got up from his chair. "I said I'd come."

Kitsy stared him in the face for maybe a minute. Then her eyelids flickered. "How do you like the devil's music?" she said. "Does it make you forget the dreary hymns you sing through your nose?"

That wasn't fair, for the preacher had a big bass voice that rumbled around deep inside him before bursting through a wide-open mouth. He opened his mouth now and laughed till the rafters shook.

"The devil may be accomplished in evil," he said, "but he can't play a fiddle worth a tinker's dam!"

For just a second it was so quiet in the cabin you could hear a cat walking. Then Old Man Grainger grabbed Kitsy by the shoulder and flung her aside.

"So I can't play the fiddle!" he shouted. "I'm the champeen fiddler of seven counties—eight if the judges hadn't of been crooked!"

He stopped then and his face tightened up and the red went out of it. He held out the fiddle to the preacher.

"Mebbe you kin do better," he said.

The preacher took the fiddle and ran his hand over the back as if he were petting a favorite dumb animal. "It's a long time since I've practiced," he said. "But if I can't play better than the devil, I deserve to go to hell."

He picked at the strings with long thin fingers and tightened up a couple of pegs. "To a sensitive ear," he said, "this fiddle is out of tune."

The preacher sat him down in the devil's chair without a by-your-leave to anyone, and slid the fiddle under his chin. The very first notes he drew, a hush settled inside the cabin, and except for the music and the flash of the bow, there wasn't anywhere sound or movement. At first the preacher played only simple things, tunes that every Scotsman knows, and all the world besides, like Annie Laurie and Lochaber No More and The Flowers o' the Forest; and some that must have come from his land's far north or maybe the Outer Islands, weird wailing melodies in a minor key that called to mind all manner of things fanciful and sad.

All the time the devil and his sons sat quiet on the floor, and the devil didn't make even a move toward the puncheon. But Kitsy crept closer and closer to the preacher's chair, till she was sitting almost at his feet. And she looked at his face as if she couldn't draw away her eyes.

The preacher untucked the fiddle and laid it across his knee. " 'Tis a strange thing, Mr. Devil," he said, "a strange thing indeed that you should play so badly the tune which in my country they say you devised. 'Tis called the Devil's Hornpipe. This is how it should go."

It was the tune men said old Raftery played the night he died—the tune the preacher heard while he climbed the path to the top of Dead Man's Butte. Wild and strange it was, with crazy trills and quavers and double-stopping even in the trills. It made you think of things that set the blood racing and the foot tapping—of things you wouldn't ever talk about to anyone, not if you wanted to be thought an honest God-fearing man.

Before the preacher had been at it a minute, everyone in the room was clapping hands in time to the music. All except the devil himself. He never twitched a muscle, but the sweat ran down his face in streams.

All of a sudden Kitsy got up off the floor. Her body swayed in time to the music, and the firelight cast queer shadows on her face. For a minute she stood in the middle of the room, swaying to the music. Then she began to dance. And that was strange, for they say that who-ever dances to the devil's music is the devil's slave forever after. But Kitsy couldn't help herself. White, strained, with the kind of look you see on people in a trance or maybe going mad. She swung her hips like a woman of the streets, and her feet twinkled so fast under her long skirt you'd have sworn sometimes they weren't there at all. And all the time the music rose wilder, faster, so that it seemed no mortal feet could ever keep time to it.

Kitsy never missed a step. Not even when she dropped her skirt from her hips and kicked it across the room. She danced then in her lace petticoat. Her slim legs flashed golden in the firelight and whenever she spun in a circle the petticoat flared out straight from her waist, showing what she wore underneath, which was little enough to make a man blush. But the preacher never flicked an eyelid and his bow never missed a note.

Like a candle flares up bright just before it goes out, Kitsy spun in a dazzling pirouette, so fast she was just a blur, and crashed to the floor. The Devil's Hornpipe snapped off short, like a broken string. The preacher crossed the room in one jump and dropped to his knees be-side the huddled heap on the floor. He slid his arm under Kitsy's shoulders and drew her close to him. Kitsy lay white and still against his chest; then her blue eyes opened and she smiled up into his face.

"Preacher," she said, "you played me down."

He gathered her up as if she were a child and set her in a chair. Then he picked up her skirt, which lay all crumpled in a corner.

"Make yourself decent," he said.

Old Man Grainger spoke in a voice so low that the preacher barely caught his words. "I never heerd the beat of it," he said, and his face worked strangely. "Go peaceable now and we'll do ye no harm."

The preacher drew himself up and his eyes flashed lightning. "I will go when my work is done!"

"What work?" You could tell from the way the old man spoke that he was afraid.

The preacher pointed to the puncheons ranged along the wall. "The destruction of the devil's brew," he said. "The brew you carry over the trails to the weak and the ignorant and afraid."

A great anger flamed in his eyes now and his voice rang out like a bugle. "Go home, old man, and pray! Leave off this trumpery masquerade which would not deceive a child, much less one armed with the Word! Go home and repent, all of you! And henceforth show yourselves not as devils, but as men!"

For a long minute the preacher and the devil faced each other, breast to breast, eye to eye. Without a word, Old Man Grainger turned away. He went out of the cabin, walking slowly—a man beaten, tired, old. The others followed, one by one, till the preacher stood alone.

He stood for a long time without moving. After a while he gathered up an armful of sticks and threw it on the fire. When the flames leaped up, he pulled bits of blazing wood from the hearth and scattered them about the room. The floor and walls caught in a dozen places.

The preacher picked up the devil's fiddle and made as if to throw it into the fire. A hand caught his arm and he whirled about.

"Kitsy!"

"Dad will miss his music," she said.

The preacher smiled. "A fine fiddle," he said, "when well played."

He led her outside then, just in time, for the fire was blazing on three sides of them. They stood together in the shadow of the trees and watched the flames in the cabin grow brighter, shoot out through the windows, the roof, toward the sky.

"The devil brews good ale," the preacher said. "It burns well."

"You're a brave man, preacher," Kitsy said. She stood close to him and her hand rested lightly in the crook of his arm.

"I'm a good fiddler," the preacher said.

"And I'm the devil's own now," Kitsy said. "For I danced his Hornpipe. But, preacher, I couldn't help it."

The preacher laughed the way he did before he took the fiddle from Old Man Grainger. You could hear his shout a mile away, above the roaring of the flames.

"Whoever dances the Devil's Hornpipe belongs to the man who plays it!" And he swept her into his arms and kissed her the way no girl had ever been kissed in Coyote Gully or maybe the whole of the West.

That night the folk had gathered in the crossroads store from as far away as the second range of foothills, for word had got round that the preacher had gone to fight the devil in Raftery's cabin on the top of Dead Man's Butte. And though they laughed loud and drank hard, you could see a great fear was on them, though maybe the fear wasn't the same for all. They stayed in the store a long time while the night wore on and the liquor sank lower in the keg.

The Scots were talkative enough at first, but after a while they were dour and silent, for they were Covenanter stock and knew that the devil was real, no matter how much they denied him when the sun shone. The Englishmen from the ranches drank more than their share and quarreled noisily with the Swedes, but after a while they, too, were quiet, and wishing they hadn't come. All the time old Lauchlan Fraser slept behind the flour barrel. Or seemed to. But every now and then his eyelids lifted and his eyes gleamed sharp in the lamplight.

When they heard horses galloping, there wasn't a man of them not on his feet, and Olaf Svenson took a double-barreled shotgun from under the counter and fingered the triggers. When the preacher came in with Kitsy behind him, there was a sound like the night wind sighing in the treetops, which was only a great gust of breath coming all at once from men's lungs, and a shout went up that rattled the crockery on the shelves. But the shout died away and men stared at the preacher, and the great fear came back. For the preacher's face was black with smoke and his eyelashes gone and his coattails singed and the smell of fire upon him. And through the open doorway they could see a blaze of light on the top of Dead Man's Butte—flames shooting to the sky and painting the clouds a fearful bloody red.

The preacher walked down the room and men gave back on either side. He stood with Kitsy beside him, and his face was dark and awesome to behold. "The devil is gone from Coyote Gully!" he thundered. "The devil and all his works!"

With one mighty sweep of his arm he hurled the keg of liquor from the counter. It was almost empty, but even so you could hear a groan rumble through the room, and men watched with anguished eyes the liquor run across the floor and form little dust-covered puddles in the worn places.

The preacher stalked back to the door, turned and stood with his long body framed in the doorway, the fire on Dead Man's Butte behind him. "I give you one week!" he said, and his voice chilled the blood of all who heard him. "One week, to make the manse fit for the minister's wife to live in!"

That was thirty years ago. The old manse is gone now, and there's a fine big new one on the best street in Coyote Gully. It needs to be big, for the Reverend and Mrs. Dugald Cameron have a large family, and besides, they're hospitable folk who keep open house nearly every night of the week. The preacher and Kitsy aren't often alone, and if you knock on their door almost any hour you're sure of a warm welcome. But sometimes if you go past the manse at night you'll hear music from the back room where the light is, and then you'll know not to knock, for there won't be any answer. It's a fiddle playing that you hear—wild, eerie music that lifts the hair on the back of your head if the night is dark. It couldn't be, of course, for it's the preacher who plays it, but if you heard that tune anywhere else, you'd swear it was the Devil's Hornpipe.

_A professor of English at the University of Saskatchewan (Saskatoon) until his death in January 1972, Edward McCourt was one of western Canada's most highly respected writers and critics. He has been described by one of his colleagues as 'a man for all seasons'. Most of his novels and stories have as their setting the prairies and people he knew and loved so well. 'Dance for the Devil' appeared in_ SATURDAY EVENING POST _(Oct. 18, 1952) and was chosen by this popular magazine as one of its best stories of that year. Mr. McCourt suggested this story as his personal favourite when we asked him to submit a story for this collection._

Here is a story from the Indian people of the West Coast told by one who knows and loves the tales of his people.
The two men in conflict may be legendary characters—
as old as man himself—
but they are also
as real as today
and as timeless as man's desires.

# ko-ishin-mit and paw-qwin-mit

George Clutesi

The Moon of many Moods had come and gone.

Kloose-mit the herring had fed the children of the land

With their glistening roe they had fed the Indian people.

The last of the drying herring eggs upon the long racks

Now sun-dried to a golden hue were stored for summer use.

The Budding Moon had arrived. The time to play was here again.

It was early spring. The young men in the village vied against each other for their own clubs in tournaments, field games, wrestling matches, races, swimming, weight lifting and many more games.

Paw-qwin-mit, the Son of Skate, was the acknowledged spear-throwing champion of the whole region. It was said that he was so light and deceptive in his feints and movements that he was impossible to hit with the tournament spear. Paw-qwin-mit was a handsome young man with broad shoulders and narrow hips and slender legs.

Ko-ishin-mit, the village boaster, thought otherwise.

"He is so wide in the shoulders that you can't help but hit him, if you are strong enough," Ko-ishin-mit would boast loudly in his croaky voice. "I myself am pretty fast on my feet and I am strong. I can throw the tournament spear as straight, and as far, as anyone else," he boasted to one and all. "Paw-qwin-mit thinks he is the best now because he hasn't thrown the spear with me," Ko-ishin-mit was loud in his bragging. "I can beat Paw-qwin-mit, I know I can." He would get so excited in his boastful talk that the older men in the village would

admonish him not to talk so foolishly but this would only serve to
infuriate Ko-ishin-mit to louder and more boastful talk.

It was during one of these loud outbursts that he let it be known he
had been training most rigidly for the spear-throwing tournament.

"I am fast on my feet. I can feint, and I am more cunning than Paw-
qwin-mit." The foolish young Ko-ishin-mit had begun naming his
imagined opponent.

Paw-qwin-mit was a good-natured young man. He took Ko-ishin-
mit's many challenges with good humour and ignored the rude remarks
thrown in his direction from the foolish and croaky voice of Ko-ishin-
mit. It was known by everyone in all the region that this was one of the
many qualities that made Paw-qwin-mit so popular as "The Spear
Thrower." Indeed he was the undisputed champion until, of course,
the foolish and boastful Ko-ishin-mit began his bragging of being a
better thrower.

It was the day of the big tournament. The other sports of the field
and water had been run and dealt with. At this particular time of the
season when the sun was warm, when the buds on all the reawakening
plants were bursting forth in their pale green crowns, and the salmon-
berry blossoms in their bright flaming red jackets swayed and beckoned
the humming-bird small to sip nectar, when the nettle shot from the
loam, the bracken unfurled its golden crown from the mossy glens and
the tree-toad voiced his cracky song—then was the spear-throwing
season heralded in.

The preliminaries had come and were finished. Now the senior and
more experienced throwers were in the field and competing with great
earnestness. The young men were many. They were all lithe, fast,
strong of arm and sure of stance. The entire village was out for this
event—the old, the young, the women with babies strapped on their
backs or cuddled in their cradles as snug as only babies can be. This
was indeed the event of the season.

Paw-qwin-mit was the chief referee of the tournament. The last bout
was on and the two contestants opposed each other in earnest. Paw-
qwin-mit stood to one side in the middle of the open arena. In his
hand high over his head was poised a sprig of evergreen, a signal for
the contestants to take their places at the ends of the open lane pro-
vided for this sport. The young men paced deliberately to their respective places, ten plus two paces apart, that was the prescribed and ac-

cepted distance for the throw. The men stood clean and lithe in their fur-seal battle shorts. They stood erect, back to back, their spear tips resting lightly on the soil directly in front of them. There was complete silence. The spring sun shone from directly overhead. These two throwers were the best, next to Paw-qwin-mit who was the undisputed champion of the entire coastal region.

"Now hear me." Both men turned slowly. "The man to my right shall throw the first spear," Paw-qwin-mit's voice was loud and clear. The contestants showed no emotion as they deliberately turned with their spears poised lightly in their strong hands.

"On your marks. Ready. Throw!"

The first spear whistled through the still air in a low, straight line. The live target deftly side-stepped and the swift shaft missed its intended mark by a scant hand. There was an audible sigh from the women of the audience.

"Throw two." The sprig of evergreen was poised overhead again.

"The man on my left will make the throw. On your marks. Ready. Throw!"

The second shaft blazed down the line chest high at a terrific speed and thudded harmlessly into the earth as the intended victim just as deftly side-stepped.

This contest was real. Each contestant was determined to win. It was certainly good enough to be next to the great Paw-qwin-mit as Thrower of the Spear. Both young men knew this and both men would surely think twice before attempting to wrest the crown from the most popular spearman of them all. Each succeeding throw seemed to come nearer to its mark but never made an actual hit. The contestants now stood face to face at all times and took their turns at the throw. It was remarkable how true the shafts sped and the speed was never diminished.

"Hear me now. Each of you have one more throw. Do you wish to rest?" Paw-qwin-mit's voice was very clear and he timed his words to come slowly as he directed his question first to one then to the other.

"No." "No." Both men declined the offer of respite.

"All right. Both men stand back to back. The man to my right will make the throw. Easy now. Turn. Ready. Throw!"

The shaft came hurtling at terrific speed towards its intended victim and again the swift missile missed its mark by a mere finger.

"The last throw. Easy. On your marks. Turn. Throw!" Paw-qwin-mit's voice was strong. It rang through the clear still spring air.

The last shaft came blazing down the line, straight for its mark it hurtled. The throng held its breath. There was no sound. This last throw would determine the outcome of the tournament. Would it find its mark?

Thud. The last and final shaft imbedded itself in the thick turf behind the broken earth of the measured arena. A full-throated cheer went up from the throng that had held its breath to bursting point, glad that neither of the young men was hit.

Paw-qwin-mit waited discreetly until the cheering had subsided to a good-natured hum before he stepped out into the arena again and his loud voice requested that the two young men step forward. In good time the two, who but a moment before were bent on hitting each other, now stood side by side facing the great crowd. They stood very close together, almost touching. The contest was over. It was evident that there was no enmity between them, both had broad smiles on their handsome young faces. They stood at easy attention with their heads held high, their eyes set well above the throng. Each had done his utmost and each had just managed to outwit the other. Both showed superb form. It was a good contest. True, there were misses but one could say that the bad throws in this contest were much too close for the other man's comfort.

This was truly a contest of nerves. At ten plus two paces it was almost impossible to hit an agile opponent unless fear became evident on the part of the intended victim. The thrower, too, must not at any moment reveal any apprehension or nervousness, however slight. It was like entering an unfamiliar village where a good watch dog comes at you snarling and showing his fangs. Show fear and the dog will surely charge. Stand if you must but speak to the dog in a commanding voice. If you show no fear the creature will not attack—a simple contest of nerves. The spear throwing then was indeed an exercise for the nerves.

"Now hear me." Paw-qwin-mit slowly turned a complete round, as he addressed the now happy throng, until he was facing the two men again. He touched the right shoulder of the one, then the other, with the evergreen sprig and in a ringing voice he declared the contest a tie. A great shout went up from the enthusiastic people. It was a popular decision made by a popular man. The two young men touched shoulders momentarily before they ran to join their companions who were still standing in the arena set aside for contestants, to be congratulated and slapped on the right shoulders good-naturedly by them all.

It was the time for any contender to step forward now and declare his challenge for the championship. The last two contestants knew better than to make such a challenge. Indeed they were very happy to be known as "Next to the great Paw-qwin-mit." According to all appearances the tournament was over. It was a successful day, there being two instead of one second best.

From the far side of the village a figure was seen approaching the field of the arena in a resolute and deliberate stride. There was a dead hush in the crowd which had been so jubilant but a moment ago. The lone figure drew nearer swiftly.

"Ko-ishin-mit!" A chorus went up from the throng, "Ko-ishin-mit! What can Ko-ishin-mit possibly be up to now?"

Ko-ishin-mit timed his appearance perfectly—the moment before the official announcement of a successful tournament. He strode directly to the centre of the arena where Paw-qwin-mit still stood and, without looking towards him, he slowly stopped his march, turned resolutely to the direction of the Chief's and contenders' platform, and in his thin croaky voice announced: "I, Ko-ishin-mit, do now, this day, hereby challenge the so-called spear-throw champion, Paw-qwin-mit, to a duel, here and now to determine who really is the champion."

"Tu-shack, tu-shack? What has happened?" was all the elders and councillors could muster in their complete surprise to this totally unexpected turn of events.

Ko-ishin-mit stood perfectly still after his brazen challenge. His beady little black eyes were fixed resolutely on the Elder. There was consternation within the ranks of the officials on the Chief's platform. Ko-ishin-mit readily sensed this and foolishly gloated over the awkward situation he had created, however temporary it may have been. For the moment he was master of the situation.

At long last, after a prolonged delay and confusion, the otherwise staid and venerable Elder stood up. There was complete silence in the great throng—not from awe nor from respect but from complete surprise. Ko-ishin-mit had timed his appearance perfectly. He was master of the situation and he knew it.

"What say you, Paw-qwin-mit? You have heard the challenge. Bear in mind that you are honour bound to defend your title." The wise old Elder spoke slowly and directly to the champion.

There was now an audible murmur from the official platform. "No, no, no. This cannot be. This must not happen. It is sheer foolishness."

Paw-qwin-mit recovered from his initial surprise. He reluctantly looked towards Ko-ishin-mit, hoping to see him show that he was only clowning.

The challenger stood his ground. He made no move. His eyes were still fixed on the now standing Elder. He was master of the situation. He gloated. Even then the champion spear thrower could not believe this awkward situation was real. His own eyes sought those of the Elder for some explanation. He was shaking his head very slowly, hoping now desperately that this display of utter foolishness was but a joke on the part of Ko-ishin-mit.

"The so-called champion spear hurler is scared. If he refuses to meet me then I am the real and rightful champion," said Ko-ishin-mit seriously.

Paw-qwin-mit's face was cast towards the ground in apparent consternation. This is real, he admitted to himself, this is real. He lifted his head slowly and sought some explanation from the Elder. "Tell me he jokes. Tell me this is not real," he said silently to himself. There was complete silence. The Elder refused to repeat his admonition to Paw-qwin-mit of a moment before. Doubtless, he too hoped that the foolish and impulsive Ko-ishin-mit was indeed joking. All knew without a shadow of a doubt that he would never have a chance as a spear hurler with the thus far indomitable Paw-qwin-mit.

Ko-ishin-mit's ego was increasing by the moment and he showed it to the best advantage. "Paw-qwin-mit, I shall stand here and await your return. Go and bring your best shaft. I will duel with you to the finish," Ko-ishin-mit spoke brusquely. He mistook the throng's silence as awe for his contempt for the champion, when indeed it was pity for his foolishness.

Paw-qwin-mit reluctantly left for his home and soon returned. In his hand he carried a short shaft with two protruding tips. It was a practice shaft—not the real throwing shaft.

"To your respective places. Do not turn until I give the command. Do not throw until the command is given to do so. The championship is at stake. Each of you must abide by the rules." The Elder was visibly not happy with the turn of events but he knew his duties. He carried them through.

Ko-ishin-mit strutted affectedly and with pomp to his chosen end. He had bedecked his person, which was completely black, with gleaming red feathers. Around his black head, around his elbows, his waist and his knobby knees and ankles were festooned arrays of red feathers. He was indeed a sight to behold.

Paw-qwin-mit did not bother to change his attire or to add any frills. He came in his natural dress, without any costume whatsoever. He walked reluctantly, almost foolishly. He felt ridiculous to have to submit to this foolhardy situation perpetrated by this known foolish and senseless person called Ko-ishin-mit.

"I throw first," Ko-ishin-mit's voice was loud and croaky. "I throw first."

Paw-qwin-mit nodded in assent, otherwise he made no reply.

"On your marks. Turn. Get set. Throw!" The Elder's voice was shaky. It was evident that he was nervous, not because of the outcome of this duel but because he had permitted it to take place.

Ko-ishin-mit had plotted out his strategy in forcing this showdown, in a manner only he could carry out, with utter folly. He leaned far back, ostensibly to impel his shaft the faster. This tell-tale and unnecessary manoeuvre of course gave Paw-qwin-mit ample time to determine the type of throw that would come. He avoided the oncoming shaft with no apparent effort. Ko-ishin-mit's shaft thudded harmlessly into the earth.

"Throw two. On your marks. Turn. Throw!"

Ko-ishin-mit suddenly became animated. "Klootch, klootch, klootch." He was jumping straight up and down in an amazing exhibition of grotesque light-footed manoeuvres. "Klootch, klootch, klootch," he sang loudly in his croaky voice, "Klootch, klootch, klootch."

No doubt this was to distract and otherwise unnerve the great Paw-qwin-mit. The champion stood motionless. His cool, sure eyes followed Ko-ishin-mit's every move, hop and jump.

Zing! The two-pronged shaft seemed to come from nowhere. It whizzed through the silent air at unbelievable speed. Before any of the onlookers realized what had happened Ko-ishin-mit was pinned to the soft earth. His two knobbly black legs were clamped solidly betwixt the twin prongs of Paw-qwin-mit's practice shaft. Ko-ishin-mit flapped gallantly to free himself but without success and soon exhausted himself with his great efforts to regain his feet. There he lay, helpless, with both feet pinned to the ground.

Paw-qwin-mit trotted lightly over and freed him, helping him to his feet. A great deafening roar came from the throng. Not for the victory but for the champion's true sportsmanship. This was what made him a great champion—together with his ability to turn with no apparent effort to show but a mere sliver of himself sideways. The handsome young Paw-qwin-mit was indeed broad in the shoulders. Sideways he was so thin he made a very difficult target to hit. So all he had to do to avoid the thrusts was to turn sideways. The foolish Ko-ishin-mit did not realize this till too late.

Paw-qwin-mit admonished Ko-ishin-mit never to jump or leap in the air. "Once your feet left the solid ground you were relatively helpless to any average spear hurler, and you dragged your feet under you so. You are lucky that you did not challenge any of the other more reckless young hurlers to a duel to the finish because I say that they would have finished you, and for good."

For once in his life Ko-ishin-mit was meek. He realized that he was indeed very lucky to escape with his life and only because of Paw-qwin-mit's good graces.

"You are the Champion," he murmured weakly.

To this day it is said that all Ravens hop-skip and jump whenever they move on their feet.

*George Clutesi is a Canadian Indian writer and artist from Vancouver Island. His collection* SON OF RAVEN, SON OF DEER (*Gray's 1967*) *was a Centennial project. In the book he presents fables of the Tse-Shant people of the west coast. We were impressed by Clutesi's ability to take the lore of his people and write in such a way that his story 'Ko-ishin-mit and Paw-qwin-mit' is applicable to all people.*

"They are not my suitcases. They are your suitcases. You admit it. Please to move your suitcases to the opposite rack, where, if they fall, they will fall upon your own heads."

The scene is a crowded train in Europe. The speaker sits in the seat facing you. You are the visitor in his land.

What do you do? Ignore him? Appease him? Argue with him?

Or do you decide to beat him *at his own game, on his own ground ?*

# we have to sit opposite

Ethel Wilson

even in the confusion of entering the carriage at Salzburg, Mrs. Montrose and her cousin Mrs. Forrester noticed the man with the blue tooth. He occupied a corner beside the window. His wife sat next to him. Next to her sat their daughter of perhaps seventeen. People poured into the train. A look passed between Mrs. Montrose and Mrs. Forrester. The look said, "These people seem to have filled up the carriage pretty well, but we'd better take these seats while we can as the train is so full. At least we can have seats together." The porter, in his porter's tyrannical way, piled their suitcases onto the empty rack above the heads of the man with the blue tooth, and his wife, and his daughter, and departed. The opposite rack was full of baskets, bags and miscellaneous parcels. The train started. Here they were. Mrs. Montrose and Mrs. Forrester smiled at each other as they settled down below the rack which was filled with miscellaneous articles. Clinging vines that they were, they felt adventurous and successful. They had travelled alone from Vienna to Salzburg, leaving in Vienna their doctor husbands to continue attending the clinics of Dr. Bauer and Dr. Hirsch. And now, after a week in Salzburg, they were happily on their way to rejoin their husbands, who had flown to Munich.

Both Mrs. Montrose and Mrs. Forrester were tall, slight and fair.

They were dressed with dark elegance. They knew that their small hats were smart, suitable and becoming, and they rejoiced in the simplicity and distinction of their new costumes. The selection of these and other costumes, and of these and other hats in Vienna had, they regretted, taken from the study of art, music and history a great deal of valuable time. Mrs. Montrose and Mrs. Forrester were sincerely fond of art, music and history and longed almost passionately to spend their days in the Albertina Gallery and the Kunsthistorische Museum. But the modest shops and shop windows of the craftsmen of Vienna had rather diverted the two young women from the study of art and history, and it was easy to lay the blame for this on the museums and art galleries which, in truth, closed their doors at very odd times. After each day's enchanting pursuits and disappointments, Mrs. Montrose and Mrs. Forrester hastened in a fatigued state to the cafe where they had arranged to meet their husbands who by this time had finished their daily sessions with Dr. Bauer and Dr. Hirsch.

This was perhaps the best part of the day, to sit together happily in the sunshine, toying with the good Viennese coffee or a glass of wine, gazing and being gazed upon, and giving up their senses to the music that flowed under the chestnut trees. (Ah Vienna, they thought, Vienna, Vienna.)

No, perhaps the evenings had been the best time when after their frugal pension dinner they hastened out to hear opera or symphony or wild atavistic gypsy music. All was past now. They had been very happy. They were fortunate. Were they too fortunate?

Mrs. Montrose and Mrs. Forrester were in benevolent good spirits as they looked round the railway carriage and prepared to take their seats and settle down for the journey to Munich to meet their husbands. In their window corner, opposite the man with the blue tooth, was a large hamper. "*Do* you mind?" asked Mrs. Montrose, smiling sweetly at the man, his wife, and his daughter. She prepared to lift the hamper on which the charming view from the carriage window was of course wasted, intending to move it along the seat, and take its place. The man, his wife, and his daughter had never taken their eyes off Mrs. Montrose and Mrs. Forrester since they had entered the carriage.

"*If* you please," said the man loudly and slowly in German English, "*if* you please, that place belongs to my wife or to my daughter. For the moment they sit beside me, but I keep that place for my wife or my

daughter. That seat is therefore reserved. It is our seat. You may of
course use the two remaining seats."

"I'm sorry," said Mrs. Montrose, feeling snubbed, and she and Mrs.
Forrester sat down side by side on the two remaining seats opposite the
German family. Beside them the hamper looked out of the window at
the charming view. Their gaiety and self-esteem evaporated. The train
rocked along.

The three continued to stare at the two young women. Suddenly the
mother leaned toward her daughter. She put up her hand to her mouth
and whispered behind her hand, her eyes remaining fixed on Mrs.
Montrose. The daughter nodded. She also stared at Mrs. Montrose.
Mrs. Montrose flushed. The mother sat upright again, still looking at
Mrs. Montrose, who felt very uncomfortable, and very much annoyed
at blushing.

The man ceased staring at the two young women. He looked up at
the rack above him, which contained their suitcases.

"Those are your suitcases," he asked, or rather announced.

"Yes," said Mrs. Montrose and Mrs. Forrester without smiles.

"They are large," said the man in a didactic manner, "they are too
large. They are too large to be put on racks. A little motion, a very little
motion, and they might fall. If they fall they will injure myself, my wife,
or my daughter. It is better," he continued instructively, "that if they
fall, they should fall upon your heads, not upon our heads. That is logical. They are not my suitcases. They are your suitcases. You admit it.
Please to move your suitcases to the opposite rack, where, if they fall,
they will fall upon your own heads." And he continued to sit there
motionless. So did his wife. So did his daughter.

Mrs. Montrose and Mrs. Forrester looked at the suitcases in dismay.
"Oh," said Mrs. Forrester, "they are so heavy to move. If you feel like
that, please won't you sit on this side of the carriage, and we will move
across, under our own suitcases, though I can assure you they will not
fall. Or perhaps you would help us?"

"We prefer this side of the carriage," said the man with the blue tooth.
"We have sat here because we prefer this side of the carriage. It is logical
that you should move your suitcases. It is not logical that my wife, my
daughter and I should give up our seats in this carriage, or remove
your suitcases."

Mrs. Montrose and Mrs. Forrester looked at each other with rage in their hearts. All their self-satisfaction was gone. They got up and tugged and tugged as the train rocked along. They leaned resentfully across the erectly sitting man, and his wife and his daughter. They experienced with exasperation the realization that they had better make the best of it. The train, they knew, was crowded. They had to remain in this carriage with this disagreeable family. With much pulling and straining they hauled down the heavy suitcases. Violently they removed the parcels of the German family and lifted their own suitcases onto the rack above their heads, disposing them clumsily on the rack. Panting a little (they disliked panting), they settled down again side by side with high colour and loosened wisps of hair. They controlled their features so as to appear serene and unaware of the existence of anyone else in the railway carriage, but their hearts were full of black hate.

The family exchanged whispered remarks, and then resumed their scrutiny of the two young women, whose elegance had by this time a sort of tipsy quality. The girl leaned toward her mother. She whispered behind her hand to her mother, who nodded. Both of them stared at Mrs. Forrester. Then they laughed.

"Heavens!" thought the affronted Mrs. Forrester, "this is outrageous! Why can't Alice and I whisper behind our hands to each other about these people and make them feel simply awful! But they wouldn't feel awful. Well, we can't, just because we've been properly brought up, and it would be too childish. And perhaps they don't even know they're rude. They're just being natural." She breathed hard in frustration, and composed herself again.

Suddenly the man with the blue tooth spoke. "Are you English?" he said loudly.

"Yes — well — no," said Mrs. Forrester.

"No — well — yes," said Mrs. Montrose, simultaneously.

A derisive look came over the man's face. "You must know what you are," he said, "either you are English or you are not English. Are you, or are you not?"

"No," said Mrs. Montrose and Mrs. Forrester, speaking primly. Their chins were high, their eyes flashed, and they were ready for discreet battle.

"Then are you Americans?" said the man in the same bullying manner.

"No," said Mrs. Montrose and Mrs. Forrester.

"You can't deceive *me*, you know," said the man with the blue tooth,

"I know well the English language. You *say* you are not English. You *say* you are not American. What, then, may I ask, are you? You must be something."

"We are Canadians," said Mrs. Forrester, furious at this catechism.

"*Canadians*," said the man.

"Yes, Canadians," said Mrs. Montrose.

"This," murmured Mrs. Forrester to Mrs. Montrose, "is more than I can bear!"

"What did you say?" said the man, leaning forward quickly, his hands on his knees.

"I spoke to my friend," said Mrs. Forrester coldly, "I spoke about my bear."

"Yes," said Mrs. Montrose, "she spoke about her bear."

"Your bear? Have you a bear? But you cannot have a bear!" said the man with some surprise.

"In Canada I have a bear. I have two bears," said Mrs. Forrester conceitedly.

"That is true," said Mrs. Montrose nodding, "she has two bears. I myself have five bears. My father has seven bears. That is nothing. It is the custom."

"What do you do with your bears?" asked the man.

"We eat them," said Mrs. Forrester.

"Yes," said Mrs. Montrose, "we eat them. It is the custom."

The man turned and spoke briefly to his wife and daughter, whose eyes opened wider than ever.

Mrs. Montrose and Mrs. Forrester felt pleased. This was better.

The man with the blue tooth became really interested. "Are you married?" he asked Mrs. Forrester.

"Yes," she replied. (We'll see what he'll say next, then we'll see what we can do.)

"And you?" he enquired of Mrs. Montrose. Mrs. Montrose seemed uncertain. "Well, yes, in a way, I suppose," she said.

The man with the blue tooth scrutinized Mrs. Montrose for a moment. "*Then*," he said, as though he had at last found her out, "if you are married, where is your husband?"

Mrs. Montrose took out her pocket handkerchief. She buried her face in her hands, covering her eyes with her handkerchief. She shook. Evidently she sobbed.

"Now you see what you've done!" said Mrs. Forrester. "You shouldn't ask questions like that. Just look at what you've done."

The three gazed fascinated on Mrs. Montrose. "Is he dead or what is he?" asked the man of Mrs. Forrester, making the words almost quietly with his mouth.

"Sh!!" said Mrs. Forrester very loudly indeed. The three jumped a little. So did Mrs. Montrose.

There was silence while Mrs. Montrose wiped her eyes. She looked over the heads opposite. The wife leaned toward her husband and addressed him timidly behind her hand. He nodded, and spoke to Mrs. Forrester.

"Well," he said, "at least you admit that *you* have a husband. If you have a husband then, where is he?"

"Oh, I don't know," said Mrs. Forrester lightly.

"No, she doesn't know," said Mrs. Montrose.

The three on the opposite seat went into a conference. Mrs. Montrose and Mrs. Forrester did not dare to look at each other. They were enjoying themselves. Their self-esteem had returned. They had impressed. Unfavourably, it is true. But still they had impressed.

The man with the blue tooth pulled himself together. He reasserted himself. Across his waistcoat hung a watch chain. He took his watch out of his pocket and looked at the time. Then to the surprise of Mrs. Montrose and Mrs. Forrester he took another watch out of the pocket at the other end of the chain. "You see," he.said proudly, "I have two watches."

Mrs. Montrose and Mrs. Forrester were surprised, but they had themselves well in hand.

Mrs. Montrose looked at the watches disparagingly. "My husband has six watches," she said.

"Yes, that is true," nodded Mrs. Forrester, "her husband *has* got six watches, but my husband, like you, unfortunately has only two watches."

The man put his watches back. Decidedly the battle was going in favour of the two young women. How horrid of us, he was so pleased with his watches, thought Mrs. Montrose. Isn't it true that horridness just breeds horridness. We're getting horrider every minute. She regarded the man, his wife and daughter with distaste but with pity.

"You *say*," said the man, who always spoke as though their statements were open to doubt, which of course they were, "that you come from Canada. Do you come from Winnipeg? I know about Winnipeg."

"No," said Mrs. Montrose, and she spoke this time quite truthfully, "I come from Vancouver." Mrs. Forrester remained silent.

"And you, where do you come from?" persisted the man in a hectoring tone, addressing Mrs. Forrester. Mrs. Forrester remained silent, she had almost decided to answer no more questions.

"Oh, do not tell, please do not tell," begged Mrs. Montrose in an anguished way.

"No," said Mrs. Forrester importantly, "I shall not tell. Rest assured. I shall not tell."

"Why will she not tell?" demanded the man. He was tortured by curiosity. So was his wife. So was his daughter.

"Sh!!" said Mrs. Montrose very loudly.

The man seemed ill at ease. By this time nothing existed in the world for him, or for his wife, or for his daughter but these two Canadian women who ate bears.

"How is it," asked the man, "that you no longer buy my trousers?"

"I beg your pardon?" faltered Mrs. Montrose. For a moment she lost ground.

"I said," replied the man, "why is it that you no longer buy my trousers?"

The ladies did not answer. They could not think of a good answer to that one.

"I," said the man, "am a manufacturer of trousers. I make the most beautiful trousers in Germany. Indeed in the world." (You do not so, thought Mrs. Forrester, picturing her husband's good London legs.) "For three years I receive orders from Winnipeg for my trousers. And now, since two years, yes, since 1929, I receive no more orders for my trousers. Why is that?" he asked, like a belligerent.

"Shall we tell him?" asked Mrs. Forrester, looking at Mrs. Montrose. Neither of them knew why he had received no more orders for his trousers, but they did not wish to say so. "Shall we tell him?" asked Mrs. Forrester.

"You tell him," said Mrs. Montrose.

"No, *you* tell him," said Mrs. Forrester.

"I do not like to tell him," said Mrs. Montrose, "I'd rather you told him."

The man with the blue tooth looked from one to the other.

"Very well. I shall tell him," said Mrs. Forrester. "The fact is," she said, looking downward, "that in Canada men no longer wear trousers."

"What are you saying? That is not true, never can that be true!" said the man in some confusion.

"Yes," said Mrs. Montrose, corroborating sombrely. "Yes, indeed it is true. When they go abroad they wear trousers, but in Canada, no. It is a new custom."

"It is the climate," said Mrs. Forrester.

"Yes, that is the reason, it is the climate," agreed Mrs. Montrose.

"But in Canada," argued the man with the blue tooth, "your climate is cold. Everyone knows your climate is cold."

"In the Arctic regions, yes, it is really intensely cold, we all find it so. But not in Winnipeg. Winnipeg is very salubrious." (That's a good one, thought Mrs. Montrose.)

The man turned and spoke rapidly to his wife. She also turned, and looked askance at her daughter. The expressions of the man, his wife, and his daughter were a blend of pleasure and shock. The two liars were delighted.

At last the man could not help asking, "But they *must* wear something! It is not logical."

"Oh, it's logical, all right!" said Mrs. Forrester.

"But what *do* they wear?" persisted the man.

"I never looked to see," said Mrs. Montrose. "*I* did, I looked," said Mrs. Forrester.

"Well?" asked the man.

"Oh, they just wear kilts," said Mrs. Forrester.

"Kilts? What are kilts? I do not know kilts," said the man.

"I would rather not tell you," said Mrs. Forrester primly.

"Oh," said the man.

Mrs. Montrose took out her vanity case, and inspected herself, powder puff in hand.

"I do not allow my wife and daughter to paint their faces so," said the man with the blue tooth.

"No?" said Mrs. Montrose.

"It is not good that women should paint their faces so. Good women do not do that. It is a pity."

(Oh, Alice, thought Mrs. Forrester in a fury, he shall not dare!) "It is a pity," she hissed, "that in your country there are no good dentists!"

"Be careful, be careful," whispered Mrs. Montrose.

"What do you mean?" demanded the man with the blue tooth.

(She will go too far, I know she will, thought Mrs. Montrose, alarmed, putting out her hand.)

"In our country," said the rash Mrs. Forrester, "anyone needing attention is taken straight to the State Dentist by the Police. This is done for aesthetic reasons. It is logical."

"I am going to sleep," said Mrs. Montrose very loudly, and she shut her eyes tight.

"So am I," said Mrs. Forrester, in a great hurry, and she shut her eyes too. This had been hard work but good fun for Mrs. Montrose and Mrs. Forrester. They felt, though, that they had gone a little bit too far. It might be as well if they slept, or pretended to sleep, until they reached Munich. They felt that outside their closed eyes was something frightening. The voice of the man with the blue tooth was saying, "I wish to tell you, I wish to tell you . . ." but Mrs. Montrose was in a deep sleep, and so was Mrs. Forrester. They sat with their eyes tightly closed, beside the hamper which still occupied the seat with the view by the darkening window. Mrs. Montrose had the inside corner, and so by reason of nestling down in the corner, and by reason of having an even and sensible temperament, she really and truly fell asleep at last.

Not so Mrs. Forrester. Her eyes were tightly closed, but her mind was greatly disturbed. Why had they permitted themselves to be baited? She pondered on the collective mentality that occupied the seat near to them (knees almost touching), and its results which now filled the atmosphere of the carriage so unpleasantly. She had met this mentality before, but had not been closely confined with it, as now. What of a world in which this mentality might ever become dominant? Then one would be confined with it without appeal or relief. The thought was shocking. She felt unreasonably agitated. She felt rather a fool, too, with her eyes shut tightly. But, if she opened them, she would have to look somewhere, presumably at the family, so it seemed safer to keep them closed. The train sped on. After what seemed to her a very long time, she peeped. The wife and daughter were busy. The husband sat back, hands on knees, chin raised, expectant, eyes closed. His wife respectfully undid his tie, his collar, and his top shirt button. By this

time the daughter had opened the hamper, and had taken from it a bottle and a clean napkin. These she handed to her mother. The wife
moistened the napkin from the bottle and proceeded to wash her husband, his face, his ears, round the back of his neck, and inside his shirt
collar, with great care. "Like a cat," thought Mrs. Forrester, who had
forgotten to shut her eyes.

The man with the blue tooth lowered his raised chin and caught her.
"You see," he said loudly, "you see, wives should look properly after
their husbands, instead of travelling alone and . . ." But Mrs. Forrester
was fast asleep again. The whole absurd encounter had begun to hold
an element of terror. They had been tempted into folly. She knew—as
she screwed up her closed eyes—that they were implicated in fear and
folly.

The two young women took care to sleep until the train reached
Munich. Then they both woke up.

Many people slept until they reached Munich. Then they all began
to wake up.

*Ethel Wilson's* MRS. GOLIGHTLY & OTHER STORIES *(1961) established her
as a leading Canadian story-teller. She lives in British Columbia and her
stories explore human feelings and inter-relationships. The story, 'We Have
to Sit Opposite', has not (to our knowledge) been anthologized before. We feel
that the story is particularly timely considering the tendency of Canadians to
travel abroad on an increasing scale.*

'They're the *familiars*. I tell you these hills are full of witches and —wizards, I think they call them.'
What is a *familiar*? Read your *Funk and Wagnalls*. That reference describes the familiar as 'a spirit which is supposed to attend and obey a sorcerer'. You don't believe it? Careful! You may be turned into a toad.

# journey home

W. T. Duncan

It was one of those dismal days when you want to be left alone. I had regretted making the trip almost as soon as I had begun, though I must say that I had been looking forward to seeing my sister for some time. The monotony of party-going, the effusive altercations of the garrulous populace, and the endless flow of noisy traffic would be left behind me. For two weeks, anyhow.

But as the train rumbled through the valley along by the river, past gloomy shacks half hidden in the labyrinth of dark green trees, with the sky barely visible because of the mountains on all sides, the environment seemed dismal. Certainly not a place that I could ever feel comfortably at home in ever again.

How would my sister greet me? She had always been against my leaving the old home, and was extremely angry when I had left some three years ago. "This is where you belong and here you must stay," she had said. We had not exactly quarrelled when I had left, but our parting had not been a pleasant one.

The sun had gone down behind one of those gargantuan mountains, and soon the air would be a little cooler. I leaned back on my seat and hoped that relaxing would rid me of trepidation at the thought of homecoming. I closed my eyes.

Until I closed them I hadn't noticed the two men sitting across from myself, but now the sound of their voices disturbed me somewhat. They were strangers, but one had made a tentative remark to the other, in the hope that he might strike up a conversation, and the other, who had been reluctant to speak at first, had put his magazine on the seat beside him and was joining in the conversation, much to the satisfaction of the first man who had engineered it.

It's not that I don't like to hear people talk, for sometimes a discussion can be pleasant and help to pass the time, especially on a journey such as this. But this particular conversationalist was another of those omniscient persons you have probably met yourself: the know-everything type who likes to let everyone else know that he does.

I opened my eyes a little to study the man. He was gesticulating and telling his travelling companion which was the highest mountain in these parts and how he knew that it was, or something to that effect. The other fellow sat tacitly listening, waiting for his chance to speak. I felt rather sorry for him. If he was good enough to join in the conversation he should at least be allowed to say his two cents' worth.

The first man—the noisy one—was a rotund little chap with a raucous voice, which did not suit his speckled countenance at all. Certainly a talkative little menace whom I wouldn't want to be stuck with for the duration of such a journey. The other man was taller and much more timid. He was merely talking to pass the time, yet most things he managed to say were reasonable, at least not offensive to my ear.

It was no use—relaxing was out of the question; the chubby man's voice would permit no rest.

"Of course there are. Haven't you ever seen any of those big birds, any cats or lizards around here?"

The taller man shook his head: "I've only been here once before. I'm only visiting. I don't know what goes on."

"Well, they're them," the speckled one insisted. "They're the *familiars*. I tell you these hills are full of witches and—wizards, I think they call them." He extended his hands to exaggerate his statement. "Full of 'em."

"Aren't they called warlocks?" the timid man ventured.

"What?"

"Wizards."

"Oh," the rotund man caught on, "warlocks, not wizards. Yes, that's right, I couldn't think of the word. Anyhow, whatever you call them, this part of the country's full of 'em."

The other man pondered a moment then argued. "Well, I was here last year and I never saw any. I was here a whole week. Never even heard about anything like it."

"That's the trouble. People won't talk. They got a spell on 'em. Most of them have. And the rest are too scared to say anything." The little man looked at me while he was speaking. Obviously he wanted to get me in on the conversation.

"Surely somebody would have said something about it if that was so," the taller man persisted. "I mean, this is a civilized world. Witches and such are just old legends kept alive." He hesitated, not wanting to hurt the other's feelings: "By the likes of yourself." He looked at me for agreement.

Although I was not in on the argument, both men were regarding me expectantly, as if asking me either to side with one or the other. I was sorely tempted to enter the conversation, if only to rescue the more helpless one. However, before I could decide for myself, the option was removed.

"Okay," the hoarse-voiced little man continued, "don't believe me. But you mark my words!" He looked directly at me. "D'you hear that? He don't believe a word I'm saying."

It was here that I was unfortunately dragged into the argument. "I suppose he has a right to air his opinion," I offered.

"Do you live around here," the man went on, barely waiting for me to say my piece.

I gave him a supercilious glance, which obviously bounced off his thick skin.

"As a matter of fact I'm visiting my sister," I informed him.

"Well, if you've got relatives around here, you must've heard something about what I've been talking about." He was hoping that I would corroborate his statements. "Our friend here," he pointed to the man he had been talking to, "doesn't believe a word I've told him."

This fat, toadish little person may have been counting on my support but I think I rather disillusioned him.

"For someone who does not know that a warlock is a male counterpart of a witch, I don't think you are in a position to expound theories such as you are now doing," I said contemptuously.

"You don't have to tell me anything," the chubby man argued. "I live around here. I know. Lived here all my life."

"Bully for you!" I yawned.

I could have become quite upset with the chap right there and then, but the train pulled into Little Holland Junction. The taller man was getting up and preparing to leave us.

"This is where I get off," he smiled at me, timidly.

I think he was quite relieved to be going, and stumbled off in a flurry of embarrassment. The moujik of a man who remained with me was a complete bore, and my only regret at the taller man's departure was that it left me the sole passenger in the car with him.

The train huffed away again and soon the familiar rumbling vibrated the carriage. I was leaning out the window, listening to the rhythm of the rumbling wheels. I did not notice my contemporary (as I shall loosely call him) sit on the seat next to mine.

"No bad feelings, you know," he assured me.

I started, for at first his voice gave me a little fright.

"My good fellow, of course not," I lied. "But I think there is no purpose in renewing our temporary—friendship, shall we say, nor is it my desire to do so." You have to be pompous to these characters, you know. I then concentrated my attention upon the passing landscape outside the window.

"No need to be so high and mighty," the voice said. "All I asked you was your opinion on witches. Just trying to be friendly."

I decided there and then I could not stand this man for another half hour, which was the time it would take to arrive at my destination. I ignored him.

"Jest how far are you going?" he went on, as though I had been complimentary instead of insulting.

"My dear sir, can you not understand? I do most emphatically not wish to talk with you," I snapped angrily. Surely this would rid me of him.

"All right, all right. You don't have to . . ."

I stood up, exasperated at the fellow's audacity.

"Sir!" I shouted. "I am a man of short patience. If you insist on directing your nonsensical utterances toward myself, I shall not be responsible for the consequences."

The fat little man opened his mouth to speak, but I let him go no further. I shook my finger at him sternly and glared at him.

"I warn you, my man, cease!"

"But who are you to . . ."

"Cease! I say cease!"

"Don't tell *me* when to cease," he was answering back, when I lost

control of my temper. I made the sign and completed the incantation with the proper words:
"HECATE'S SEEDS I SOWED: TURN THIS MAN INTO A TOAD."

There was a puff of green smoke. The air soon cleared, and sitting on the seat in the place of the little man was a fat green toad. I was quite pleased with myself. Time had not marred that magic touch.

Silence! At last, how pleasant. I picked up the toad and examined it; *perfect*, I muttered to myself as I dropped it out the window. Then I noticed the big blackbird flying alongside the train. It swooped gracefully to where I dropped the toad and I heard a distinct screeching. Of course, the big blackbird was my sister's *familiar*. How kind of her to greet me after all these years.


*Duncan's story, 'Journey Home' was first broadcast over CBC radio and was selected by John Drainie for his collection, STORIES WITH JOHN DRAINIE. We particularly enjoyed this story because Duncan explores, in an entertaining fashion, an area not often touched by Canadian writers.*

Few men know how many times the world has been on the verge of a nuclear holocaust since the atomic age became a frightening reality.

But we do know that the mushroom cloud has hovered over us . . . and will continue to do so.

The warning comes suddenly.

You make your preparations.

And you wait . . .

And what if you survive?

# after the sirens

Hugh Hood

They heard the sirens first about four forty-five in the morning. It was still dark and cold outside and they were sound asleep. They heard the noise first in their dreams and, waking, understood it to be real.

"What is it?" she asked him sleepily, rolling over in their warm bed. "Is there a fire?"

"I don't know," he said. The sirens were very loud. "I've never heard anything like that before."

"It's some kind of siren," she said, "downtown. It woke me up."

"Go back to sleep!" he said. "It can't be anything."

"No," she said. "I'm frightened. I wonder what it is. I wonder if the baby has enough covers." The wailing was still going on. "It couldn't be an air-raid warning, could it?"

"Of course not," he said reassuringly, but she could hear the indecision in his voice.

"Why don't you turn on the radio," she said, "just to see? Just to make sure. I'll go and see if the baby's covered up." They walked down the hall in their pajamas. He went into the kitchen, turned on the radio and waited for it to warm up. There was nothing but static and hum.

"What's that station?" he called to her. "Conrad, or something like that."

"That's 640 on the dial," she said, from the baby's room. He twisted the dial and suddenly the radio screamed at him, frightening him badly.

"*This is not an exercise. This is not an exercise. This is not an exercise,*" the radio blared. "*This is an air-raid warning. This is an air-raid warning. We will be attacked in fifteen minutes. We will be attacked in fifteen minutes. This is not an exercise.*" He recognized the voice of a local announcer who did an hour of breakfast music daily. He had never heard the man talk like that before. He ran into the baby's room while the radio shrieked behind him: "*We will be attacked in fifteen minutes. Correction. Correction. In fourteen minutes. In fourteen minutes. We will be attacked in fourteen minutes. This is not an exercise.*"

"Look," he said, "don't ask me any questions, please, just do exactly what I tell you and don't waste any time." She stared at him with her mouth open. "Listen," he said, "and do exactly as I say. They say this is an air-raid and we'd better believe them." She looked frightened nearly out of her wits. "I'll look after you," he said: "just get dressed as fast as you can. Put on as many layers of wool as you can. Got that?"

She nodded speechlessly.

"Put on your woollen topcoat and your fur coat over that. Get as many scarves as you can find. We'll wrap our faces and hands. When you're dressed, dress the baby the same way. We have a chance, if you do as I say without wasting time." She ran off up the hall to the coat closet and he could hear her pulling things about.

"*This will be an attack with nuclear weapons. You have thirteen minutes to take cover,*" screamed the radio. He looked at his watch and hurried to the kitchen and pulled a cardboard carton from under the sink. He threw two can openers into it and all the canned goods he could see. There were three loaves of bread in the breadbox and he crammed them into the carton. He took everything that was wrapped and solid in the refrigerator and crushed it in. When the carton was full he took a bucket which usually held a barbage bag, rinsed it hastily, and filled it with water. There was a plastic bottle in the refrigerator. He poured the tomato juice out of it and rinsed it and filled it with water.

"*This will be a nuclear attack.*" The disc jockey's voice was cracking with hysteria. "*You have nine minutes, nine minutes to take cover. Nine minutes.*" He ran into the dark hall and bumped into his wife who was swaddled like a bear.

"Go and dress the baby," he said. "We're going to make it, we've just got time. I'll go and get dressed." She was crying, but there was no time for comfort. In the bedroom he forced himself into his trousers, a second pair of trousers, two shirts and two sweaters. He put on the heaviest, loosest jacket he owned, a topcoat and finally his overcoat. This took him just under five minutes. When he rejoined his wife in the living room, she had the baby swaddled in her arms, still asleep.

"Go to the back room in the cellar, where your steamer trunk is," he said, "and take this." He gave her a flashlight which they kept in their bedroom. When she hesitated he said roughly, "Go on, get going."

"Aren't you coming?"

"Of course I'm coming," he said. He turned the radio up as far as it would go and noted carefully what the man said. "*This will be a nuclear attack. The target will probably be the aircraft company. You have three minutes to take cover.*" He picked up the carton and balanced the bottle of water on it. With the other hand he carried the bucket. Leaving the kitchen door wide open, he went to the cellar, passed through the dark furnace room, and joined his wife.

"Put out the flashlight," he said. "We'll have to save it. We have a minute or two, so listen to me." They could hear the radio upstairs. "*Two minutes,*" it screamed.

"Lie down in the corner of the west and north walls," he said quickly. "The blast should come from the north if they hit the target, and the house will blow down and fall to the south. Lie on top of the baby and I'll lie on top of you!"

She cuddled the sleeping infant in her arms. "We're going to die right now," she said, as she held the baby closer to her.

"No, we aren't," he said, "we have a chance. Wrap the scarves around your face and the baby's, and lie down." She handed him a plaid woollen scarf and he tied it around his face so that only his eyes showed. He placed the water and food in a corner and then lay down on top of his wife, spreading his arms and legs as much as possible, to cover and protect her.

"*Twenty seconds,*" shrieked the radio. "*Eighteen seconds. Fifteen.*"
He looked at his watch as he fell. "Ten seconds," he said aloud.
'It's five o'clock. They won't waste a megaton bomb on us. They'll save
it for New York." They heard the radio crackle into silence and they
hung onto each other, keeping their eyes closed tightly.

Instantaneously the cellar room lit up with a kind of glow they had
never seen before, the earthen floor began to rock and heave, and the
absolutely unearthly sound began. There was no way of telling how far
off it was, the explosion. The sound seemed to be inside them, in their
bowels; the very air itself was shattered and blown away in the dreadful
sound that went on and on and on.

They held their heads down, hers pushed into the dirt, shielding the
baby's scalp, his face crushed into her hair, nothing of their skin ex-
posed to the glow, and the sound went on and on, pulsing curiously,
louder than anything they had ever imagined, louder than deafening,
quaking in their eardrums, louder and louder until it seemed that what
had exploded was there in the room on top of them in a blend of
smashed, torn air, cries of the instantly dead, fall of steel, timber and
brick, crash of masonry and glass—they couldn't sort any of it out—all
were there, all imaginable noises of destruction synthesized. It was like
absolutely nothing they had ever heard before and it so filled their
skulls, pushing outward from the brainpan, that they could not divide
it into its parts. All that they could understand, if they understood anything, was that this was the ultimate catastrophe, and that they were
still recording it, expecting any second to be crushed into blackness,
but as long as they were recording it they were still living. They felt, but
did not think, this. They only understood it instinctively and held on
tighter to each other, waiting for the smash, the crush, the black.

But it became lighter and lighter, the glow in the cellar room, waxing
and intensifying itself. It had no color that they recognized through
their tightly-shut eyelids. It might have been called green, but it was
not green, nor any neighbor of green. Like the noise, it was a dreadful
compound of ultimately destructive fire, blast, terrible energy released
from a bursting sun, like the birth of the solar system. Incandescence
beyond an infinite number of lights swirled around them.

The worst was the nauseous rocking to and fro of the very earth
beneath them, worse than an earthquake, which might have seemed
reducible to human dimensions, those of some disaster witnessed in

the movies or on television. But this was no gaping, opening seam in the earth, but a threatened total destruction of the earth itself, right to its core, a pulverization of the world. They tried like animals to scrabble closer and closer in under the north cellar wall even as they expected it to fall on them. They kept their heads down, waiting for death to take them as it had taken their friends, neighbors, fellow workers, policemen, firemen, soldiers; and the dreadful time passed and still they did not die in the catastrophe. And they began to sense obscurely that the longer they were left uncrushed, the better grew their chances of survival. And pitifully slowly their feelings began to resume their customary segmented play amongst themselves, while the event was still unfolding. They could not help doing the characteristic, the human thing, the beginning to think and struggle to live.

Through their shut eyelids the light began to seem less incandescent, more recognizably a color familiar to human beings and less terrifying because it might be called a hue of green instead of no-color-at-all. It became green, still glowing and illuminating the cellar like daylight, but anyway green, nameable as such and therefore familiar and less dreadful. The light grew more and more darkly green in an insane harmony with the rocking and the sound.

As the rocking slowed, as they huddled closer and closer in under the north foundation, a split in the cellar wall showed itself almost in front of their hidden faces, and yet the wall stood and did not come in on top of them. It held and, holding, gave them more chance for survival although they didn't know it. The earth's upheaval slowed and sank back and no gaps appeared in the earth under them, no crevasse to swallow them up under the alteration of the earth's crust. And in time the rocking stopped and the floor of their world was still, but they would not move, afraid to move a limb for fear of being caught in the earth's mouth.

The noise continued, but began to distinguish itself in parts, and the worst basic element attenuated itself; that terrible crash apart of the atmosphere under the bomb had stopped by now, the atmosphere had parted to admit the ball of radioactivity, had been blown hundreds of miles in every direction and had rushed back to regain its place, disputing that place with the ball of radioactivity, so that there grew up a thousand-mile vortex of cyclonic winds around the hub of the displacement. The cyclone was almost comforting, sounding, whistling, in whatever stood upright, not trees certainly, but tangled steel beams and odd bits of masonry. The sound of these winds came to them in the cellar. Soon they were able to name sounds, and distinguish them from others which they heard, mainly sounds of fire—no sounds of the dying, no human cries at all, no sounds of life. Only the fires and cyclonic winds.

Now they could feel, and hear enough to shout to each other over the fire and wind.

The man tried to stir, to ease his wife's position. He could move his torso so far as the waist or perhaps the hips. Below that, although he was in no pain and not paralyzed, he was immobilized by a heavy weight. He could feel his legs and feet; they were sound and unhurt, but he could not move them. He waited, lying there trying to sort things out, until some sort of ordered thought and some communication was possible, when the noise should lessen sufficiently. He could hear his wife shouting something into the dirt in front of her face and he tried to make it out.

"She slept through it," he heard, "she slept through it," and he couldn't believe it, although it was true. The baby lived and recollected none of the horror.

"She slept through it," screamed the wife idiotically, "she's still asleep." It couldn't be true, he thought, it was impossible, but there was no way to check her statement until they could move about. The baby must have been three feet below the blast and the glow, shielded by a two-and-a-half-foot wall of flesh, his and his wife's, and the additional thickness of layers of woolen clothing. She should certainly have survived, if they had, but how could she have slept through the noise, the awful light, and the rocking? He listened and waited, keeping his head down and his face covered.

Supposing that they had survived the initial blast, as seemed to be the case; there was still the fallout to consider. The likelihood, he thought (he was beginning to be able to think) was that they were already being eaten up by radiation and would soon die of monstrous cancers, or plain, simple leukemia, or rottenness of the cortex. It was miraculous that they had lived through the first shock; they could hardly hope that their luck would hold through the later dangers. He thought that the baby might not have been infected so far, shielded as she was, as he began to wonder how she might be helped to evade death from radiation in the next few days. Let her live a week, he thought, and she may go on living into the next generation, if there is one.

Nothing would be the same in the next generation; there would be few people and fewer laws, the national boundaries would have perished—there would be a new world to invent. Somehow the child must be preserved for that, even if their own lives were to be forfeited immediately. He felt perfectly healthy so far, untouched by any creeping sickness as he lay there, forcing himself and the lives beneath him deeper into their burrow. He began to make plans; there was nothing else for him to do just then.

The noise of the winds had become regular now and the green glow had subsided; the earth was still and they were still together and in the same place, in their cellar, in their home. He thought of his books, his checkbook, his phonograph records, his wife's household appliances. They were gone, of course, which didn't matter. What mattered was that the way they had lived was gone, the whole texture of their habits. The city would be totally uninhabitable. If they were to survive longer, they must get out of the city at once. They would have to decide immediately when they should try to leave the city, and they must keep themselves alive until that time.

"What time is it?" gasped his wife from below him in a tone pitched in almost her normal voice. He was relieved to hear her speak in the commonplace, familiar tone; he had been afraid that hysteria and shock would destroy their personalities all at once. So far they had held together. Later on, when the loss of their whole world sank in, when they appreciated the full extent of their losses, they would run the risk of insanity or, at least, extreme neurotic disturbance. But right now they could converse, calculate, and wait for the threat of madness to appear days, or years, later.

He looked at his watch. "Eight-thirty," he said. Everything had ended in three-and-a-half hours. "Are you all right?" he asked.

"I think so," she said, "I don't feel any pain and the baby's fine. She's warm and she doesn't seem frightened."

He tried to move his legs and was relieved to see that they answered the nervous impulse. He lifted his head fearfully and twisted it around to see behind him. His legs were buried under a pile of loose brick and rubble which grew smaller towards his thighs; his torso was quite uncovered. "I'm all right," he said, beginning to work his legs free; they were undoubtedly badly bruised, but they didn't seem to be crushed or broken; at the worst he might have torn muscles or a bad sprain. He had to be very careful, he reasoned, as he worked at his legs. He might dislodge something and bring the remnant of the house down around them. Very, very slowly he lifted his torso by doing a push-up with his arms. His wife slid out from underneath, pushing the baby in front of her. When she was free she laid the child gently to one side, whispering to her and promising her food. She crawled around to her husband's side and began to push the bricks off his legs.

"Be careful," he whispered. "Take them as they come. Don't be in too much of a hurry."

She nodded, picking out the bricks gingerly, but as fast as she could. Soon he was able to roll over on his back and sit up. By a quarter to ten he was free and they took time to eat and drink. The three of them sat together in a cramped, narrow space under the cellar beams, perhaps six feet high and six or seven feet square. They were getting air from somewhere although it might be deadly air, and there was no smell of gas. He had been afraid that they might be suffocated in their shelter.

"Do you suppose the food's contaminated?" she asked.

"What if it is?" he said. "So are we, just as much as the food. There's nothing to do but risk it. Only be careful what you give the baby."

"How can I tell?"

"I don't know," he said. "Say a prayer and trust in God." He found the flashlight, which had rolled into a corner, and tried it. It worked very well.

"What are we going to do? We can't stay here."

"I don't even know for sure that we can get out," he said, "but we'll try. There should be a window just above us that leads to a crawl-space under the patio. That's one of the reasons why I told you to come here. In any case we'd be wise to stay here for a few hours until the very worst of the fallout is down."

"What'll we do when we get out?"

"Try to get out of town. Get our outer clothes off, get them all off for that matter, and scrub ourselves with water. Maybe we can get to the river."

"Why don't you try the window right now so we can tell whether we can get out?"

"I will as soon as I've finished eating and had a rest. My legs are very sore."

He could hear her voice soften. "Take your time," she said.

When he felt rested, he stood up. He could almost stand erect and with the flashlight was able to find the window quickly. It was level with his face. He piled loose bricks against the wall below it and climbed up on them until the window was level with his chest. Knocking out the screen with the butt of the flashlight, he put his head through and then flashed the light around; there were no obstructions that he could see, and he couldn't smell anything noxious. The patio, being a flat, level space, had evidently been swept clean by the blast without being flattened. They could crawl out of the cellar under the patio, he realized, and then kick a hole in the lath and stucco which skirted it.

He stepped down from the pile of brick and told his wife that they would be able to get out whenever they wished, that the crawl space was clear.

"What time is it?"

"Half-past twelve."

"Should we try it now?"

"I think so," he said. "At first I thought we ought to stay here for a day or two, but now I think we ought to try and get out from under the fallout. We may have to walk a couple of hundred miles."

"We can do it," she said and he felt glad. She had always been able to look unpleasant issues in the face.

He helped her through the cellar window and handed up the baby who clucked and chuckled when he spoke to her. He pushed the carton of food and the bucket of water after them. Then he climbed up and they inched forward under the patio.

"I hear a motor," said his wife suddenly.

He listened and heard it too.

"Looking for survivors," he said eagerly. "Probably the Army or Civil Defense. Come on."

He swung himself around on his hips and back and kicked out with both feet at the lath and stucco. Three or four kicks did it. His wife went first, inching the baby through the hole. He crawled after her into the daylight; it looked like any other day except that the city was leveled. The sky and the light were the same; everything else was gone.

They sat up, muddy, scratched, nervously exhausted, in a ruined flower bed. Not fifty feet away stood an olive-drab truck, the motor running loudly. Men shouted to them.

"Come on, you!" shouted the men in the truck. "Get going!" They stood and ran raggedly to the cab, she holding the child and he their remaining food and water. In the cab was a canvas-sheeted goggled driver, peering at them through huge eyes. "Get in the back," he ordered. "We've got to get out right away. Too hot." They climbed into the truck and it began to move instantly.

"Army Survival Unit," said a goggled and hooded man in the back of the truck. "Throw away that food and water; it's dangerous. Get your outer clothing off quick. Throw it out!" They obeyed him without thinking, stripping off their loose outer clothes and dropping them out of the truck.

"You're the only ones we've found in a hundred city blocks," said the soldier. "Did you know the war's over? There's a truce."

"Who won?"

"Over in half an hour," he said, "and nobody won."

"What are you going to do with us?"

"Drop you at a check-out point forty miles from here. Give you the scrub-down treatment, wash off the fallout. Medical check for radiation sickness. Clean clothes. Then we send you on your way to a refugee station."

"How many died?"

"Everybody in the area. Almost no exceptions. You're a statistic, that's what you are. Must have been a fluke of the blast."

"Will we live?"

"Sure you will. You're living now, aren't you?"

"I guess so," he said.

"Sure you'll live! Maybe not too long. But everybody else is dead! And you'll be taken care of." He fell silent.

They looked at each other, determined to live as long as they could. The wife cuddled the child close against her thin silk blouse. For a long time they jolted along over rocks and broken pavement without speaking. When the pavement smoothed out the husband knew that they must be out of the disaster area. In a few more minutes they were out of immediate danger; they had reached the check-out point. It was a quarter to three in the afternoon.

"Out you get," said the soldier. "We've got to go back." They climbed out of the truck and he handed down the baby. "You're all right now," he said. "Good luck."

"Good-bye," they said.

The truck turned about and drove away and they turned silently, hand in hand, and walked toward the medical tents. They were the seventh, eighth, and ninth living persons to be brought there after the sirens.

*Hugh Hood lives in Montreal and most of his stories portray a vivid view of contemporary life in Canada's largest city. His stories have been collected in two books—*FLYING A RED KITE *(1962), and* THE FRUIT MAN, THE MEAT MAN AND THE MANAGER *(1971). Hood's reputation as one of Canada's leading short story writers has been steadily growing.*

"The ties that bind man and his dog can be of many strengths, but the ties which bound Arnuk to old Maktuk were beyond human strength to break."

Canada's north can be a cruel and savage land. Man, animal, and the elements are so inextricably linked together that to mention one without the others is meaningless. Few writers illustrate this fundamental truth better than Farley Mowat does in this exciting and moving story about the dog Arnuk.

# the last husky

Farley Mowat

So the people built the little igloo and departed into the wastelands. They went from the place singing the laments for the dying, and they left nothing behind them except the old man. They even took Arnuk, the dog, for that was the old man's wish, and Arnuk was the last and most precious gift that an old man could make to his son and to his grandson and to his people.

It had been a bitter season; the long hungry months before the spring, and in the camp of the people there had been endless cries of children who were too young to know that starvation must be faced in silence. There had been death in the camp, not of men, but of those who were almost as important to the continuance of human life. For the dogs had died, one by one, and as each one was stilled in death so did man's hopes for the future shrink. For in the stark plains country of the Barrenlands men and dogs are one in their need for each other.

Yet though it had been a bitter time, there had been no word spoken against the folly of feeding one old and useless human body. Maktuk, the son, had shared his own meagre rations equally between his aged father, and his starving child who also bore the name that linked the three together. No word was ever spoken, but on a dark April day, the old man raised himself slowly from the sleeping ledge and gazed for a little while at his grandchild, and out of the depths of a great love, and greater courage, old Maktuk spoke these words.

"I have it in my heart," he said, "that the deer await you at the Western Lakes. Go quickly to them, else you will remain in this empty place forever. Go when morning comes, and I will stay. And you shall take Arnuk with you that in the years ahead you will remember me and not forget to leave the spirit gifts upon my grave."

There had been no discussion and no argument, for even an old man has his rights, and this is his final one. In the morning the people were gone, and behind young Maktuk's sled the dog Arnuk tugged convulsively at her tether and turned her head backward to the small white mound of the abandoned igloo, rising shadowless against the endless snows.

Arnuk had been born in the preceding spring in the lean times that always grip the land before the deer return. She was the seventh pup of the litter, and there was no food for her. And if an old man had not taken it upon himself to feed and care for her, she would have died before her life began. Yet she saw summer come and knew the pleasures of long days spent romping with the other young dogs by the side of the great river where the summer camp was pitched. When she grew tired, she would come to the skin tent and push against the old man's knees until he opened his aged eyes and smiled at her.

And so she grew through the good summer months and the people in the camp gazed at her almost with awe, for she became beautiful and of a size and strength surpassing that of any other dog in camp. And when the winter came she thrust her shoulders into harness with the other young dogs, and she gave freely of her strength to men. In the winter evenings she came into the igloo, and this was permitted by Maktuk the son, for he knew the comfort that his father took from the feel of her thick fur against his ancient body. Maktuk the elder gave her the name she bore, Arnuk—The Woman—for she was wife and mother to him in the last winter of his years.

Because there can be no death while there is birth, old Maktuk himself insisted that his dog be mated in the late winter days when the moon stands still and the wild dogs, the great white wolves, howl of their passion to the flickering northern lights. So it was arranged, for Arnuk bore within her the promise of a strength that would be the people's strength in years to come. And when Maktuk, the elder, felt the throb of new life in the womb of The Woman he was content. For his love for the dog was very great, and her life was his life too.

The spring hunger had already begun before Arnuk was mated, and the famine grew with the passing days. The older dogs died first, yet near the end even Arnuk's littermates lay stiff and silent in the snows. But Arnuk's strength was great, and when there was some scrap of bone, or skin, that the people could spare, she received it—for in her womb lay the hopes of many years to come.

This was the way of things when the people turned from the lonely igloo and dragging the sleds with their own failing muscles, set their faces to the west.

The ties that bind man and his dog can be of many strengths, but the ties which bound Arnuk to old Maktuk were beyond human strength to break. Arnuk went with the people, but resisting fiercely. And on the third day of the journey she gnawed through the rawhide tether and before dawn she had vanished into the swirling ground drift of the windswept darkness. In the morning Maktuk, the son, held the frayed tether in his hand and his face was filled with the sorrow of foreboding. Yet when he spoke to his family it was with these words.

"What must be, surely cannot be denied. The Woman has gone to my father and she will be with him when the Snow Walker comes. But my father's spirit will know of our need, and perhaps the day will dawn when he will return The Woman to us, for if she does not come the years ahead are dark."

As for Arnuk, she reached the little igloo before dawn broke that day, and when the old man opened his eyes to see if it was the Snow Walker at last, he saw the dog instead. And he smiled and laid his bony hand upon her head, and once more he slept.

The Snow Walker was late in coming, but on the seventh day he came, unseen, and when he passed from the place the bond was broken. Yet it was not broken, for Arnuk lingered with her dead for three days more and then it was the wind perhaps, that whispered the unspoken order. "Go to the people, go!"

When she emerged from the igloo she found her world had been obliterated beneath a heavy blizzard. For a while she stood in the pale winter sun, her golden coat gleaming against the purple shadows, then she turned her face with its broad ruff and wide-spaced amber eyes, toward the west, for that way lay her path. And within her the voices of the unborn generations echoed the voice of the wind, but with a greater urgency. "Go to the tents of men," they told her. "Go!"

With her head down, and her great plume held low, she moved westward into the pathless spaces, and only once did she pause to turn and stare for a long minute at her back-trail, waiting for some final sign. There was no sign, and at length she turned away.

This was the beginning of her journey. Death had severed the bonds that held her to one man, but she was still bound fast to men. Through untold generations the fate of her kind had been one with that of men, back through the long dim sweep of time even before the Eskimos drifted west across the island chain from Asia. Arnuk was one with the people, and her need of them was as great as their need of her.

And in this hour her need was truly great, for through the long days in the igloo she had eaten nothing, and now her hunger was six-fold, for within her the new life waxed on the substance of her body. She was in a desperate hurry to renew the links with men, and so she drove herself.

She did not halt even when darkness swept the bleak plains into obscurity. At midnight she came to the place where she had chewed her way free of young Maktuk's sled. She knew it was the place only by an inner sense, for the snow had levelled all signs, and had drifted in all trails. She circled amongst the hard drifts, whining miserably, for terrible doubts had begun to seize upon her. She climbed a rock ridge to test the night air for some sign that men were near. Scents came to her. The acrid odour of a white fox unseen in darkness, and the unbearably desirable odour of an arctic hare that had fled into invisibility at her approach. But there was no scent of man.

Her whines rose to a crescendo, a wild pleading in the darkness, but there was no answer except the rising moan of the wind. And at length, worn into stupor by the weight of her hunger, and by her loneliness, she curled up in the shelter of a drift and lost herself in dreams.

So the dog slept in the heart of the unfathomable wilderness. But as she dozed uneasily, a profound change was taking place in the secret places of her body. A strange alchemy was at work. She lay with her nose outstretched on her broad fore-paws and her muscles twitched with erratic impulses. Saliva flowed to her mouth, and in it was the taste of blood. In her mind's eye she laid her stride to that of the swift deer, and her teeth met in the living flesh and she knew the savage ecstasy of the last quiver in a dying prey.

From somewhere out of time the ageless instincts that lie in all living cells were being re-born, so that the dog, and the new life within her, would not perish. And when Arnuk raised her head to the dawn light, the thing was done, the change complete.

The dawn was clear, and Arnuk, her perceptions keenly sharpened by the chemistry of change, tested the wind. When she found the warm smell of living flesh, she rose to seek it out.

Not far distant, a Snowy Owl, dead white and shadowless in the pre-dawn, had earlier swept across the plains with great eyes staring. The owl had seen, and fallen so swiftly on a hare, that the beast had known nothing until the inch-long talons clutched his life and took it from him. It was a good kill, and the owl felt pleasure as it perched above the corpse. The great bird savoured the weight of its own hunger, and while it sat complacent, crouched above the hare, it did not see the flow of motion on a nearby drift.

Arnuk was a weasel creeping up upon a mouse; a snake slithering upon a sparrow. Skills she had never known, skills that had come to her in all completeness from forgotten half-beasts lost in the dimmest aeons, were hers now. Her belly dragged on the hard snows and she inched forward. When she was a dozen feet away, the owl raised its head and the yellow eyes of the bird stared with expressionless intensity full into Arnuk's face. Arnuk was the stillness of death, yet every muscle vibrated in the grip of a passion such as she had never known before. And when the owl turned back to its prey, Arnuk leapt. The owl saw the beginning of the leap and threw itself backward into its own element with a smooth thrust of mighty wings. But those wings were a fraction slow and the hurtling form of the dog, leaping six feet into the air; struck flesh beneath the feathers.

It was a brief battle. Three times the talons of the bird drew blood, and then they stiffened, and relaxed in death.

Arnuk slept afterwards while white feathers blew into the bleak distance, and tufts of white fur moved like furtive living things in the grip of the wind. And when she woke again the agony of her hunger was at an end and the savage drive of her new instincts was momentarily dulled. Once more she was man's beast and lost.

She woke, and without a glance at the red snow beside her, set out again into the west, unconscious, yet directly driven.

The people whom she sought were wanderers on the face of a plain
so vast that it seems limitless. The dog could not conceive of the odds
against her finding them, but in her memory was the image of the summer camp where she had spent her youth, and with an unerring perse-
verance she set her course for that far distant place.

A day and a night, and nearly a hundred miles of scarred rock ridges
where the snow-demons rose and whirled like dancing spirits, separated her from the place of the owl before weariness brought her to a
halt again. And in all that space she had seen no trace of men. Few
were the beasts or birds that moved upon that sullen desolation and
the world seemed empty of all forms of life except the dog. Yet this
was an illusion, and Arnuk, sleeping fitfully in a snow-hollow, was
roused to reality by the new senses that had quickened in her. She sat
up abruptly and the long hair of her ruff lifted stiffly. The white dawn
was breaking, but this time it brought no promise of food. Instead it
brought cold fear.

Arnuk could not tell how she had been warned, and yet the warning
was implicit. Her ruff was a flag of her courage, and she growled deep
in her broad chest. There was nothing to be seen, or heard, or smelled—
and yet she knew. Leaping from her snow bed she raced toward the
long line of a gravel ridge that had been burnished clear of snow by the
winter gales.

The light was breaking when she reached the high ground and there,
where two huge rocks stood up like tombstones, she took her stand,
facing her back trail. And at last she saw the shadows, four of them,
weaving and fading in the dim light, but drawing always closer.

She knew them. Many times, while she still lived in the security of
men's camps, those shadows had circled beyond the fire-light, singing
their blood-stirring songs. And the dogs of men had lifted their heads
and flung back the challenge with an hysterical ferocity. For the dogs of
men and the dogs of the wilderness walk apart, theirs being the hatred
of brothers who have denied their common blood.

Arnuk was afraid. She crouched close to the rocks and waited while
the shadows flickered in the rising dawn, drew closer, and halted
silently a dozen yards away.

Dimly Arnuk understood that a law had been broken, and that when
she had come unannounced into the territory of the wolves she had
invited death. Hatred of the "others" welled up within her. The new

forces that had come to her gave her a savage will to live. Her lips drew
back and her white teeth glistened as she tensed herself for war.

It must be that miracles are not reserved for men alone, for a miracle
came to pass upon that wind-swept ridge when the leader of the wolves,
a gaunt and greying giant, stood and tested the dawn wind. He faced
Arnuk, his grizzled muzzle wrinkling in a strange perplexity, and after
one dreadful moment of poised immobility, his straining muscles
eased, and, incredibly, from his massive chest there came an almost
plaintive whine. The wind blew gustily and a veil of driven snow rolled
up the ridge. And when it passed, the dog Arnuk was alone. The wolves
had vanished utterly, swallowed by the anonymity of night, and the
dog understood that she was spared. Perhaps she may have understood
that there are many laws amongst the 'others' and chief of all is the one
which gives immunity to a female ripe with new life, even though she
be an outlander from a different world. The wolves had known, and
Arnuk once more took up her journey, aware that there was peace between her and the wild ones whose land this was.

The days passed and after each the sun stood a little higher in the
sky. Space lengthened under the dog's feet and the explosion of spring
disturbed the world. The snows grew soft and the Barrens' rivers, freed
from their chains, thundered angrily across the plains. In a white and
glaring sky flights of ravens hung like eddies of burned leaves and on
the opening ponds geese mingled with the raucous flocks of gulls.

The awakening of life was in the deep moss, where the lemmings
tunneled, and it was on the stony ridges where cock ptarmigan swag-
gered before their mates. It was in all living things and in all places,
and it was within the womb of the dog Arnuk. Her journey had been
long, and her broad paws were crusted with the dried blood of a hundred stone-cuts. Her magnificent coat was matted now, and lustreless
under the spring suns. Nevertheless she drew upon hidden strengths
and upon her own indomitable will, and she went forward into the
western plains.

Gaunt, hot eyed and terribly exhausted, she brought her quest to an
end on a day in early June. Breasting a long ridge she saw before her
the brilliant light of sun on roaring water and she recognized the River.
She had come home.

Whining with excitement she ran clumsily down the slope, for her
body had grown awkward in these last days. And soon she was

amongst the rings of weathered boulders where, in the summer that was past, men's tents had stood.

The tents were gone. There was no living man to welcome the return of the lost one. Only on the nearby ridges the motionless piles of rocks that the Eskimos call Inukok, Men of Stone, were there to see the coming of Arnuk. They, and the hidden piles of bones under rock cairns near the river, the old graves of forgotten people. Arnuk understood that the place was empty of living men, yet for an hour she refused to believe it. Pathetically she ran from old tent-ring to old meat-cache, sniffing each with a despairing hope, and finding nothing to give her hope, and when realization became inescapable, the dog curled herself in a depression beside the place where old Maktuk had once held her at his knees, and she gave herself up to her great weariness and to her bitter disappointment.

Yet the old camp was not as empty as it looked. While Arnuk made her fruitless search she had been too preoccupied to know that she was being watched. Had she glanced up the river to a low cliff she might have seen a lithe shape that followed her every move with eyes that held in them a hunger not born in the belly. She would have seen and recognized the wolf, and her hackles would have risen and her teeth been bared.

The wolf was almost as young as the dog. Born the preceding spring he had stayed with his family for a full season until in the early spring of this year, the urge to wander had come over him and he had forsaken his ancestral territory. Many adventures had befallen him, and most had been bitter ones for he had learned, at the cost of torn flanks, and bleeding shoulders, that each wolf family guards its own land and there is no room for a stranger. His tentative offers of friendship had been met with bared teeth in the lands of three wolf clans before at last he came to the river and found a place where no wolves were.

It was a good place. Not far from the empty Eskimo camp the River flared angrily over a shallow stretch of rounded boulders to lose itself in the beginning of an immense lake, and at the shallow place the caribou had made a ford in their spring and summer migrations. They crossed the river here in untold thousands, and not all escaped the river's anger. The drowned bodies of dead deer lay amongst the rocks at the river mouth, and there was ample food for a great population of arctic foxes, ravens, and white gulls. But the wolves of the area did not visit the place for it belonged to man, and that which man claims to himself is forbidden to the great wild dogs.

Knowing nothing of this prohibition the young male wolf had taken up his home by the river, and here he nursed his loneliness. Perhaps even more than dogs, wolves are social beasts, and the 'lone wolf' is only a legend. Companionship in the hunt, and in the games that are played after the hunt, are vital to the happiness of the great white beasts. Isolation from their own kind is purgatory for them, and they can know a loneliness that eats away the heart.

It had been so with the young wolf, and when he saw and smelled the dog Arnuk, he was filled with conflicting emotions. He had seen no dog before, yet he sensed that the golden coated beast below him was not quite of his blood. The smell was strange, and yet it was familiar. The shape and colour were strange, and yet they roused in him a warmth of memory and desire.

He had been rebuffed so many times before that he was cautious now, and when Arnuk woke from her sleep of exhaustion she did not at first see the stranger, but her nostrils told her at once of the nearness of deer meat. Her hunger was savage and overpowering. Without caution she leapt to her feet and flung herself upon a ragged haunch of caribou that had been dragged to within a few yards of her. Only when she had satisfied her first desperate hunger did she glance up and meet the still gaze of the young wolf.

The wolf sat motionless a hundred feet from the dog, nor did he so much as twitch an ear as Arnuk's hackles lifted and the threat took form deep in her throat. He remained sitting, yet tense to spring away, and after a long minute Arnuk again dropped her head to the meat, satisfied that the wolf meant her no harm.

This was the way of their first meeting, the wolf and the dog. And this was what came of it.

With the mockery of this second deserted camp before her, Arnuk gave up her search for men. She could no longer fight against the insistant demands of her heavy body, and there was no more time for searching. Now once again, in her hour of despair, the hidden force within her took command. Before that first day was out her mood had changed magically from deep dejection to a businesslike alertness.

Ignoring the young wolf, who still kept his distance, Arnuk made a quick tour of the familiar ground beside the river. She carefully ex-

amined the carcasses of five drowned deer, and from each of these she
chased the screaming gulls and gutteral ravens, for this meat was hers
now by right of greater strength. Then, satisfied with the abundant food
supply, Arnuk left the river and trotted briskly inland half a mile to
where a rock outcrop had opened its flanks to form a shallow cave.
Here, as a pup, Arnuk had played with the other dogs of the camp.
Now, as a full grown female, she examined the cave with more serious
intent. The place was dry, and protected from the winds. There was
only one thing wrong, and that was the smell of the cave. It was pervaded by a potent and unpleasant stench that caused Arnuk to draw
back her lips in anger and distaste—for no animal upon the face of the
great plains has any love for the squat and ugly wolverine. And a
wolverine had clearly used the cave during the winter months.

Arnuk's nose told her that the wolverine had been gone for several
week's and there was little likelihood that he would return until the
winter winds forced him to seek shelter. Arnuk scratched earth and
sand over the unclean floor, then set about dragging moss into the
deepest recess. And here at last she hid herself and made surrender to
her hour.

Arnuk's pups were born on the third day she spent in the cave, on a
morning when the cries of the white geese were loud in the spring air.
It was the time of birth, and the five squirming things that lay warm
against the dog's fur were not alone in their first day of life. On the
sand ridges beyond the river a female ground squirrel suckled the
naked motes of flesh that were hers, and in a den by a ridge a mile distant an arctic fox, already greying into summer coat, thrust his alert
face above the ground while the feeble whimpers of the pups his mate
was nursing warned him of the tasks ahead. All living things in the land
by the river moved to the rhythm of the demands of life new born, or
soon to be born. All things moved to this rhythm except the outcast
wolf.

For the three days that Arnuk remained hidden, the young wolf felt a
torment that gave him no peace. Restless and yearning for things he
had never known, he haunted the vicinity of the cave. He did not dare
go too close, but each day he dragged a piece of deer meat within a few
yards of the cave mouth, and then drew back to wait with pathetic
patience for his gift to be accepted.

On the third day, as he lay near the cave snapping at the flies which

hung about his head, his keen ears felt the faintest tremors of a new
sound. He was on his feet instantly, head outthrust and his body
trembling with attention. It came again, so faint that it was felt rather
than heard—a tiny whimper that called to him across the ages and
across all barriers. And in that instant his loneliness was done. His
great unease was at an end. He shook himself sharply, and with one
quick, proprietary glance at the cave mouth, trotted out across the
plain—no longer a solitary outcast, but a male beginning the evening
hunt that would feed his mate and pups. So, simply and out of his deep
need, the young wolf filled the void that had surrounded him through
the torturing weeks of spring.

Arnuk did not easily accept the wolf in the role he had chosen to
play. For several days she kept him at bay with bared teeth, although
she ate the food offerings he left at the cave mouth. But before a week
was out she had come to expect the fresh meat; the tender ground
squirrels, the arctic hares, and plump ptarmigan. And from this it was
not really a long step to total acceptance of the wolf who, by his every
action and by his whole demeanour, expressed his self-imposed devotion to his adopted family.

The neighbour fox, a grey shadow on the rocks above the cave, was
the only watcher on the morning when Arnuk sealed the compact with
the wolf. The little fox watched with his usual curiosity as the big dog
paused by the carcass of a fresh-killed hare, then glancing past it saw
the sleeping form of the young wolf. The fox watched as the dog stepped forward one slow pace at a time until she was standing close to the
exhausted hunter. And the fox watched as the husky's brush wagged
slowly, as the wolf raised his head, and as the two great beasts touched
noses.

In the days that followed, the fox saw much of the happenings at the
cave, for he was a fearless little beast, and he knew that the wolf regarded him with disinterested neutrality. Coming back to his own kits
after a mouse hunt, he would sometimes detour to pass close to the
cave and then he would pause and bark sharply at the sight of the five
golden pups that flung themselves over the inert body of the wolf,
snapping at his tail and ears, and scratching sand into his half closed
eyes.

Often the fox followed the wolf on the long night hunts—but at a
discreet distance, for this was business and it was unsafe to come too

close to the great hunter. They were long hunts, for the wolf had marked out for his adopted family a territory of nearly a hundred square miles, and each night he circled his domain harvesting the food that was now his by right.

As for Arnuk, her life was without complaint. There were no fears to bother her, and there were no empty spaces in her heart. As the pups grew larger she weaned them, and then for a few hours each day she was free to enjoy the somnolent pleasure of a sunny hour lying still as death beside a lemming's run, waiting for the sweet morsel of flesh that might be her reward for patience.

Occasionally she visited the empty camp of men, but she no longer felt the old longing tugging at her. Her life was full.

So the days passed until the pups were in their seventh week. Midsummer in the Barrens, and the herds of deer were drifting southward once again. The crossing place was once more thronged with caribou, and the young calves grunted beside their ragged mothers while the old bucks, their velvet covered antlers reaching to the skies, followed aloofly in the van.

And then one evening a desire for the long chase came over Arnuk, and in the secret ways that men know nothing of, she made her restlessness and her desire apparent to the wolf. When the late summer dusk fell, Arnuk went out alone into the darkening plains, secure in the knowledge that the wolf would stay behind to guard the pups until her return.

She did not intend a long absence, only a few hours at the most, but near the outskirts of the territory she came on a band of young buck deer. They were fine beasts, and fat, which at this time of year was a mouth-watering oddity. Tired of too much lean meat, Arnuk knew a sudden surge of appetite and she circled the resting herd, filled with an ardent hunger.

An eddy of the uncertain breeze betrayed her, and the startled deer sprang to their feet and fled. Arnuk was hungry, and the night was a hunter's night. She took up the long chase.

So the hours drove the brief night from the land and when the hard early winds of dawn rose in the north the young wolf roused himself from his vigil by the cave-mouth. A sense of dim foreboding made him turn to the den and thrust his head and shoulders into the entrance. All was well, and the pups were rolled together in a compact ball, whimpering and jerking their stubby legs in sleep. Yet the feeling of uneasiness persisted in the wolf's mind and he turned toward the river where the grey light picked out the long roll of distant ridges.

Perhaps he was worried by the long absence of the dog, perhaps he had been warned by senses that remain unknown to us. His uneasiness grew and at last he trotted away from the den following the cold trail of Arnuk, hoping to see her golden form approaching from inland.

He had gone no more than a mile when the vague sense of something evil took concrete form. A vagrant eddy brought the north breeze to his nostrils and instantly he knew what had disturbed him when he woke. He turned back toward the cave with startling speed and broke into a hard gallop.

As he breasted the slope beside the den, the stink of wolverine rose like a foul miasma in his nostrils and the young wolf was transformed in the instant into a savage thing, distrait with the most elemental rage. He came down the slope in half a dozen gigantic leaps, his ears flat to his skull and his great throat rumbling with incoherent hate.

The wolverine, old and wise from a long life of slaughter, had winded the young pups in his old winter lair from a great distance off. He had not known any desire to revisit the foul winter den as he made his way slowly up-river, but the smell of the pups tempted him. Perhaps he would have ignored the temptation, for though he feared no living thing, he had no particular desire to meet the fury of a female wolf defending her young. But the night had been empty for him, and his cavernous belly rumbled with hunger. His temper, always vile, was edged by hunger and so in the grey dawn-light he turned from the river and circled cautiously upwind until he found a rock out-thrust that gave him cover, and from which he could observe the den. Here he waited with a terrible patience until he saw the young wolf trot from the den mouth toward the inland plains.

Still cautiously, the wolverine left his cover and slowly moved in upon the den, pausing for long moments to reassure himself that the pups were undefended. His squat, massive body hugged the rough ground as he drew closer, and now fully certain of success, he could already taste the pleasure of the killing, and the salt warmth of blood.

There was blood enough for him to taste that dawn. But it was not to be the blood of Arnuk's pups.

The young wolf's savage rush was so swift that the wolverine had only sufficient time to slew about and take the weight of the attack upon his side. It was enough to save him for the wolf's white teeth sank through the tough skin, but missed their promised hold upon the throat, and met in the sinews of the killer's shoulder. On any other beast it would have been a good hold, leading to victory, but on the wolverine it was not good enough. The wolverine knows neither fear nor pain, and its squat body is possessed of a strength equal to any beast three times its size. A weasel by blood with all the weasel's capacity for fury, the wolverine has the body of a bear, and such is its vitality, that life remains in it until that body has been literally torn apart.

So it was with the old beast at the cave mouth. He did not feel his injury, but instead was aflame with an insane anger. He swung his fifty pounds of bone and gristle into a savage counter-thrust.

Had the wolf been older, and more experienced, he might have side-stepped that lunge, but he was young, and blinded by the allegiance that he had freely given to the pups that he had never sired. He held his grip and did not slacken it as the wolverine's teeth raked his unprotected flank.

They fought in silence. The sun, red on the eastern rim, was pallid beside the glare of blood upon the rocks. The fox watched the terrible duel for an instant from its distant den, and then, appalled by the fury of that struggle, slunk into the dark earth and lay beside his mate and kits, in trembling fear . . . .

It was the gulls that warned Arnuk. From afar off as she came wearily homeward in the warmth of the the morning she saw them circling, and heard their strident screams. They eddied above the rocks where the den lay, and weary as she was she mustered her strength and came on at full pace. And so she found them, the murderer torn to bloody fragments before the murder was begun. And so she found the wolf, his throat ripped raggedly across, and his still body stiffening beneath the rising sun.

The bodies still lay near the cave when, a week later, the voices of men echoed once more along the shores of the river. And they still lay by the cave a little later on when the young man called Maktuk bent down to the dark opening and very gently thrust his hand under the frightened pups, while Arnuk, half wild with old emotions, stood trembling by his side. Maktuk was a man of the great plains and he could read much that cannot be written, so that he knew all there was to know of what had taken place beneath the ragged rocks.

And it was because he knew, that on an evening in late summer he took his son to the bank of the river, and placed the boy's hand on the head of the golden dog, and spoke these words.

"Maktuk, my son. In a little time you shall be a man and a fine hunter, and all the wide plains will know your name and skill. And in those days to come you will have certain friends to help you in the hunt, and and of these the greatest you shall always call *Arnuk*, and then my father will know that we have received his gift, and he will be at ease. And in those times to come all beasts shall fall to your spear and bow— save one alone. For never shall you lift your hand against the white one, against *Amarok* the great white wolf—and so shall our debt be paid."


*The controversial Farley Mowat submitted 'The Last Husky' to us on the condition that the anthology be totally Canadian. Although Mowat is not principally known as a short story writer, his story leaves no doubt that he is a fine story-teller. The story originally appeared in* Saturday Evening Post *in 1955. Mowat's love of and concern for Canada's north and its people is evident in this story, as it is in many of his books. Mowat lives in Port Hope, Ontario.*

When someone announces that he is about to die, the immediate family is understandably upset. It is a very serious matter.

When Uncle Desmonde tells his family that his death is imminent, *they certainly are upset* . . . but not for the reasons you might expect. They are prepared for the fact that Uncle Desmonde must die, *but not for the manner in which he chooses to die.*

As Uncle Felix says, 'Consider the scandal . . .'

# six beauties

Robert Fontaine

**M**y Uncle Desmonde announced abruptly one day that he expected to die presently. This was a common announcement in our family, of course, and no one paid much attention.

Desmonde, however, persisted, and in time we began to consider his case with a certain amount of seriousness.

"It is true," Papa said, "that the blood pressure of Desmonde is greatly elevated."

"That's dangerous," *Maman* said. "You never can tell in cases like that. I hate to mention it, but you remember Jean Dubuc went like that."

"Jean Dubuc," Papa observed, "went *comme ça* only after he had filled himself with ale and fallen into a lake."

"Still," *Maman* insisted, "if his blood pressure had been low . . ."

She shook her head as if to say we might still have had Jean Dubuc with us.

"The sideboard of Desmonde is forever empty," I said.

"Yes," my father agreed. "He eats all the time. Still, it is better than robbing a bank or marrying a woman with twelve children."

"Who is doing that?" *Maman* inquired nervously.

"No one," Papa replied. "I merely make a comparison."

"Anyway," *Maman* said, "to eat so much rich food as Desmonde does is to encourage sudden death."

A few days later, surely enough, Desmonde had a fainting spell. He fell suddenly to the floor while reaching for a bottle of *vin ordinaire*. For a while we left him undisturbed, thinking him merely tired.

Soon Papa noticed, as did I, that Desmonde's face had become a peculiar color, and we called the doctor.

The doctor immediately ordered Desmonde to a diet of wet toast and warm milk plus, here and there, a mushed egg, barely cooked.

It was like taking wings from a bird.

"Begone, vulture!" Desmonde exclaimed. "The medicine is worse than the malady."

"Take my word for it," the doctor said. "Your blood pressure is like the weather in Ecuador."

"Go! faker, quack, medicine man."

The doctor shrugged and fastened up his small black bag.

"My fee is four dollars," he said coldly.

"Why?" Desmonde inquired with narrowed eyes.

"Why?" the doctor repeated, puzzled.

"Yes. Did I steal your stethoscope?"

"Very well," the doctor agreed. "Three dollars. Let us have no arguments. I don't feel very well myself."

Desmonde handed him two dollars.

"You may keep the change," he explained, leading the medico to the door.

"Believe me," said the doctor, "I hope you drop dead before I get home."

When the doctor was gone, Desmonde regarded us all plaintively.

"Why," he inquired, "does he not wish me to eat hay, which will dry me up and make my blood pressure zero?"

He continued to eat highly spiced foods and to drink too much wine and to insist daily that he was dying and that he did not care since to live on wet toast, warm milk, and mushed eggs was a fate worse than death.

After a while the wine and the food and the pressure seemed to rise to Desmonde's head, because he began to confide to us the strange manner in which he wished to die. Only my mother, whom he did not wish to shock too much, remained innocent of his dream.

We promptly called a family conference.

Desmonde was not present, so we spoke freely around the table with the red-fringed cloth.

"Consider," Uncle Felix announced, after the preliminaries had been dispensed with, "the scandal."

"The scandal," Papa replied, "is more important to you than the death of your brother. Consider *this*. If he remains quietly seated on the wet toast and mushed eggs he will live perhaps to a great age. If he attempts to carry out his plan, his teeth will surely stop aching permanently!"

Felix stretched out his hands helplessly.

"Make no mistake; he will kill himself, anyway. Is it necessary he do it with such fervor and publicity?"

He looked at me, as if for help. I shrugged.

"I don't know," I said. I did not know much about these things and I was interested only in the outcome, as at a cinema serial.

My mother spoke now, gently: "If he is bent on dying, then he should have his last wishes granted, I think."

Uncle Louis scratched his red nose.

"*J'en suis tout bleu,*" he said.

I sat up at this. For Uncle Louis to be flabbergasted was indeed a rarity.

"It is also doubtful," Felix explained, pointing a fork at Papa, "that Desmonde can find six of the most beautiful girls in Canada for such a venture."

"Pouf!" Papa scoffed. "Desmonde can hire artists' models. Who is more beautiful? What is the difference to an artists' model if she poses for a picture or eats dinner? It is enough if she receives her fee and is not harmed in any way. *N'est-ce pas?*"

"Why," I inquired earnestly, "should Desmonde harm anybody?"

"You are too young," Papa replied. "How old are you?"

"Haha! *Mon père!* He asks me how many years I have!"

"I cannot remember everything," my father said. "Anyway, beyond a doubt you are too young to know."

Uncle Louis ran his fingers around the curves of his ears.

"And Desmonde is too old," he said. "So we do not have to worry about that."

"Desmonde is not so old," *Maman* observed from across the room.

"He is past one hundred in the glands," Felix said. "With a tree it is the rings of the trunk, with a horse it is the teeth, with a man it is the glands."

"And with a woman?" *Maman* laughed.

"A woman," said Papa, "is never over thirty-nine. If she is your wife, she is never over thirty."

"Anyway," said *Maman*, flushing with pleasure, "Desmonde is not so old. He is still young enough to enjoy the normal activities of life. I don't see him in a wheel chair."

"Listen to her sing!" Papa chuckled. "She does not know of what we are speaking, yet she sings and sings. She is like a bird. A bird sings and has no idea of what it is singing."

"Then *tell* me," my mother said coldly. She put down a pair of my knickerbockers she was mending. "I know, of course, that there is a secret."

My father looked around carefully at the others. There seemed to be no objection, so he said: "Desmonde has it in his head to die, as you know. He now has arrived at the point where he wishes to die in style. It is not enough for my brother to merely die. With him there must be a pageant."

"If he dies in the true Christian manner what is the difference?" *Maman* asked.

"Sing on!" Papa laughed. "The true Christian manner, eh? 'The Beautiful Ending,' eh? Do not imagine any such thing to yourself, my hummingbird."

"Hummingbirds," I said, "do not sing."

"With their feet," Felix corrected, "they sing."

"Are we," my father asked, somewhat irked, "to discuss the beautiful death of Desmonde or the feet of hummingbirds?"

Everyone was silent. My father spoke once more to my mother: "Desmonde wishes to have a fine dinner on his last day on earth. The main dish of this dinner will consist of brook trout, whole brook trout cooked in wine and served with iced grapes. There will also be hot cheesecake, truffles, leek soup, and so forth. The Last Menu is quite complete, believe me!"

*Maman* moistened her lips.

"It sounds good," she said.

"The rest," said Papa ominously, "does not sound so good."

He looked around at the others, and they all smiled mysteriously.

Papa's glance fell on me again and he raised his brows with a certain hesitation.

"How old did you say you were?"

"Since I have no glands," I laughed, "what difference?"

"Hmm," murmured my father. "Well, you are too young for this to harm you. Eh, *mes frères*?"

He looked around at the others again. They nodded in agreement. I took a deep, satisfactory breath.

Papa went on: "Desmonde wishes, you understand, to have a wine with each course. The finest wines, and the most correct. He has not yet named the wines, since he is not on certain ground when it comes to the wines, which must be exactly right. This banquet, you see, is to be exquisite in all respects. How many times in his life does a man die? Eh?"

"I myself," interrupted Felix, "am a good judge of wines. It is a wonder Desmonde does not consult me. To judge wines one needs a tongue of the rarest sort. To judge exquisite wines one needs an exquisite tongue."

"One needs also the exquisite wines," Papa laughed.

"To tell you the truth," *Maman* said. "It all sounds quite pleasant to me."

"Ah, but wait . . . wait, my dove. Imagine *this* to yourself! Desmonde wishes as his dinner companions the six most beautiful girls in Canada. Or perhaps not the six most beautiful. Perhaps six *of* the most beautiful. Anyway, six beauties to dine with him while he overeats, elevates the blood pressure, and dies. Ha!"

"And why not?" *Maman* smiled. "Beautiful girls, I understand, are the best appetizers at dinner."

"And why not!" my father mocked, leaning back in his chair and winking at the others.

"Listen to her!" Felix chided.

"Oho!" said Uncle Louis, "they are moving the furniture out of her head. Soon will come in the butterflies!"

Papa now spoke softly and mysteriously.

"It is the way Desmonde wishes the beautiful girls to dress!"

"And how is that?" *Maman* encouraged.

My father took a deep breath and swallowed hard.

"They must wear," he said in a precise tone, "a large picture hat of the garden-party type. The hat they must keep on while eating."

He spoke slowly, relishing the details of his presentation.

*Maman* said: "That is the old fashion, but it is, nonetheless, charming."

"Ah, charming, eh? So! Imagine this, then: they must wear long black gloves which reach up past the elbows, and long black silk stockings of what is called the opera length."

He showed with a gesture on his trousers about where the stockings would reach.

*Maman* became slightly pink, but she spoke gaily: "It all sounds very delightful. What else?"

"What else what?" Papa asked, grinning broadly.

"What else must the beautiful girls wear?"

"Haha!" laughed Felix. "What else!"

"Oho!" said Louis. "What else!"

I squirmed in my chair anxiously.

"Well," I demanded, "*what* else?"

"You are too young," Papa said.

Everybody laughed at this, except, of course, *Maman*.

"I do wish you would tell me what else," she remarked crisply.

Papa leaned back and downed a large glass of red wine. When he was finished he wiped his lips slowly with the serviette and replied calmly: "Nothing."

"Nothing?" *Maman* repeated.

"Nothing," said Papa, Louis, and Felix in unison.

There was a long silence. *Maman* spoke after a while and without looking at us.

"Perhaps," she suggested uneasily and with a sharp and wondering glance at me," perhaps we had better have the Reverend McKintosh speak to Desmonde."

"McKintosh?" repeated Felix. "McKintosh? There was a McKintosh who invented a mechanism for tipping the hat at a lady without removing the hands from the pockets. It worked, I believe, by steam. Although this seems impossible. Then there was . . ."

"The minister of the Presbyterian church, of course," *Maman* stated.
"Where *bibi* used to go to Sunday school. *Bibi*, perhaps, had better start
again."

"In the winter," I agreed. "When come the Christmas parties."

"No McKintosh," Papa said. "*Mais non!* McKintosh will drone to
Desmonde that he must live the rest of his life on scones and breakfast
tea and read, every day, a dozen chapters from the New Testament.
To sit on wet toast first . . . and then to lay on scones and tea, reading
the New Testament . . . bah! Why should a man live at all if that is what
he must do? Also, a Presbyterian would not be expected to know about
the subtleties of wines, truffles, hot cheesecake, and beautiful girls in
picture hats and opera-length, black silk stockings."

"Who then?" asked *Maman.*

"Only a priest," my father replied, "would know if this is good. A
priest is compassionate. A priest has the understanding of human
frailty without the dryness in the heart of the Protestant clergy."

"Ah. *Bon! Bon!*" exclaimed Felix. "Always, in the history of the
world, the priest has stood . . ."

"Good," interrupted Louis. "Father Sebastian!"

"Father Sebastian it is," agreed Felix. "Father Sebastian knows
everything . . ."

"Except which is the right way to Paradise," Louis amended.

"Tomorrow, then," Papa said, "I will invite Father Sebastian to discuss with us Uncle Desmonde's farewell banquet."

We were, of course, all gathered together while my father told the
story to Father Sebastian.

The Father listened attentively, solemnly tapping a finger to his
under lip every now and then, and murmuring frequent "ahs."

"And so," my father concluded, "we wish your advice. What do you
think of it? Is it bad? Is it an evil thing to do? Or is it good?"

The priest reflected a long time, crossing and uncrossing his legs,
tapping his mouth thoughtfully, looking often into nowhere, dreamily,
a faint smile flickering on his shining face.

"Hmmmmmm," he murmured finally. I tugged nervously on my
stocking. My mother moistened her lips. Papa lit a cigar, and Felix and
Louis stared fixedly at Father Sebastian.

"Hmmmmmmmmmmmmmm!" he repeated. "Wine . . . brook trout

... truffles ... hot cheesecake ... iced grapes ... and so forth. Hmmmm ... picture hats ... black gloves to the elbow ... stockings of the opera length ... Hmmmmmm."

"So?" questioned my father, eagerly and solemnly. "Will it be good?"

"It will all depend ..." Father Sebastian ordained at length.

"On what?" asked my father nervously.

"On the choice of wines," Father Sebastian concluded.


*Robert Fontaine lived in Ottawa as a young boy; his personal recollections of his bilingual family background have given us the highly delightful book,* THE HAPPY TIME (1945). *Many stories from this entertaining account of Fontaine's boyhood have been anthologized. Similar reminiscences of Fontaine's were published in magazines like* MACLEAN'S: *one such story, 'Uncle Geralde and the Green, Green Grass' was included in* STRAWBERRIES AND OTHER SECRETS (*Nelson, 1970*).

# two sisters

Markoosie

I have travelled all over the North and have seen some of the old bones left by our ancestors. But there was one old whale bone that was so far away from the sea that I just had to ask a friend of mine why it was so far from the shore. We were fishing at the time so he told me he would tell me about it when we returned to the settlement. A few days later he told me this story:

"Long ago there were two beautiful sisters who had many admirers. Several men wanted to marry them but their father did not want to lose his daughters and would not give them permission. The sisters were happy that their father did not want to part with them, as they did not wish to get married.

"One day however, the father finally consented to the marriage request of one man. The two sisters were very sad and threatened to run away. But the old man did not believe them and would not change his mind.

"The next morning when the old man woke up he was shocked to find that his daughters had gone. He immediately called upon all men to search for them and promised that the first to find them would have his choice of the two girls.

"Naturally all the young men answered the call and the great search began.

"At first they followed the girls' tracks but after awhile they lost them as they had become buried in new snow. The search went on for many days and weeks without a sign of them. Finally a year went by and the men began to return one by one.

"Then the father was really worried and kept asking people to search but they were tired of looking. The old man had to start looking on his own. After travelling for many months and finding no trace of his daughters he had to admit they were dead.

"Sometime later a stranger came to the settlement. He had a strange story to tell. He said that many years before while hunting caribou he spotted two people in the distance. As he approached them he was surprised to see that they were women.

"When he asked them where they were from they were unable to tell him. He noticed a great uncut dead whale near a lake and wondered aloud how such a big animal could be so far away from the sea. The two women said they had killed the whale and had dragged it up to the lake. The man did not believe them and said nothing more. The two women then invited him to their small hut of rocks and moss for dinner. When he stepped inside he saw many fish in one corner. He was curious and asked where all the fish had come from. The women pointed to the lake and indicated that they had come from there. The man was shocked because he had tried unsuccessfully to catch fish in the lake many times and he told them so.

"Calmly one of them said that fish would come by the thousands if one poured blood from an animal into the lake. The man told them he did not believe their story. But the women said they would prove it to him while he watched, so he went along with them thinking he would have a good laugh.

"The women took some blood from the dead whale, went to the lake and poured the blood into the hole where they had fished. Thousands of fish swarmed around the blood and the women scooped them up. The man couldn't believe his eyes. The women told him that they had great strength and that was why they were able to drag the dead whale inland from the sea. Then the man became frightened and went away.

"When the old man heard this story he was sure these two women were his long-lost daughters. So the next day he asked the stranger to take him to the place where he had last seen them.

"Days later they reached the lake and found the dead whale and some fish but the women had left. They found their tracks which led to some nearby hills. As they were following the tracks a strange thing happened.

"Suddenly one of the human tracks became the footprints of a wolf. Further along, the other human track also turned into that of a wolf. Then the two men were sure that the two sisters had turned into wolves and they never looked for the women again."

Here ends the story. But that old bone near the lake, which I saw, was part of this tale. And many natives will tell you everytime you go fishing in that lake that you will hear a wolf crying in the distance. And when there are no fish to be found in the lake do not be surprised to see an Eskimo pour blood into it.

*This talented Eskimo has the distinction of being not only the first commercial pilot among his people, but also the first widely known Eskimo writer, author of the best-selling* HARPOON OF THE HUNTER. *He was the subject of a CBC television program on the 'Telescope' series. A native of Resolute Bay, Markoosie writes uniquely of his people and he has explored situations verging on fantasy and science-fiction. We chose 'Two Sisters', which originally appeared in* NORTH (1971), *because of the apparent simplicity, yet definite subtlety, with which Markoosie entertains his reader.*

The universe may hold many life forms
—some of an order higher than man.
Is there also universal justice? Systems
of law? Love? Compassion?
A baby is born among the stars.
What father would give it as a gift?
What man would accept it?

# a grain of manhood

Phyllis Gotlieb

She was lying formless; the contour of her body was lost except for the white ring of pain that worked its way downwards every so often like a wedding ring over a swollen knuckle. All her other miseries were encompassed by this masterpiece of nature, a force at one with lightning and thunder, the hurricane, the great reach of the four-thousand-year-old sequoia.

In the intervals she was a person again, and she turned her eyes to James, who was standing at the window watching white peaks rising out of the shadow of night. She asked for the first time, "James, what will you do when this is over?"

"I don't know." He spoke through the window to the sky. In spite of the unexpected hurry to the hospital he was wearing his dark suit, pressed and fresh, and a tie knotted with painful neatness.

"Why do you always call me James?" he asked suddenly. "Why not Jim or some other kind of short thing?"

She would have said, Why not, it's your name, but she was too miserable for even the feeblest humor. "I don't know. You always looked like a James to me. Hair parted neatly, folded handkerchief in pocket, buckled briefcase." And on Earth perhaps a bowler hat and tight furled umbrella. "It seemed suitable."

"You mean stodgy and prissy."

"No, James, just suitable. It's right for you, and I've always liked you as you are."

But he kept his lips compressed and his eyes on the white peaks.

The hospital lay in the crater's plain circled by the mountains of
Axmith's Territory II. Not a person in the whole of the Community
who did not know them, and all he had ever wanted was to dissolve
among them like a grain of salt without much more color or savor. She
liked him as he was—and what she had done to him!

"You never did explain—" he began.

"Oh, James, let it go!" She tensed on the bed and then tried to make
herself limp and slide under the coil of pain. "You wouldn't let me, all
those awful months. Now I don't want to."

Light reflected back on his face from the mountains of Axtu, and for
a moment it showed open and vulnerable. She set her hands warily over
the frenetic writhing in her belly and said with bitterness, "A virgin
birth would have seemed more reasonable to you."

He said in the precise way she claimed she had never hated, "There
are at least three people on Axtu besides us who know I am sterile."

*Shut up! Shut up! You married me because there was a good job for a
married man out here! Shut up!* "And of course no-one could want me
but you, James, you're pretty sure of that." Perhaps not. She stared
at the pale green ceiling, green walls, palely enameled night-table,
water-pitcher, callow-colored with the uncertain light reflected from
the western wall of the pumice crater. All things sullen, solid, a hard
shine to them. In her mind colors flickered, shifting pure prism-hues,
only paled and whitened by pain, till she opened her eyes to the noth-
ingness of reality.

She said, "What's there to explain? The old story . . . ."

He opened his mouth and closed it. Then he said, "When *that* is
born—"

"I'll go away, if you like. You'll never have to see me or it again."

"Don't be foolish. It can't be hidden now. Damn it, why couldn't you
have gotten rid of it, like any other woman?"

"Why couldn't you have had children like any other man?" she said
softly. It drew the blood to his face. Could she ever have pretended to
love this man, who used so much nastiness to cover his vulnerability?
With an effort she kept her voice gentle. "When we found we couldn't
have children, I couldn't help being restless . . . all the money we'd
saved with my working, and I hadn't seen my people for three years
. . ." The time-old tale of alien grain. No use saving money for the
child, and she used it to visit Earth.

But she had forgotten that life on Earth was what she had married to get away from. There was nothing for her, and all she had was the return fare to Axtu, and she started back.

But the shipwreck changed it.

She shared the liferaft with the mutilated body of an old woman who had taught her the Italian hemstitch a few hours before; it took three days till the boat homed on a safe planet and landed battered and useless on the rocky shores of a lake. The equipment seemed crushed. The radio had told her that the air and water were usable, but now it was silent, and she had no idea whether it was still sending the automatic SOS, nor how to repair it or use it.

She crawled outside at last, poising on jagged rocks that bruised her feet, and looked out over the grey expanse of the lake, flat and sunless.

*Nothing worse than the hell I've always lived in.* She grinned in despair and went back into the boat to salvage food.

The lake was in a crater-like depression, a stony saucer of water, and she was unable to see beyond the rim. When the boat landed she had been asleep and had not seen the planet's face—a grim tumbling sleep with the consciousness of the blanket-wrapped body beside her, the vacuum of loneliness in an old woman who had died without her descendants around her. There was only one other blanket. She stuffed it into a canvas bag with some concentrates and a canteen and slung it over her shoulder. There was not much to eat. Even if there were her survival would be only a matter of inertia.

She stared around once more. There was no sign of movement, not a wind carrying gull-cries, scuttling run of lizard, or oozing of any alien life she might have imagined. The air and water might be all right, but the planet gave no sign of being any more generous than that.

There was a tinge of chill to the grey air; she wiped sweating palms on her skirt and began to climb the rim. Once her foot dislodged a stone; it rolled downward for a few feet, and that was the first sound she heard beyond the beating of her own heart.

She climbed, and before she reached the top she began to hear something more: the trill of a pipe so faint and uncertain it might have been the singing of blood in her brain. But it grew and paced her as she stumbled on; it traced the whorl of her ear.

Light grew overhead, palely, and then burst into a burning sun; the sky became blue, as if she had risen out of a cloud. The points of the rocks dulled, the ground softened. She was walking on clipped green turf.

She stopped, took off her shoes, and stood with her toes pressed in the grass, dropping the canvas bag from her shoulder. The piper was walking beside her, fingering the stops. His scales were blue, green, amber and silver; colors writhed on him like the lights on a peacock's neck.

The unfluid walls of plaster and fiber-board faced her, and the falsely soothing colors of metal-frame tables. "That was Kolanddro," she said. "I didn't have to explain anything to him. He knew already."

"The way I never did," said James, and added half under his breath, " —and never will."

She remembered the months of nights she had lived alone with the half-formed creature in her, screaming in nightmare that it was clawing and ripping its way out through the frail membranes of protection that were all she had been able to give it—or maintain against it . . .

The former face of the planet had crumbled like a clay mask. Here there were heavy-leaved trees; grass grew damp and cool beneath them. But in the sunshine the strange people who lived there had raised gaudy paper pavilions of pure color. They came at the sound of the pipe and gathered round her. She would have said that they were dressed, but they were wearing only the fur, scales, or bat-wings their curious nature had given them, and there were no two alike.

They were humanoid, but flat-nosed and narrow-jawed; it was hard to find the form beneath the skin. Some of the feathered and crested ones looked like the Eighteenth Century Romantic's idea of the Noble Savage, but she was able to find neither nobility or evil in their faces.

The scaled man beside her said, "This is Nev; I'm Kolanddro, and you see these are my people. You came from the wrecked boat."

"I did. How could you have learned my language?"

"I translate alien tongues. I'm the Interpreter." That explained it to him, perhaps.

He lowered his shining lids with the effect of a smile. "You'll understand it later."

"I see. You people are telepathic."

"No. *I'm* telepathic. That's why I'm the Interpreter."

"And I don't have to tell you that my name's Lela Gordon, and I'm from Earth, etc."

"Nor ask to see anyone more important than I, because no-one will understand you."

She smiled, then sighed. "It doesn't seem very easy to leave here. Can you help me?"

But he had turned to speak to someone, and she looked around at the Nevids who had approached her. They returned her interest with a kind of inoffensive curiosity, and when they had seen enough left to go about their business. Kolanddro brought her a bowl of fruit and fresh bread.

"We don't make this kind of thing with our grain, but we baked it when it became evident that you would be with us."

"Are you clairvoyant too?"

He made a glittering gesture. "I have great range. There's little I can't do here." He blinked. "No, I can't repair your boat. We haven't any hard metals—and we don't need them." He pointed out a winged man who resembled the Spirit of Communication which for centuries had graced the telephone book. "We have Messengers." He tapped his head. "We have Interpreters." Recognizing the panic rising in her he said anxiously, "Please eat. You won't come to harm here."

She said, "I believe you . . . but the strangeness . . . is overpowering." But she calmed herself enough to eat her meal under the tossing shade. The bread was rather heavy, but good enough for having had the recipe deduced from a fleeting picture in a sleeping mind.

Kolanddro blinked and asked, "What is lemon souffle?"

"Something I'm glad I didn't dream of while I was sleeping," said Lela. She added very gently, "I really don't like having my mind read."

"While you are staying here you will have to get used to it."

*But I don't want to stay here.* She was uneasy with the strangeness, the sense of having already become completely integrated into the life of the planet in an hour's time. She thought of the old woman dead in the boat who might have been happy to spend the last years of her age under this sun, and brushed crumbs from her skirt.

"I think I'd better stay near the boat in case the signal's working."

He stared at her with his black and green eyes. "You'll never reach the boat without my help," he touched the pipe, "and if you go you won't come back, or even remember all this. There'll be no more food or shelter for you."

She said slowly, "Open Sesame?"

"The connotation's unclear . . . I see, an old story (perhaps you'll tell it to me sometime?) — yes, something like that."

"Kolanddro," she spoke to his still shadow on the grass, ". . . are you an illusion?"

"You will have to decide that for yourself."

The chill that crimped her skin was not an illusion, at least not more so than the whole cosmos of matter. Where in relation to this place were the grey lake and the overcast sky?

"There's nothing to be afraid of. Believe me." He ran a pearl nail around the rind of a yellow fruit and halved it. "But if you stay here you must live as one of us. We like privacy and we don't let anyone leave us who'll endanger it."

"It's beautiful here," she said reluctantly.

"It is. And we know what kind of things aliens will bring us. We've had experiences with them." He stood up. "I'm busy now, but most people like to rest in the heat of the afternoon. I think you will be glad of a rest; you may have my house." He pointed out a particularly vivid pavilion of crimson and purple. He swallowed the rest of the fruit, spat out four green pips into the palm of his hand, and cast them to the winds.

"Four more zimb trees," he said.

"You had already forgotten me by then," said James.

"James, I thought you would have been glad to forget me . . . they wouldn't have taken your job away from you here just because your wife was lost in space."

"That wasn't why I married you."

"If there was another reason it was because feeling so trodden on yourself you had to have someone to hurt in return."

"Don't, Lela. I never meant to hurt you."

But she was thinking of the last few months of sullen meals, crushing silence and loneliness. *What in hell are we going to do with a little bastard who looks as if he'd escaped from a prism, no matter how appealing he may be aesthetically? How can we keep him here? Where can we hide him?*

*The color flows on you like the broken light of a prism.*

"All you people," she said to Kolanddro, "have the same form basic-
ally—I think—but no two of you are alike on the surface. That seems
impossible."

"Not when our germ plasm is almost infinitely tractable."

"What do you mean?"

"We can take in any form of intelligent alien life. The children become
pure Nevids within three generations."

"How?"

"All psychokinetic faculties on Nev don't rest in the Interpreters—
although I will say," he added complacently, "that most of the intelli-
gence does. All Nevid parents have a choice in deciding before the
child is born what form it will take—externally, not in the vital organs."

"And the child has no choice in the matter?"

"No. His happiness depends on how well he lives with the shape we
give him."

"And if he doesn't?"

"He'll have an unhappy but interesting life."

She shivered. "I don't think I'd like that for my children."

He waved his arm at the Colony and the multicolored flow of the
strange people and the windrippled walls of their houses. "A quarter of
these people are descended from aliens. We've found for every alien
an Interpreter who could bring him into the life of the planet. I don't
think any of them have been unhappy."

"I can't believe I could ever be a part of your life."

"I'm no more part of the life here than you are. The Interpreter is born,
not made by the longings of his parents, and he comes no more often
than"—he searched her mind for the parallel—"the true genius on your
planet. Man or woman, he gives up private life."

"Your laws are cruel."

"Only as cruel or weak as the people who live by them. Do I seem
that way to you?"


She never really knew the shapes of their souls or the range of their
emotions, and only had rare glimpses of the mines and orchards,
weavers and goldbeaters, that produced what she used and ate. Sometimes she thought she had glimpses of city spires beyond the forests,
and though she knew that the Colonies often shifted with the seasons,
there was no change as long as she was with them, and she never found

out what they traded for with coins or feathers, or if they sacrificed the living on stone altars, nor the names of their strange gods.

She woke late one morning after a restless night; she was queasy and aching, and was struck with the sudden fear that she was going to have a child. She made breakfast, and when Kolanddro came in and stood silently looking at her, her teeth began to chatter. He only smiled, and loosening a strand of her hair laid it across his green-white palm, where it lay very black, as if he were matching samples of material.

"I can't go through with this," she whispered.

"You've accepted the conditions . . ." he became hesitant and faltering for the first time since she had known him, ". . . I have had to accept them." But she turned away. What had he had to give up?

Late afternoon when the sun was falling toward the west, a woman dropped down from the sky. She did not come directly into the encampment where the cooking-fires were going, but folded her wings and waited at the edge of the clearing, searching in the shifting colored frieze her people made of their most commonplace actions.

Kolanddro noticed her and moved forward; Lela turned from her task to watch them as they spoke, soundless shadows in a green shade. Something in their attitudes made her very still, though her halting command of the language would not have allowed her to understand them even if she had heard their voices.

The Nevid woman pointed toward the west; her downy hands flickered and her head lifted urgently to his calm face.

Then she turned away and came into the clearing where there was a late gold patch of sunlight lingering; she stopped and stood with her head bent down, almost as if to thrust it under her wing. Soundless and motionless she waited for the desire for flight to thicken her wings with blood. When the great delicate membranes opened she rose against the sun in a blaze of heraldic red, diminished and was gone.

But Lela soared with her in imagination over thickets and rolling hills, perhaps past stone towers and shimmering rivers, half-blinded by the deep light that warmed the clear air, and without pleasure in the flight.

A voice murmured in her ear that the meat was scorching, and she felt both foolish and sick: she recognized Kolanddro's sacrifice to the laws of Nev. When she looked again, he was gone. He came out of the pavilion a few minutes later; he was wearing an obsidian dagger.

It was not until after supper that she saw the stranger emerge along the forest trail from the same direction the woman had come. He was a crested and feathered man as splendid of his type as Kolanddro; Kolanddro washed his face and hands in a basin and went out to meet him.

They faced each other in a pantomime of tense hieratic gesture; Kolanddro spoke, unfastening his belt with the dagger and laying it on the ground. He moved his hands in a wide gesture, as if to erase whatever angers were between them, and they turned and separated.

Lela sat waiting for him in the pavilion. The sun had almost set and the evening air had thickened to sweet dusk heavy with the smells of flowers and fruit. Indoors was the heart of a rose. The simple dress the Nevids had made for her slid over her body in rich folds; the sky was mauve and pearl flowing with the last of the sun.

Kolanddro came in, his mind so full of his own affairs it was quite blind to hers. He murmured, "That was a long journey for nothing."

"I think he'll make it again," she said. "I'm going back."

He stared at her. She went on falteringly, "I know it will be a lot of trouble to put things right—but they will be right . . . I thought I could be a moral person simply by accepting the inevitable. Now I no longer believe it's inevitable."

"If you leave we can't take you back—you understand?"

"I understand—the kind of law that lets you risk death fighting a rival even when you're the most important member of the community."

He said, "A superman on your world would have to live by the same laws as the rest."

"I agree. I don't think your laws are unjust, or even inflexible—but they aren't sensitive." The word conjured James, with his capacities for loneliness and self-laceration and suddenly time, even a lifetime, seemed very short. "They've gotten stunted along the way, and on Earth they're always reaching, like a tree, for the ultimate justice—not only in lawcourts, but in relations between persons . . . this justice, it's a clumsy, top-heavy thing, full of stupid mistakes and dead ends— but it grows."

"If people on Earth are much like you they must make themselves terribly miserable for nothing."

"They do. Will you let me go?"

"No-one may ever find you out there."

"I have enough food for a while, and there's water."

"My son?"

"I think you'll have other sons. Please."

"What can you and your husband make of him on Earth?"

She winced. "Perhaps someone who can love both Earth and Nev."

"No. He won't know anything of Nev." He watched her gravely a moment, and she waited. He said, "When everything is quiet I'll take you back to the boat. I'll break the law, for you."

*When the night was dark and quiet I took off the dress the Nevids had made for me and put on the one I came in. Render unto Caesar. We went down along the smooth grass and the colors shimmered on him even in the dark. All I could think of, feeling so foolish and sick, was that he was going to kill that splendidly feathered man, or be killed, and there was nothing to say, because I'd told him what I thought of his laws.*

*"But we don't fight to the death."*

*"Thank you."*

*"Our law would never allow anyone to leave as cold and unprotected as you are doing. I must bring you food and clothing."*

*"No . . . they'd make me feel worse."* But there was one thing I wanted from him. I knew he guessed it, but I said it anyway.

*"Kolanddro. Don't make me forget Nev."*

*I found my canvas bag. It was weatherproof, but the shoes were rotted from nights of dew and days of hot sun.*

*He put his pipe to his mouth, and I had one glance of his fingers glittering on the stops and then the stones* cut her feet. She stood on the sharp edges like the transformed mermaid who walked on knives of pain as long as she had legs. She thought she could hear a last thin echo of the pipe, but it faded into the hollow lapping of the waters on the shore under the night wind.

There was no clear memory of how long she waited on the shore, days and nights. She ate concentrates when hunger became painful, and drank water when her tongue rattled in her throat, and nightmares chattered around her. She wondered that the baby lived, but it clung fiercely to the fetal stalk and thrived, walled away from her terrors.

She could hardly move when a loud bleep sounded in the boat at last, and she crawled into the terrible place on hands and knees to pick away at the wreckage and find the source, and push the switch that told them she was there. When the rescue ship lifted, she was in a bunk tossing with fever; she never saw the face of the planet.

"Lela."

She was fastened in one clench of force. "Please call the nurse now, James," she whispered. He pressed the buzzer.

"You came back, even when you could have died out there—"

"James, I could fall downstairs on my head any time, or pull a hang-nail and get septicemia; it's a chance. But I don't care now. I just want to die."

"Don't talk like that! I want you to live and be happy. With me, whatever happens! I love you, Lela . . ."

But the mist was rising before her eyes, red as the blood in the wings of the Nev woman against the sun.

She opened her eyes once out of the chaos of pain and sound; a rubber-gloved hand was holding a shining thing by the heels, a baby gleaming with the last detritus of amniotic fluid. She sank back.

He was a complete and perfect replica of James, down to the last neat lock of dark hair on his forehead. A stranger in the world, he lay beside her; his arms and legs trembled, his face crumpled, his pink hands moved aimlessly with unconscious grace.

"I can't understand it," James said, ". . . but he is beautiful. Lela, I have to tell you this now; I thought I could get away with it, but I can't. I knew I was sterile before we were married."

"I guessed it," she said. "That was really why I went away. I was going to leave you. But it doesn't matter now."

"But you did come back."

"Yes. I didn't expect much." The months gone, the long slow growth of a child in her; the woman's right she had wanted so deeply—eclipsed in bitterness and recrimination. She smiled without joy. "The tie that binds."

But he said quietly, without arrogance, "No. This depends on us."

She bent to smell the newness of the child's flesh, and to feel the hands on her face. "All right, James."

The white sun of Axtu was very clear and warm in the room. She moved her clean drained body under the sheets, grateful enough to have her breasts ripening with milk, the baby in her arm, and James beside her with the faint pulsing of hope between them.

*Phyllis Gotlieb has published several volumes of poetry in Canada. However, with the publication of the novel* SUNBURST *in 1964 she established herself as a writer in the science-fiction field. Her many science-fiction stories have been published in various sci-fi magazines. We selected ' A Grain of Manhood' from a number of stories which she submitted to us because we felt that this story well illustrates the skill with which Mrs. Gotlieb uses the exotic setting of the science-fiction genre to explore basic human emotions. Mrs. Gotlieb lives in Toronto.*

# acknowledgements

The publishers have made every effort to acknowledge copyright;
any errors or omissions are unintentional and we would be glad
to learn of them.

Stories

"The Sound of Hollyhocks", © by Hugh Garner 1968, 1971, is
reprinted with the kind permission of McGraw-Hill Ryerson Ltd.

"Gentlemen, Your Verdict" by Michael Bruce originally appeared in
*Maclean's Magazine*, Jan. 1, 1947.

"A Few Notes for Orpheus" by Don Bailey is reprinted from *Fourteen
Stories High* by permission of Oberon Press.

"The Fall of a City" by Alden Nowlan is reprinted by permission of the
author.

"The Painted Door", from *The Lamp at Noon and Other Stories* by
Sinclair Ross, is reprinted by permission of the author and The
Canadian Publishers, McClelland and Stewart Limited, Toronto.

"The Firing Squad" by Colin McDougall originally appeared in
*Maclean's Magazine*, 1953, and is reprinted by permission of the author.

"Two Fishermen", copyright 1959 by Morley Callaghan, is reprinted by
permission of the Harold Matson Company, Inc.

"The Late Man" by Andreas Schroeder is reprinted from *Fourteen Stories
High* by permission of Oberon Press.

"Always a Motive" by Dan Ross is reprinted by permission of the
author.

"Dance for the Devil" by Edward McCourt is reprinted by permission of
the late author.

"Ko-ishin-mit and Paw-qwin-mit" by George Clutesi is taken from *Son
of Raven Son of Deer*, Gray's Publishing Ltd., Sidney, B.C., 1967,
pages 99-110.

"We Have to Sit Opposite" by Ethel Wilson, from *Mrs. Golightly and
Other Stories*, is reprinted by permission of The Macmillan Company of
Canada Limited and Macmillan London and Basingstoke.

"Journey Home" by W. T. Duncan, from *Stories with John Drainie*, is reprinted by permission of the author.

"After the Sirens" is from *Flying a Red Kite* by Hugh Hood, The Ryerson Press, by permission of McGraw-Hill Ryerson Limited.

"The Last Husky" by Farley Mowat originally appeared in *Saturday Evening Post*, April 2, 1955, and is reprinted by permission of the author.

"Six Beauties", from *The Happy Time* by Robert Fontaine, is reprinted by permission of Lurton Blassingame, the author's agent. Copyright © 1945 by Robert Fontaine. Published by Simon and Schuster, Inc.

"Two Sisters" by Markoosie originally appeared in *North* (1971), and is reprinted by permission of the author.

"A Grain of Manhood" by Phyllis Gotlieb is reprinted by permission of the author and her agents, Scott Meredith Literary Agency, Inc., 580 Fifth Avenue, New York, N.Y. 10036.

Photographs

2, Michael Semak
3, Rudi Haas (Information Canada Photothèque)
4, Michael Semak
5, R. Jacques (Information Canada Photothèque)
6, Miller Services
20, Miller Services
26, Jack Long (Information Canada Photothèque)
40, Miller Services
59, Vivienne (Miller Services)
66, Miller Services
68, Malak (Information Canada Photothèque)
88, Michael Semak
106, Ted Grant (Information Canada Photothèque)
116, G. Hunter (Information Canada Photothèque)
117, Michael van Elsen
    Miller Services
118, Michael van Elsen
119, Michael Semak
120, Gar Lunney (Information Canada Photothèque)

152, Michael van Elsen
158, Hale Observatories
170, Photo of Karasea's Silver Nikki II
194, "Igloo Dwellers" by Lucy, Cape Dorset
198, MGM, "2001: A Space Odyssey"

The cover illustration and design are by Paul Kaufhold.
The book's design is by Michael van Elsen.

This book is set in eleven-point Garamond and twenty-point
Helvetica by Moore Type.
Printing and binding is by T. H. Best.
Printed and bound in Canada

1234567890CM82109876543